Praise P9-BYM-362

'Fowler writes devilishly clever and mordantly funny novels that are sometimes heartbreakingly moving.'
Val McDermid, *The Times*

'Christopher Fowler is an award-winning novelist who would make a good serial killer.'
Time Out

'An imaginative fun house of a world where sage minds go to expand their vistas and sharpen their wits.'
New York Times Book Review
on the *Bryant & May* books

'Fowler repeatedly challenges the reader to redraw the boundaries between innocence and malevolence, rationality and paranoia... He has the uncanny ability to invoke terror in broad daylight.'
The Guardian on *Demonised*

'His sentences zip along, wonderfully funny or moving – sometimes both.'
The Independent on *Paperboy*

'The climax is truly spectacular... this would make a great piece of cinema. It has everything that you could ever want from a thriller.'
The Eloquent Page on *Roofworld*

Also by Christopher Fowler

Roofworld
Rune
Red Bride
Darkest Day
Spanky
Psychoville
Disturbia
Menz Insana
Soho Black
Calabash
Breathe
Paperboy
(Autobiography)
Film Freak
(Autobiography)

COLLECTIONS
The Bureau of Lost
Souls
City Jitters
More City Jitters
Flesh Wounds
Sharper Knives
Personal Demons
Uncut
The Devil in Me
Demonised
Old Devil Moon
Red Gloves

BRYANT & MAY
Full Dark House
The Water Room
Seventy Seven Clocks
Ten Second Staircase
White Corridor
The Victoria Vanishes
Bryant & May On the
Loose
Bryant & May Off
the Rails
The Memory of Blood

PLASTIC

CHRISTOPHER FOWLER

SOLARIS

First published 2013 by Solaris
an imprint of Rebellion Publishing Ltd,
Riverside House, Osney Mead,
Oxford, OX2 0ES, UK

www.solarisbooks.com

ISBN: 978 1 78108 125 9

A CIP catalogue record for this book is available
from the British Library.

Designed & typeset by Rebellion Publishing

Printed in the US

FOREWORD
Joanne Harris

EVERY YEAR, A million books never see publication. Some are rightly ignored; some die; some are just not saleable enough. Some receive rave rejections before being thrown onto the trash pile. And sometimes one splendid, heroic book fights its way to the top of that pile, bites its thumb at the corporate, commercial world of publishing and announces to the world at large: Read me, or else.

Plastic is one of these. I was lucky enough to read it in manuscript form some seven or eight years ago. From the first page I was hooked. Dark, compassionate, violent, wise and wittily razor-edged – if Quentin Tarantino had decided to collaborate with Alan Bennett to rewrite *Bridget Jones' Diary*, then surely the script would have been something like this. I already knew the author to be the master of urban unease, but to me this new novel went further still. I loved it, raved about it to everyone I knew and assumed that it would just be a matter of time before it became a bestseller.

In a world where credit rules supreme, where images of unattainable perfection are held up to women as not only achievable, but absolutely necessary, where nobody looks beyond the surface, where to be on TV is everyone's fantasy and where the acquisition of yet another handbag, yet another pair of shoes, might hold the key to happiness, *Plastic* has an uncanny resonance. The heroine, June Cryer, whose description of herself as 'a dead housewife' comes frighteningly close to home, is the existential Everywoman of the consumer generation. Unloved, unhappy, overweight, she is filled with confusion about the world around her; about her husband, who is leaving her; about the dreams she used to have.

'When I was young I would kneel on my mother's threadbare sofa and watch snowflakes dissolving against the warm lounge windows, I would stare into the frozen streets as white and muffled as the inside of a pillow and think of a distant future when I would become important to someone. Even in winter my life was sunlit, one giant possibility. How far did I end up from that dream?'

Her displacement activities, her preoccupation with trivia, with TV, and particularly with shopping as a desperate means of filling an inner void, will strike many a chord amongst those of us who know what it's like to speed-shop through Selfridges, wielding the plastic with deadly intent, and to return triumphant with the sense of a job well done and a shopping bag full of assorted items that only an obsessive-compulsive on crack would think made any kind of sense…

All of us have been there. All of us know what it's like. June speaks for all of us when she says of a visit to Selfridge's:

'I arrived in front of the building like Caesar at the gates of Rome and swept past the doorman with a look that said 'I'm about to jag a spike in the monthly national consumer index, so don't even *think* of fucking with me'.

But such pleasures as this have consequences. And as events unfurl with the breathtaking inevitability of a row of collapsing dominoes, June suddenly finds herself on the dark side of consumerism, in a world of shopping at gunpoint, a world in which human flesh is just another commodity to be traded, and where even such a mundane object as a potato peeler may be given a new and sinister role...

However, in spite of all this, the publishing world was not convinced. Whilst admitting the book was terrific (I don't think any manuscript has ever been so widely – and furtively – read in-house), editor after editor pronounced it "tricky to sell". A thriller about shopping, narrated by a housewife? From Sophie Kinsella, from Kathy Lette – from any female writer, in fact – it would have been acceptable. But from Christopher Fowler? Tricky.

And so *Plastic* continued to circulate under a series of different titles, acquiring converts wherever it went like some literary underworld movement – a secret Campaign for Real Fiction.

Finally, here it is, in all its subversive glory.

Read it with the light on.

'*Our houses are not in the street anymore.*
The street is in our houses.'
Charles Gounod

CHAPTER ONE
Dead Housewife

THERE'S BLOOD EVERYWHERE, and none of it's where it's supposed to be.

On the carpet. On the curtains. All over me. And I know it won't wash out because this shirt is pure silk. If you don't want to ruin silk, never sneeze in a Starbucks with a mouth full of blueberry muffin. As I sit here I keep thinking *if only I could go back to my old life.* I could head into the kitchen and start going through the ironing again, except that the iron is now sticking out of the TV screen.

My name is June Cryer, and I am a dead housewife.

To put it another way, I am a pelmet-vacuuming, Tesco-shopping, voucher-clipping, dishwasher-loading, Radio Heart-loving dead housewife who should have stayed home instead of getting into a fight with the kind of men who feature on crime programmes with blurry boxes over their faces.

I'd like to comb my hair and put on a bit of lippy, make myself presentable, but I can't get up. The man standing guard over me is entirely devoid of manners. He has a foil-wrapped burger in his fist, and takes ruminative lumps out of it while he's deciding where to dump my body. The meat juice is running over his knuckles like blood. My God, we've come a long way from Raffles, the Gentleman Thief.

How the hell did I ever get here?

All I can think is that I must have fallen into a deep sleep the day I got married, like some character from a fairy tale, except Sleeping Beauty was out cold before she met her prince, and he fought a dragon and slashed his way through a forest of poisonous thorns to get to her, whereas Gordon just said 'I suppose I should marry you if you're not going to have a termination', and instead of the Kiss of True Love bringing me to my senses it was his unrepentant affair with the bitch next door.

I look up at the Burger-Muncher and realise I am *way* out of my depth. By the time my neighbours hear about me I'll be gone. I'll turn up on the news, found in the long grass of a railway embankment, or floating face-down in the Thames, just another unidentified torso sucked along by the tide. My severed head will be discovered in a freezer bag in the high street, only to be replaced with bunches of lurid garage flowers still wrapped in plastic. Why don't people take the plastic off? When Princess Diana died it looked like several tons of Quality Street had been dumped outside her house. But that's how I'll be found, scattered across the city in half a dozen binliners, recognised by my ankle-chain or the piercings in my ears.

So much for the dignity of death.

I'll probably make the local edition of the six o'clock news. My disapproving neighbours will be interviewed around the corners of their front doors; 'She was a quiet woman, kept herself to herself, never went out much.' My best friend will use my disappearance as an opportunity to impose herself on athletic television cameramen. My mother will telephone my husband

and commiserate: 'Well, Gordon, you can't say I didn't warn you. I always said she was a bolter. The signs were there, it's just a shame your name had to be dragged into it.' Eventually, in death as in life, I will be totally forgotten. And I'll only have myself to blame.

As soon as my captor has finished his burger, I'm done for. He still has a quarter left but I can tell he's sizing me up for removal. *Will she go in the lift or do I have to saw her head off first?*

I once had hopes for something better than this. When I was young –

– when I was young I would kneel on my mother's faded turquoise sofa and watch snowflakes dissolving against the warm lounge windows, I would stare into the frozen streets as white and muffled as the inside of a pillow and think of a distant future when I would become important to someone. Our TV was always showing The Little Mermaid *or* Sleeping Beauty, *and we always had the colour turned up too bright. I wanted to live in a sunlit glade and find my prince. Was I so wrong for wanting that? I'm not ashamed. But how did I end up so far from those dreams?*

But I can't just forget what's happened because this has been the most memorable weekend I've had since I was seven, when our caravan got wedged under a car park barrier on the Isle of Sheppey. And I can't go back because my old life has gone forever. The last couple of days have been a, well I wouldn't use the word *nightmare*, because you recover from bad dreams, don't you?

Sorry, I know I'm rambling. I think it's shock.

They need some decent curtains on the windows in this room. Heals are having a sale, they could get it out of petty cash and keep the receipt because you never know, the colours might clash. Do thugs get expenses?

I don't feel well. I think I'm going to be sick.

I don't deserve to be in a situation like this. I can no longer make sense of the world. Nothing is in its right place anymore. There are shadows everywhere. Life can cloud over as fast as a spring morning, and suddenly everything becomes hopeless. It seems unfair, like being told you're seriously ill by a cheerful, harrassed doctor.

Let me start at the – you know.

CHAPTER TWO
Mrs. Bloke

MY FULL NAME is Penelope June Cryer, only I changed my Christian and middle names around because no-one wants to be called Penny Cryer, it sounds like a Victorian newspaper.

First of all, let me get this straight, I never meant to get involved in anything violent. It's not like me. I'm too unfashionable. I'm nice. I always buy tea-towels from those boys who call at the front door trying to better themselves. I'll always put a woolly glove on the railings. I stop and listen to charity muggers until they look for a chance to get away. But nice people finish last, don't they?

I know that being a housewife is as boring as a Post Office queue. I wanted something more, but not this. They say loss of innocence is irreversible. Well, my consciousness has been raised. I've finally found out what I've been missing, and it's way too much information, I can tell you.

Look, I'm trying to keep everything together so I can explain, but it's not easy.

Today is Sunday, but my descent into chaos goes further back to… well, my old life, my life up to the end of last week, but it's hard to pinpoint exactly where… although I'd say handwriting.

I did calligraphy at school and have a wonderful signature, with a sweeping Arabic flourish on the end of the 'Y' like I'm signing my name to a painting after years of work. I could show you a hundred signatures and they'd all be identical. I could make a biro work upside down, like spacemen. I got married and when the marriage disappointed, I started shopping. I was ready to use my signature in the nation's stores, and what happened? They introduced pin numbers, which aren't the same. Signatures were personal. Nobody sees my signature now. It was all I had, damnit. Now I'm just an arrangement of digits in someone's databank.

Credit was easy, not really money at all, just tapping out four numbers. I carried no cash. My mother said cash was the filthiest thing you could ever hold in your hand because of all the other people it's been through. Obviously she'd had little experience of penises.

I've never been good with money. I got a parking fine every single time I moved the car. We're all supposed to ride bicycles now for the environment, but my mother was a district nurse and says all bicycles ever gave her was saddle-rash and an aversion to wicker.

I suppose the whole thing *really* started last Christmas. That was the first time I realised I had a problem.

I have shopping glands. The only thing I love more than shopping is reassessing my purchases. You know, when you get them home and lay them all out and see exactly what you've bought? Remember that great feeling?

Between December 18th and 24th I spent over £9,450 on presents. The national average is £700. And I don't even have anyone to buy for except my husband, my mother and a friend who lives down the street. When the bills came in I thought they'd got it wrong, then realised that I didn't remember the shopping trip at all. I'd parked the car in Selfridges, I'd driven home with the boot and the back seat full of bags, but the bit in between was a complete blank.

I'd bought electrical goods I would never use, sweaters in triplicate, a yogurt-maker, night-goggles for God's sake. I'd ordered a cat. Some rare breed with evil, wonky eyes and overactive sweat glands that you have to keep wiping down with a damp cloth; I don't know, it must have been on TV. Last year I bought a home defibrillator. It's still in its box in the spare room.

The realisation of what I had done spoiled Christmas for me. I hid the bills from Gordon until I could figure out what to do. He spent the afternoon slumped in front of the telly performing eating rituals peculiar to the season, peering inside brazil nuts and chewing dried figs on a plastic fork. I bunged a Butterball into the oven but barely touched any of it myself. I had a bottle of Bombay Sapphire, three valiums and a packet of dry-roasted nuts, and sat in the kitchen fretting.

He went mad at me when he found the bills, but grudgingly paid up. He could afford it. Gordon places such importance on looking normal that it really becomes quite strange. He's the sort of man who wears a tie to a funfair. When I was a kid, I used to stick Welsh flags in seaside sandcastles; thinking about it, it's really odd, you know? I did it because the Welsh flag always came in a packet with the other flags when you bought a bucket and spade, that's all. So it was the normal thing to do. Gordon thinks eating dried figs one day a year is normal, but it's just what you're used to.

We all do what we're used to, and I'm used to Gordon. He was always kind to me, in a vague, thoughtless English way. He often came home with garage carnations (why is one always bright blue?) and a box of Black Magic. Men called Gordon do things like that, they have to live up to the name. He allowed me to assume that he would always be there for me. He made sure our life together was cloaked in common sense.

That's how things were with us. We didn't lead the empowered lives you read about in magazines. People in magazines are only in magazines because they're not remotely normal. Me, I'm used to being invisible. The kids in our street called me Mrs. Bloke because that's what I was, the wife of some man they saw going to work every morning, leaving the house with a briefcase. If I was on a soap opera I'd be billed as Woman Carrying Sainsbury's Bags, Woman Examining Refrigerated Desserts, Woman Peering Crossly Out Of Garden Window.

I feel special now, singled out for attention after years of transparency, but when you see what I've had to go through in the last couple of days, you'll understand why.

CHAPTER THREE
The Betrayal

I REALISED I had a problem with spending money. Getting it was easy enough, because I had an allowance from Gordon. He's always had the same job – he works for Selway, the biggest shoe company in Croydon, no designer labels, just generic menswear, black Oxford toecaps, trainers, workboots, the kind of shoes you see on salesmen who smell like hot cows after two months in the same footgear. Middle-aged men wear belts that are slightly too tight, just as women do with brassieres. Any sales assistant will tell you there's hardly a woman over thirty who chooses the right bra size. Gordon is nine years older than me, and Head of Regional Sales. He makes good money and was always generous, but when the men in his family hit thirty-five they all start to look like something out of Sofa World, and only notice you when you stand in front of the football and lift their legs to vacuum.

Gordon and June. Our names went together like Marks & Spencer or Burke & Hare. One never appeared without the other. Before we got married, Gordon didn't behave like a Gordon. He was more of a Dan or Jack. He was full of grand ideas. He gave me the impression that he wanted to get tattooed and spend a year in Goa before owning a chain of stores that sold personalised sound systems, but after one sniff of an air-conditioned office he was ready for a nameplate on his desk. I didn't have any grand plans, but I wanted a baby boy. The pregnancy was a surprise and he married me because his mother insisted, and he forgot he ever had dreams, but he remembered to blame me.

Everything continued to stay normal until just over a month ago, when our son would have been ten. That was when we had the really big fight. I thought I knew all there was to know about a man. They didn't appear to be much more complicated than video recorders, it was just a matter of programming them correctly. It turns out they're more like Swedish ovens; certain buttons used in combination produce entirely inexplicable effects.

It was a special occasion, and I wanted to buy Gordon something special to mark the day, so I decided to borrow the car because the trains were playing up. He kept a spare key inside the mallard. We have this china duck on the mantelpiece. Gordon won't let me drive his car, not because he thinks I'm a bad driver, he just thinks I'll crash it and kill someone, so I've always taken the train, but they were running late so I risked his new Vauxhall.

I didn't tell him I was going to borrow it. I thought he wouldn't find out if I put the seat and mirror back. I like shopping in London even though the parking is enough to make you stab a traffic warden through the eye, but I decided to head to Croydon because I get bored driving. Except when there's a radio play on, and even then the sound effects annoy me, especially opening doors and tinkling tea-things.

The Vauxie's air conditioning made a terrible rattling noise when I turned it on. I lay down on the seat and shone a torch through the vent on the passenger side but couldn't see anything, so I unscrewed the panel under it and disconnected the hose. I know how to do basic car maintenance because my father ran a garage and I used to watch him. I still couldn't see what was making the noise, so I connected the nozzle of my vacuum cleaner to the hose and put it on blow. I was looking down the vent, which was probably a bad idea because something shot out and hit me in the face.

More accurately, it stuck in my forehead. I felt blood trickling into my eyes. I went back into the house and ran to a mirror. It was a diamond earring, elegant setting, a good-sized blue-white oval stone, and it wasn't mine. And it was stuck between my eyes. I looked like an Indian woman.

How does a strange diamond earring get into the air vent of a car only driven by your husband?

Let me tell you about Gordon. He's insensible to the grace of living. Desk and office, house and garden, no mysteries that can't be solved with the contents of a toolbox. I suppose I'd always known about his affairs. It wasn't the first time he had been unfaithful. He's not particularly attractive, he's a little overweight and drifting within range of Pringle jumpers, so I think when the offer of sex came up he just took it.

He believes everything he reads in the tabloids, especially about immigrants ruining the country. I've always wondered what would happen if he met a sexy immigrant, he'd probably blow a fuse puzzling over the paradox. He travelled a fair amount, so there were hotels, and of course his car, which functioned like a combination office and bedroom. I'm pretty sure they were doing it in the Vauxhall because once I searched the glove box and found an empty foil disc of birth control pills and a luggage receipt for Antwerp. But I still couldn't imagine him being unfaithful – even with all the weird phone calls.

They were weird because he took the cordless into the shed even when the temperature was below zero, and he had the kind of peculiar strangled conversations men have when they're trying to hide something. I'd stayed in denial because I wanted our marriage to work, which is an unfashionable view when you see all those trendy women in car commercials kicking men out of their loft apartments. But life wasn't like that for me, it was about bleach and Hoover bags and quietly crying after midnight so as not to let the neighbours hear. Gordon said we had to talk problems over, but he always managed to talk me out of anything I wanted to change.

I cleaned the cut on my head and was standing by the garden gate with the earring in my hand feeling a bit dazed when Hilary, my next door neighbour, walked past and spoke without stopping to engage her brain. Hilary is tall and wears a shade of coral gloss lipstick I'm sure they've discontinued everywhere except Africa.

'Oh you've found it,' she said, 'thank God, I've been looking everywhere.'

She thought I'd just picked the earring up in the street. Then she realised the truth and changed colour. Hilary makes herself taller with pinned-up hair that needs a better conditioner than the complimentary kind she hoards from air-crew hotels. Hilary is a BA flight attendant who knows how to blow a whistle for attracting attention, which is something she looks like she's had a lot of practice at.

I didn't know what to say. I numbly handed her the earring, and as I did I had a clear mental picture of Hilary with her tights off and her Zara skirt hiked up astride Gordon in the passenger seat, banging her head against the windscreen. What was so galling is that she's older than me, one of those old-school British Airways bulldog-women in Belisha-beacon makeup who's born to wear a Hermes neck scarf with horseshoes on it.

I had a deal going with Gordon; he always paid for his infidelities. But this was so blatant that as I grabbed the car keys I thought to hell with Croydon, it's time for Selfridges and Harvey Nicks, the point being that in one afternoon I planned to revenge-shop myself into a coma. If I hadn't decided to do that I wouldn't have seen the shoes and I'd never have ended up here, covered in blood.

I was only going to go shopping, and now I have to die for it, how does that one work out?

CHAPTER FOUR
Birth Of An Addiction

BEFORE I MOVED to Hamingwell, I lived with my parents in one of those yellow-brick Edwardian terraced houses that provided a dream-memory of order and safety for its inheritors.

Our quiet sidestreet was a warm-walled canyon where children played ball games in the road and went to bed while it was still light in the summer months. My parents had been children during the confused decades after the war, and raised me without religion, politics or convictions of any kind in the hope that I would make up my own mind. After their weekly fight they would buy me a small gift to make amends for what I had seen and heard.

Over the years, the gifts got bigger.

By the time I was seventeen there was no cupboard space left in my bedroom for new clothes, and I couldn't take any more of their fighting, so I left home and moved into the flat over the shoe shop where I had a Saturday job. I dated the manager, but when I finished with him he had me thrown out of the flat.

I knew Gordon because he visited the store as a sales rep, and I started seeing him because he wouldn't leave me alone. After my marriage I was transferred to Kimberley Road, Hamingwell, where the children were posted indoors at their games stations and arguments were whispered because they could be heard through the walls.

The streets were as silent as those of my youth, but now they were filled with people-carriers, experimental parking layouts and signs on poles explaining penalties. Burglaries and car thefts and waves of graffiti rhythmically appeared as if a high, dirty tide of rebellion had risen and receded in the night. The residents organised teams to watch houses, to secure gardens, to scrub off the effluvium, fighting to maintain the area's postcard appearance, but the communal effort robbed us of community, and we retreated suspiciously into our homes. We grew sick of digging sharpened screwdrivers out of high street flowerbeds.

After that, the only time I glimpsed the city again was looking out of department store windows. I couldn't see that marriage was shrinking my world. You don't notice changes when they happen incrementally.

The only existing postcard of the town where I spent ten years of married life shows a yellow brick parade of shop-fronts, a laundrette, a butchers, a newsagent, a green bus garage and a length of empty black tarmac beneath an improbable blue sky. The card had been produced when the parade was newly built and the town just completed. There's a sense of bareness in the picture, of infant exposure to the world. Constructed on the expanding border of Kent and Greater London, Hamingwell sprang up fully formed. One day it was a mud-tracked building site, a black gap on an aerial night photograph, the next it was an official destination-board, a hotspot of shimmering yellow lights, its junctions freshly marked, its young trees nested in, its starter homes filled with slightly puzzled strangers, and I had been one of them.

I was nineteen when I arrived there, two months a wife and six months pregnant. It was the first time I had been any distance from my parents' house. I'm twenty-nine now, one week away from thirty, a birthday I won't live to see.

If you lower the postcard and reveal the scene behind it all these years later, you'll find the laundrette boarded up, the butchers turned into a charity shop, and only the newsagents remaining in a dingy enervated version, its cracked windows pasted with faded lottery stickers. The bus garage is now a tower block and the road is full of fat-wheeled Japanese jeeps. The meadow from which the town took its name has been concreted over as a one-stop shopping plaza, and that, too, has failed. Thanks a bunch, credit crunch.

The town lost its innocence; a schoolgirl was raped, a toddler went missing. The hopeful couples who came to Hamingwell moved on when the economic downturn hit, but up until three days ago I was still there. Ten years married and still childless, still cemented to the same man. My unborn boy had died, and the infection damaged my ovaries enough to make Gordon lose faith in fatherhood. In towns like Hamingwell, to be without children after a decade is to hang a sign around your neck saying 'Incomplete As A Human Being'. With a little rearrangement, the town's name spells 'Am In Hell.'

People stand up in meetings and admit I'm an alcoholic, I'm a shoplifter, I'm a Binge Eater. For ten years I was a Housewife – I'd tell anyone, not that anyone asked. On the rare occasions that I voiced any dissatisfaction, Gordon reminded me that at least he had married me, meaning that he might equally not have bothered. For years I kept the postcard on my bedroom table, to remind me that I was once as hopeful as the scene in the picture.

I kept a clean house; scratch that, I kept an eerily immaculate house, so tidy it looked like a show home, because it had never been stained by emotion. Spotless sofas, price stickers on my wine glasses and yellow tie-tags on my scented bin-liners. I realised I was in a rut when I noticed that our cat's diet was more varied than mine. At least his dried food came in three types. I kept busy. My husband worked late. My sinks smelled of pine. My surfaces shone. My days were full and my nights were bloody quiet, I can tell you.

I used to be kind, but I became indifferent. No longer sentient. Once I looked up the antonym of 'sentient' in my dictionary and it simply said 'dead'. Finally I turned into someone else entirely, someone as beaten as a piece of veal, as boring as a supermarket leaflet. How long does it take for a life to change beyond all recognition? Try ten years and a fistful of days. You could say I only had myself to blame, that there are women twenty years older than me who are still cool and slender and sexy, but they always knew how to be like that. When I was nine my mother told me that I would never be able to survive without a man. Thanks a lot, Ma.

Sorry, where was I up to? I wish I could have a cup of tea, perhaps some plain digestives or a Hobnob. It would calm me down. I'll tell you everything, I promise. Just the plain simple facts from now.

CHAPTER FIVE
The Art of Speed Acquisition

ON THAT FISH-tank-grey autumn afternoon when I discovered the earring, I went shopping. Actually, the term 'shopping' hardly seems adequate. I couldn't have done more damage to my credit cards if I'd driven over them. What I did was blast through Selfridges like an armed witch on a mission. I arrived in front of the building like Caesar at the gates of Rome and swept past the doorman with a look that said 'I'm about to jag a spike in the monthly national consumer index, so don't even *think* of fucking with me.'

Spending money is an intimate thing for me, so I made sure I knew the entire history of the places where I shopped, just as it was a point of honour to memorise the names of all the assistants who offered me their services. I was such a familiar face in Selfridges that the store detectives kept an eye on me, thinking I must be part of some long-term thieving reconnaissance party. I didn't look poor, of course, so they suspected me less. I always dressed for shopping as if going on a date, smart beige patent-leather heels and a sleek chocolate-toned skirt, never jeans or trainers, because I was anxious to be noticed and treated with respect.

It was not a good idea to shop in a highly emotional state. I was one thin step away from sitting down in the middle of the street and screaming. Convinced that shopping in quantity released pheromones, I tick-tacked at a furious speed across the marble floors, ankles flashing back and forth, charm bracelet jangling, begging the buzz to kick in.

The remains of the summer season fashions had been left on the shelves like hard centres discarded in a ravaged chocolate box, the sales staff as listless and fractious as children trapped in class. As I circumnavigated the territory, a hunter-gatherer on a search for hangered prey, I pushed ever deeper into the undergrowth of my desires.

It was a good way to spend the day.

Lately I had become fascinated with the textures of fashion fabrics, and as I walked I mentally alphabetized them into alpaca, astrakhan, batiste, brocade, cotton, calico, cambric, cheviot, chiffon, chenille, crepe de chine, cretonne and corduroy. By the time I arrived at damask, denim and dimity I had already made my first purchase and lost my place in the lexicon of luxury.

It's never a good idea to shop when you're angry; you're liable to buy a kitten just so you can have the option of strangling it. As I agonized over proof of Gordon's infidelity I got close to collapsing onto a stressed-leather browser-sofa to gulp noisy sobs into a Kleenex. Shopping only works as a displacement activity if you do a lot of it, so I metronomed at speed through the city-block-sized department store, brandishing my handbag like a Spartan shield.

I covered the territory as thoroughly as a soldier flushing out snipers, a hunter-gatherer on a search for spangled prey to flay and wear. I had no fashion agenda in mind. If I was subconsciously looking for a new look, it was to look as invisible as possible. There are women who want to be mistaken for celebrity WAGs, those tanned Twiglets who can prevent their skin from drying up but not their column inches. Fame wasn't for me; I wanted to be mistaken for one of those Knightsbridge trophy wives who have nothing better to do with their days than creep around retail outlets haranguing staff before heading off to rabbit-nibble a handful of greenery and pine nuts at the kind of restaurant where you can actually smell the hatred of the waiting staff. I just needed to fit in. Somewhere. Anywhere. I have control issues. I am a very, very, angry... I can't... I want...

Wait. Calm. Count to ten... where was I? Oh yes, killing – but first, shopping.

I refuse to buy from the internet. Clicking and dragging isn't a sensual experience. Shopping at Selfridges is a hot bath, a cool rain, a sudden flush of heat in the cervix. I love the ceramic faces of the cosmetic clerks, underlit by ice-blue counters. The frozen tableaux these vacuous mannequins form at their work stations make me feel like the heroine in the stage-play of my life. The lives of salespeople are probably even duller than mine, but I can see the attraction of their job. How could you resist the dramatic tungsten spots and arctic sets that effortlessly place you at the heart of a noir thriller? When that shopgirl was shot dead by her boyfriend in Selfridges a few years back, an act that would have seemed grotesque anywhere else felt entirely appropriate in such a location.

The cyclamen zephyrs that drifted over me from the perfumery inflamed my membranes. The staff drifted about me with testers and face brushes as if wielding sacrificial tools in some arcane, forgotten rite.

In housewares, the hanging crescendos of copper pots tightened my chest muscles until I could barely breathe. There were no stains in these stage-kitchens because no food was ever cooked. Sometimes I pulled open the counter drawers and breathed in their emptiness. I studied the beds covered with purple-beaded casbah cushions, the pastel French cotton sheets imprisoned in plastic as smooth as plate glass, the polished maple dining-tables laid for guests who would never ruin everything by turning up. When I touched the smokily elegant vases too slender to hold grocery store flowers but perfectly designed for a single aurum lily, I felt safe in the arms of manufacturers.

After shopping, I always wanted a cigarette and a soapy wash, because obviously the entire process was about sex. Buying an inappropriate dress is the equivalent to a thoughtless one-night stand, whereas designer shoes constitute a long-term commitment filled with recrimination and at least one decent orgasm. I hadn't been penetrated for over eighteen months. At first the dull ache of desire would not go away, but after a while it no longer bothered me. These days my clitoris was located somewhere near the top of Harrods.

As I swept through Oxford Street's great cathedral of expenditure, I pondered on the verb 'to spend'. It had a sexual connotation, of course, to empty the juices, to flush out, but I wondered why people talked about 'spending days', as though everything was currency. I felt spent. The world felt spent.

On I went, past the TV monitors of starved catwalk girls dipping at the turn of the runway, up into menswear, a square acre of wood, chrome and marble where everything smelled of citrus, musk and leather, all the things I never smelled on Gordon, who only smelled of cigarettes and computers. Soon I was carrying so many purchases that the bag ropes left Japanese-prisoner-of-war marks on my arms.

On through the food hall with its aged hamhocks hanging like the thighs of long-dead chorus girls, past rows of shocked fish arranged on ice like jewelled purses, past the jars of exotic pickles as mysterious as foetuses in a medical museum, to the perfume counters patrolled by women like bony cats, where I stood paralysed, breathing deep the smell of frangipani, honeysuckle, gardenia, jasmine, lavender, carnation, eucalyptus, lemon, sandalwood and ambergris. The atomisers, sprays, sachets, pomanders, powders, potpourris, balms, gels, oils, soaps, lotions, sticks and fixatives pumped such a sweet cacophony into the air that the hall shimmered and slipped in my vision.

On through departments of casual wear that looked as though the clothes had been randomly assigned pages of a Pantone colour chart, through to the designer collections so monochrome that I wondered if my eyes had suddenly switched to cat-and-dog vision. By now I was carrying enough purchases to stock a third-world department store.

I made it home, and set about cooking a meal to calm my nerves, a plastic M&S box containing a chive-coated fish-brick surrounded by concrete yellow sauce. I heard Gordon stop in the hall to check the bags I had dumped inside the front door. The longer he took to examine the dresses, shoes, CDs, jewellery, makeup, underwear and the furry rabbit pyjama-cases I'd bought for no reason at all from a shop in Kensington Church Street, the more I knew we were in for a fight.

I could tell he was angry by the way he walked into the kitchen, with his heels going down first. I hoped he wouldn't see the rest of the bags wedged under the table.

'You can't control it anymore, can you?' he said. The last time he had pointed this out, I'd tried explaining to him that shopping was citizenship, an essential part of belonging to the consumer society. It didn't wash then, either. I knew we were about to have the kind of fight all addicts have with their partners. 'This time you're going to take every last one of them back.'

'No,' I told him, affronted, finding things to do in the kitchen, keeping busy, rearranging spoons with all the dignity I could muster. 'I can't return them.'

'You can, June. You'll have to. I've had enough of this.' He strutted out of the kitchen and into the lounge like an angry Methodist. If he'd been a pipe smoker, he would have whipped it out and tamped it by the fireplace.

Gordon was in the wrong for having an affair and I wanted to corner him about it this time, even though the exposure would damage us. As I'd handed back the earring earlier that day, I had looked into Hilary's eyes and known that this tangerine-faced woman was Gordon's lover. Hilary had studied me with the inner-knowledge one woman has when she's been told secrets by another woman's husband. I was mortified to be watched in such a way, a way that said *I know all about your unsatisfactory sex life and your problem ovaries, your tendency to fat around the tops of your legs and that ill-advised butterfly tattoo you now regret*. Gordon was in the wrong and I was the one hiding in the kitchen.

I forced myself to go after him. I had another reason for doing so. A few days earlier I had finished a new set of hospital tests, and much to my surprise the results indicated that I now had a 50/50 chance of maintaining pregnancy to full-term. It was news I had stopped hoping for, and it couldn't have come at a worse time.

Gordon was wearing a grey suit that was two years too tight. It was one he owned for wearing at work, but lately he had taken to wearing it at weekends as well. We had bought the suit together at Bluewater. The whole purchasing process had lasted less than ten minutes, although it had taken an hour to get out of the car park.

I stalked him into the lounge. I meant to say: 'I'll take everything back tomorrow and try to be more careful in the future.'

What I said was: 'You're shagging her, aren't you?'

He thought for a moment, and chose his words carefully so that there could be no mistake. 'I'm having sex with her because I'm in love with her, June, and we're good for each other. I'm not in love with you any more because we're not.'

A gentleman would at least have come up with a few pathetic and unconvincing denials.

He made as if to leave the room, but returned to me in a fury. 'Ask yourself why I should bother to stay with you, June. Look at you. You've let yourself go. For someone who spends so much of my money on clothes, you're in a terrible state. The more time I spend with Hilary, the less I want to spend with you. Look at this house. Every square inch filled up with dolls and dogs and lamps and crap you stick on my account for the sake of shopping, just because you couldn't have a baby. I daren't turn around for fear of breaking something, all these bloody bows and ribbons hanging down.' I knew what he meant. The place was like Elton John's bedroom. 'You're frightened of leaving a blank space anywhere. They had more room to manoeuvre on board the bloody MIR space-station, for Christ's sake.' He waved his hands hopelessly at me, then at the room. 'I can't live with all this – upholstery.'

He didn't understand because we had never properly talked about the problem. For years Gordon had kept quiet and paid the bills, and I had turned a blind eye to his perambulations, but now the unspoken truce between us evaporated in a raising of war standards. Except that I couldn't fight back. I had nothing to fight with. I had never won an argument with a man in my life. All I did was provide my husband with an apparently reasonable excuse for ending a ten year marriage.

'Where are you going?'

He shook his head in disgust, slammed the door and was gone. I watched him from the lounge window, growing smaller and more feeble with each passing moment. He hopped over the low brick wall to Hilary's house like Atlas released from his burden of the world. I had never seen such a look of relief on a man's face. I had never seen him hop before.

My fingers closed around my charm bracelet, an adornment to which I took pride in adding pointlessly expensive dangly-baubles. The latest was a miniature version of the Qu'ran encrusted with 18 carat diamonds. To understand how pointless my purchase of this item is, you have to remember that I'm Church Of England.

It's not about buying expensive things, it's about wielding power. Although it's probably not as much fun if you're over a size 12, and the assistants in Gucci are as intimidating as bouncers, which, let's face it, is what they are.

Gordon came back at eleven o'clock. Clearly, he was unable to make the jump to staying out all night. We slept at opposite edges of the bed, like children who had fallen out over a board game.

The next day I went shopping again.

And that was how things continued for most of the month, while the rainy gales of a London autumn scoured the streets and slapped leaves over the car, and the house grew so cold that only our anger could startle it back to life.

Gordon stayed out, and my spending increased. But the pleasure it gave me gradually disappeared. Drug addiction would have been a healthier option; at least I'd have lost weight and got regular sex from strangers.

CHAPTER SIX
Cancelled

WHEN YOU'VE HEARD that Lady Gaga song about telephones for the fortieth time on tinny shop speakers it becomes inaudible, like the wheels of a train or aircraft engines. As the song finished, I reached the end of the floor and snapped a vacant sales assistant, who had been leaning on the counter studying the ends of her hair as if noticing them for the first time, out of her reverie.

She asked me how I would like to pay. I whipped out my Visa card and placked it onto the counter with a sound like the snap of a gynaecologist's glove coming off. The assistant rang everything up, then waited, tapping at the sides of her loose perm and staring into the middle distance in what was clearly an intermittent attack of mental aphasia. She glanced down at the till readout and winced.

'Do you have alternative credit?' she asked, returning it. 'You might want to call your bank about this one, it's probably just a fraud check.' She didn't believe it for a second, and wanted me to know that she didn't, despite the necessity of maintaining customer service policy. I knew her type. Only a tenth of her emotion showed above the surface, like an iceberg.

Insolvency was a new experience for me. I casually riffled through my purse and submitted a less scorched card, and when that didn't work, a third. In a mounting state of mortification, I went through all seven of my credit cards, but none of them registered. I was forced to explain to the assistant that she would have to put everything back.

My shopping rush climaxed and faded. I felt cold and sticky. It wasn't as though I'd been looking forward to taking everything home – that part of the process was a post-coital duty, like remaking the bed – so I mumbled some excuse about having accidentally demagnetised my strips and fled. I suddenly felt like my mother, who passed her entire life in a miasma of embarrassment.

Out on the street, I felt stripped bare. My purse yielded a handful of change, not enough for a taxi, so I was forced to use the Tube. I hated being packed in like pencils and arrived home veiled in a sheen of sweat, to sit in the kitchen staring at the spot where my crisp, calm white cardboard bags should have stood. What could have happened?

Gordon walked through the door and went straight upstairs to change, as he always did these days. I listened to the shower pattering as he washed Hilary's intimate deodorant from his loins. A few minutes later I heard him emerge from the bathroom and make a phone call. My heart was beating too fast to follow his conversation. I hovered in my usual position by the sink, randomly moving cups and plates, picking at my nails, unsure what to do next. The call went on for ages. I fancied a drink, and had lately taken to keeping vodka and orange pre-mixed in a bleach bottle under the sink, a trick I had learnt from Lou, my neighbour, but now I needed a clear head.

I've read about domestic violence, seen it often enough on the soaps, but it was never a part of our marriage, although I had once thrown a slice of wholemeal bread at Gordon. My husband specialised in injured sighs and low-volume sniping, but mostly avoided confrontation. We had barely spoken for a month. Finally the atmosphere was so bad that I wondered if he was going to come in and slap me. Gordon's family comes from the south coast; his parents are the kind of people who still tut when they see more than three black people standing together in the street, and whose exaggerated respect for money prevents them from buying anything luxurious. For them, I had brought the concept of financial embarrassment colourfully to life. The longest they ever stayed on a visit was forty-seven minutes. They couldn't understand why their son would ever give me access to his bank account.

I waited for Gordon to enter the room, but when it became clear that he wasn't going to, I forced myself to head for the lounge. He pretended I hadn't come in, but couldn't resist making huffing-noises intended for an audience. Finally he spoke without looking up. 'Well, I've finally taken care of your little problem.'

'What do you mean?' I asked timidly, dreading the answer.

'I've cancelled all your cards and reported your purse lost to the police.'

'My purse isn't lost.'

He threw the wall a look of theatrical astonishment. 'I cannot believe I was paying off seven separate accounts.'

'You weren't. I was paying some.'

'The joint M&S and your fitness card, the rest are billed to me. I've stopped the lot, all except the Connect

41

card for your personal current account, which you've hardly anything in.'

'You can't do that.'

'Can't I? I should have done it a long time ago. When my mother was younger it was still illegal to put a woman's name down on a hire purchase agreement. Now I know why. And I know why you do it, you can't help yourself, it stops you from thinking about anything important. Now you'll have to do some thinking.'

'Gordon, I'm sorry, I don't mean to do it but perhaps I'm under more stress than I realised, I mean about us –'

'You were doing this when you had no stress at all, June. God, all you have to do for a quiet life is make the bed and vacuum occasionally, buy a few bits of shopping. It's not brain surgery, is it?'

My immediate reaction was to wonder if Gordon would force me to pay my debts. All I had in my current account was what I entered by standing order every month. I had spent all my savings. I had no idea how much I owed. The thought that I was suddenly accountable was frightening because I had seen the shoes on my last little outing.

They weren't Jimmy Choos or Manolo Blahniks, just a French designer I'd never heard of. But they were the most beautiful pair of shoes in the world, pearlised stilettos, a catwalk one-off in my size. I knew I was too fat-legged for them, and had nowhere to wear them anyway. Logical thinking doesn't belong in the world of women's footwear.

The electronic shutters were already coming down in the shop window, and in the time I took to prevaricate over this podiatric pulchritude, the store shut. They weren't even expensive – although now, of course, they were far beyond my downgraded purchasing power. There aren't many perfect things created in the world, but the sight of them gave me hope for humanity. Men have as much chance of understanding the sex-appeal of impractical shoes as I have of grasping quantum physics, all that stuff about the non-binary existence of numeric multiples. Actually, I did watch some programmes about that.

I didn't want the shoes. I needed them. It was like crack. And now I would never have them. I would remain a housewife only more so, shopping at discount supermarkets and buying clothes in economy shops while my husband doled out housekeeping and openly philandered and I'd never own anything nice again, and all the lack of stress in the world wouldn't make up for being turned into a prisoner. I don't know much about prisoners, but I know they don't have lots of nice things to compensate for being incarcerated.

'Go and get me the kitchen scissors,' Gordon instructed.

He sat in front of me cutting the credit cards in half and then in quarters before dropping them in the bin with a flourish. I managed to keep one back because it was tucked in my bedside drawer. Unfortunately it was a World Of Wood discount card, due to expire in a month's time, but until then it was good for all my urgent beech flooring needs.

'I'm leaving you, June.'

'Is it because of her?'

'No, it's because of what's happened to us.'

'But we've never tried to talk about our problems.'

'There's nothing to talk about. I'm selling the house. I made an appointment with an estate agent.'

'You've already put this place on the market?' I was aghast.

'I'll be showing the first prospective buyers at six o'clock tonight. They've got a Chinese name, but you can't have everything.'

'You can't just suddenly do that. This is my home. We need to talk about it.'

'I've been thinking about it for some time, I was just looking for an opportunity to tell you.'

'I've been here. You're the one who's always working late. I can't believe you could do this.'

'I've been having money troubles. There's been a credit crunch on, or haven't you noticed? The pound's in the toilet, nobody's buying our shoes.' His defensiveness returned to anger. 'Why did I put up with this for so long? How could I have been so stupid?' He indicated the white china clowns, silver-plate candlesticks, opalescent leopards and poodles, the little glass windmills and water-wheels, the ruffled regency ladies and dandies I had made it my duty to collect and keep clean, and managed to sound hurt and betrayed. 'You are not the little girl I married.'

'No, Gordon, I'm a woman.'

'You're not, you're – I don't know what you are anymore.' He glanced distastefully around the room, as though wondering if I might possibly be a representative of the Franklin Mint, but I knew that he meant I was childless and therefore as unfinished as Schubert's eighth symphony. Hilary had a teenaged son. Her lack of depth was offset by her childbearing hips and her success as a single mother.

When you become a pilot, the hardest part is learning to trust your instruments, apparently. You have to ignore the information your senses feed you and rely solely on readings. I always imagined that being a good mother required the same ability. Hilary had put theory into practice and raised a child by herself, while I had been left behind on the ground without a flight manual. I should have used the extra free time to strengthen my personality, but I hadn't, and now it was too late; I had gone into retrograde and someone else had stepped in.

'Try fending for yourself for a while, see how you get on. You've never had a job in your life. You're going to need one now. I'm through doing everything for you, June. Do you have any idea how much you owe?' He threw the card pieces on the floor in disgust.

'No, how much?' I asked in a tiny guilt-ridden voice.

'Enough for any right-minded judge to grant us a divorce in seconds,' he snapped, unable to lay his hands on any figures. 'You'll thank me in the long run. A new perspective will do you good.'

I dropped down into an armchair and saw a world of safety and comfort roll tipsily away from me as I realised that he had been waiting for months to say this. 'But what will I do?' I asked hopelessly, ashamed by my own lack of strength.

'You should have thought of that earlier.' He scooped his car keys out of the mallard and headed toward the door.

No more credit. I felt like Samson after he'd had his hair cut off, even though I couldn't see Samson desiring French heels.

So I went to see Lou across the road.

Lou had given up on her marriage long ago, and only the dream of finding new ways to spite her husband and son kept her from cutting her own throat. She disliked her family in the same way that some people avoid feral cats; she put food down for them occasionally but generally stayed out of their way.

She also had a bad habit, but it was fitness, not shopping. Yoga, spinning, aerobics, rowing, weight-training, she had to be the best at everything and she fought all the way. Once her husband had tried to throttle her in a restaurant, and she actually fractured his wrist. I was amazed they were still together. Lou used to work at a feminist bookshop in Bloomsbury, and discovered the limits of female solidarity when she got pregnant and they changed her job description to fire her. She was my only friend, and the last person in the world you would ever go to for advice.

I went to see her because there was no-one else who would understand.

CHAPTER SEVEN
Lou

APART FROM BEING a little attention-deficit, I'm not very modern. Lou says I'm a 'Housewives' Choice' throwback, whatever that means. She's older than me, so she would know. She says I'm a living cliché, the kind of wife all those go-ahead London career girls love to sneer at. Well, now they can all laugh and say they were right; I should have stuck to what I know, then I wouldn't be in this mess.

Lou lives across the street. She smokes because it annoys her family, and has to empty out her handbag looking for her Tesco Club card at the checkout, and when other women in the queue start sighing and fidgeting she tells them to fuck off and die. Lou has a son she named Hadrian because it was the only way she could take revenge for getting pregnant and having to leave London. Everyone agrees that her husband Darren is an absolute sweetheart who dotes on her, but the gentler and kinder he is, the more she detests him. He sells office partitions and keeps showing Lou Excel spreadsheets to explain his job, not that she's remotely interested. His company motto is 'Dividing The World', and he doesn't even see that it's funny.

It's surprising Lou remains so fit, what with the chain-smoking indoors and the way she starts drinking at around eight in the morning. She leaves cigarette butts in egg yolks, toilets and beds, and was once thrown out of her local spa's flotation tank for smoking in it. She sunbathes naked in the garden because it annoys the neighbours, takes ages at tills because it annoys the staff and lights up in restaurants just to watch the look of horror on diners' faces. These days non-smokers react to cigarette smoke as if they've just been involved in a Sarin gas attack.

Lou's husband has a number of gastric disorders that require him to pick at small amounts of food all day, so she never needs to prepare food for him at night, which is just as well because the only thing she can do is scrambled eggs. She likes them because they're a food source you actually have to destroy to cook.

Her son Hadrian was expelled from school for selling grass on his mobile during lessons, and not being bright enough to come up with coded text. He's supposed to take tuition at home. He's spent the last two years locked in his bedroom online-gaming and running some incomprehensible and potentially illegal business on the internet because he finds it less embarrassing than talking to real people, so Lou is able to spend the day alone nurturing her bitterness.

She treats the fitness centre like church, repenting with leg-weights for several hours every morning, but then she comes home and sins again, hitting the drinks cabinet so hard that she's usually crocked before the evening news. She drinks with a level of vengeful chastisement that you usually only find among nuns.

Lou doesn't usually bother with people she feels sorry for, but I'm a special case. She once told me that she'd seen me through the window of her house months before we ever spoke, and wondered what the hell I was doing, because sometimes I stood frozen in the middle of our cluttered lounge staring at each of the walls in turn. Lou assumed I was watching television and had some kind of slipped disc that required me to stand upright all the time.

One day she came across the road armed with recruitment leaflets for her gym. As I answered the door and stumbled about for replies, caught off-guard, Lou realised how rarely I had spoken to strangers, and at that point made it her mission to act as my lifeline.

She told me that when she first entered the house and saw that it was cocooned with quilts, cushions, festoons, bows and tie-backs, all covered in tiny patterns intended to provide pleasure for someone much older, it was obvious to her that nothing really bad had ever happened to me in my life. There was she, carrying out acts of petty terrorism on the neighbourhood, and here was I, talking about people on television as if they were my friends. I admit it; I believe magazine articles about stranded housewives who are empowered by makeovers. I talk about cleaning products, and once crossed the road to show Lou a new fabric conditioner. I might have surrendered to my soft furnishings but the unsettling of my hands and the nervous flicker of my eyes clearly suggested a life waiting to be lived, because Lou felt she should rock the boat a little to give me a fighting chance.

'A woman at the gym told me about this game where you devise your porno movie name by taking the name of your childhood pet and joining it to the street you grew up in,' she said.

'That makes mine Tiffany York,' I said.

'Mine is Wobbles Albania – what kind of a porno name is that, for fuck's sake?' Lou sucked hard at her fag and blew smoke everywhere. She practised being a messy smoker. 'Nothing ever works for me. I should have left this shithole while I still had a chance. There's nothing to stay here for. When Darren's home he follows me around like a dog, leaving little gifts with cute messages attached. I bury them in the garden. I want a man, not a fucking spaniel. Hadrian doesn't leave his room unless I leave a message on his website saying that I'm going to disconnect the broadband. It's like having a government official in the house. He threw out all my books because he told me he wanted to live in a paper-free environment. I got my own back; I put superglue on his ethernet port and stuck a gonk over it.'

'Cicero said a house without books is like a body without a soul.'

'Yeah, but what did she know? Fucking Italians. You're too clever to be living here. You need to get out before you get permanent brain damage. I mean it. It's too late for me – save yourself.'

'I stayed because of Gordon.'

'You should try living with a man who smiles at you all the time. At least your husband behaves like any normal totally disgusting fanny-chasing creep.'

'He's having an affair with Hilary next door.'

Lou sat at her breakfast bar stirring a cocktail with the end of an apostle spoon. 'You mean Hilary 'Boarding From The Rear' Cooper?'

'That's her.'

'My God. I always wondered what kind of man she went for. Now I know; someone who's wetter than a whale's willy. Have you spoken to her about it?'

'Not exactly.'

'You should tell her she's welcome to him. It's a fatherhood issue. He wants to impregnate something before he dies. He thinks he's a king who needs an heir.'

'We once discussed adoption, but he hated the idea.'

'Of course. He wants to grow something with his face on it. The few remaining single women around here are just as bad; they'd kidnap a homeless man, fuck him and burn his body in the bathtub if they thought he had good genes. What do *you* want?'

'I don't know. I used to think I did, but now… Gordon talks about his job so much, and he obviously wants freedom, otherwise he wouldn't be seeing someone else.'

'Listen, June, you can't save your marriage once a husband starts fucking around. If you let him make up with you, he'll begin seeing her on the side and you'll be stuck at home while he's working through his second adolescence. He'll ignore you except for clean socks.' She shifted forward. 'I'm going to tell you an ugly truth. Men don't bother talking to ladies they don't want to fuck. That's why so many middle-aged women have gay friends. If you get divorced he'll declare himself bankrupt rather than pay years of maintenance. You'll have to duke it out in court.'

I'm inclined to think that Lou's drinking makes her cynical, and she'd been on Rum Sours since breakfast. The last time she did this she attempted to cut her own hair, but made such a mess of it that I was called over to repair the damage, and she ended up looking like Bette Davis in *The Anniversary*.

'There's someone coming to see the house tonight. Gordon told the estate agent that it's fully furnished and ready for occupancy.'

'Can he do that?'

'I don't see why not. He owns everything. Do you think I should go next door and talk to Hilary?'

'It's not like she stole him away from you. He's the one who wandered off. She just took what was being offered. Why do wives always blame the other woman? See if there's any ice cream in the freezer, would you?'

'I still can't believe that Gordon would –'

'He would and he did, and she wasn't the first, either.' She studied me pitilessly. 'Can't you tell? Didn't you ever notice?'

'No,' I lied, rooting in the freezer and passing her a Ben & Jerry's Very Halle Berry. She tore off the lid, prised out a lump with the end of a meat thermometer and dropped it into her drink.

'I don't suppose you did. Love is not just blind, it's very, very sick. I could see unfaithfulness in his eyes the day I met him. You've made his day, bringing it out in the open. He's one of those men who divides all women into two groups: your allies and possible shags. You married too young and he's taken the best years of your life, your good body-gravity years. Nobody with a brain gets married at nineteen, and you do have a brain, even if you seem to have stuffed it inside a needlepoint cushion. I'm making another Rum Sour, do you want one?'

'Can I have a beer?'

'Spirits would be better for you at this point. They always worked for me, even when I was pregnant. I was still chain-smoking and drinking Rum Sours when my water broke. It was great. Hadrian was born so underweight I didn't get any stretchmarks.'

'I'm not sure you're right about Gordon. He had some good qualities.'

'You're already talking about him as if he's dead. That's a good sign. Budweiser, Heineken, Tiger, Stella or Special Brew? Have the Special Brew, it must be good if tramps drink it. Name three qualities, then.'

'All right.' I thought for a moment. 'He's good with money.'

'Look where that's got you. I'm talking about physical qualities.'

'I liked the way his arms suddenly stopped being hairy just above the elbows. The way his stomach touched my back when we did spoons.' I unfocussed my eyes and thought hard. 'I'm sure there's a third thing. We've been married a long time.'

'Fantastic sex?'

'I don't think so. It was always over very quickly. I mean I've never had –'

'Orgasms, it's okay, they say it on morning TV.'

'–much chance to make comparisons.'

'Oh, sorry. I assume all women are sexually experienced. There was a year when I slept with every man under twenty-five in Nottingham who asked me. Darren's idea of warming me up in bed is to rub his hand on my crotch so hard you'd think he was sanding a door.' Lou pulled a face, opened two cans of Special Brew, chucked me one and disconsolately necked the other before returning to her rum.

'Gordon started wearing his underpants to bed once he realised that I didn't stare at his groin in awe,' I told her.

'I suppose my parents avoided killing each other for the sake of the kids,' Lou sighed. She and her brother Nick had been a disappointment to her folks. Lou had undergone an abortion at fifteen. Nick had spent his twenties in prison for manslaughter. It sounded more glamorous than it was; there had been a drunken fight in a pub over the throwing of beermats. 'The best thing you can do is to hit him where it hurts. Give in to your wildest urges and do some serious damage to his plastic.'

'He's taken away all my credit cards.'

'What about your Connect?'

'There's hardly anything left in my account. I've still got my World Of Wood discount card. I'm overdrawn by eleven thousand pounds.'

'Holy shit. Well, that does it.' She drained her glass and made a face as the nutmeg hit her. 'You're on your own. Burn the house down and we'll do a Thelma & Louise.'

'The awful thing is, I'd probably take him back.'

'You're going to make me violent if you talk like that. Haven't you got anything you can sell?'

'Everything's in his name – *everything*.'

'How did that happen? Did you learn nothing from Guy Ritchie and Madonna?'

'I'm his wife,' I explained, 'love, honour –'

'–and get everything you can lay your hands on. Expecting cashback isn't much to ask for ten years of terrible sex. Actually, you told me about the sex on the night of my thirtieth birthday.'

'I remember. We drank two bottles of Slivovitz in the garden and you were sick into our fishpond. I wish I'd never found that earring.'

'It's better than having to pretend you still love him.'

'But I do still love him.'

'Darling, he was draining his dick into the flying waitress before slipping home and pressing it into the small of your back. We can take him down.'

Lou was happy to take revenge for all the wives in the world if necessary. She cracked the cap from another beer, slid it across the counter and patted my arm comfortingly. The radio DJ began to play Love Is In The Air. 'God, this song's such shit. Love songs are all lies. There's only suffering and death in the air once a woman stops looking like she's fun. That's why you spend all your waking hours cruising malls, because you let shop-smiles replace the respect of a husband. If he ever showed you any.'

'He did. It's just... he's busy and angry all the time. I'm at home, so I don't have the kind of problems he deals with.'

'Of course you do, you just don't see them, sitting over there in your frilly little house full of frilly little things, burying yourself in books and TV shows. I'm not being rude, darling, but you've got absolutely no fucking idea about what's really going on in the world. It's changed a lot since you were locked up in the marital penitentiary.'

'I've wasted my life. Seneca said that there's nothing so ruinous to good character than idling away time at spectacles.' I always remember things I've read when I start to get drunk. 'Although I imagine he was talking about gladiatorial games rather than shopping.'

Lou started mixing a fresh cocktail. 'If you'd spent as much time on a StairMaster as you have reading, you'd be able to split walnuts in your butt-crack by now instead of quoting somebody who's been dead for fifty years. I really don't get it. You're the smartest person I ever met, you know shitloads of really long words, you could have been anything you wanted. I've seen you get a couple of drinks in you and go all lyrical and passionate, quoting Byron and shit, it's like a cloud that comes over you. You could have done something special. You could have got out. Yet you settled for this. I just don't understand.'

I stopped listening to Lou. Her words wavered past me like moths. I knew that once Gordon had made a decision there would be no negotiation with him, and that without money I would have to find a job. But I had no skills to fall back on. I didn't dare go and see my mother, because she was waiting for affirmation that I had failed to keep my marriage together. When she heard that I had lost my baby boy, she called me and said: 'If you can't give him children, you can't expect him to stay with you.' Besides, Ruth was becoming lost inside her head. She tried using the phone to change TV channels, and put catfood in the washing machine. Her mother had been a cold Englishwoman of the old school. Ruth had confused distance with privacy and would let no-one, especially me, help her.

'I don't even want to go back to the house,' I told Lou.

'Well, darling, you can't stay here. Mr. Charisma will be home in an hour, and I've got a fight booked with him.'

'I don't have the talent to hold down a real job. I'll have to work in McDonalds or something.'

'You'd be the oldest person there. They only employ easily duped children.'

'Then I'll do something part time. Something from home.'

Lou tipped the remains of the blender into her glass. 'This isn't the Victorian era, you can't sew dolls for sixpences. Besides, you haven't got a home any more, you haven't got any money and you haven't got a marriage. He's got it all, including a new sex life. What are you going to do, go back and stand in the middle of the room again?'

Alarmed, I looked at the tiny gold watch Gordon had given me as a wedding gift. 'I have to go home and cook his dinner. Just in case he comes back.' I climbed down from my stool and made my way unsteadily across the road.

'I want you to know you're being pathetic,' Lou stood in the middle of her front lawn shouting after me. 'Stand up for yourself. Give him the divorce he wants, then get yourself a good lawyer. Have a massage and a joint an hour before the hearing, lie your tits off in court, I'll coach you through it and we'll split whatever we make. If you don't, you'll just stay here with a wandering husband and no money until you end up like one of those old dears who creep around Sainsbury's with a fucking tartan wheelie-basket complaining about the price of fish, except that most of those are still happily married because they snapped up the last decent men in the sixties. I'm serious, June. You're thirty next week. It's a sign from God. This could be your last chance to get out alive. Don't fuck it up!'

But I had already closed my front door.

CHAPTER EIGHT
The Proposition

THE HOUSE HAD changed. The pastel rooms with their bright corners, as soft and decorative as patterned paper towels, now looked alien and comfortless. It was like going back to someone's house after attending their funeral.

When you're just a housewife, you end up watching too much television, and I've watched a lot: celebrity makeovers, comedy quizzes, Top 100s, reality TV, chat shows that consist of TV personalities with the depth of balloon animals. I could run a restaurant or an airline from the knowledge I've gained. Worst of all, I got addicted to documentaries. Secrets Of The Pharaohs, Killers Of The Serengeti, Unexplained Weather, Jet Engines Of The 20th Century, Hitler's Flying Saucers, The Boy Whose Skin Exploded, The World's Heaviest Teen Mother. I've watched so many pseudo-science documentaries that I feel like I've been to a third-rate university. I leave the rolling news on all afternoon. I'm sure they interview the same people every day. Woman Outside School, Fat Girl On Sofa, Man In Shop Doorway, Welsh Pensioner In Strange Hat. I see the Sky anchorman reporting from Africa and think 'horrible John Lewis shirt', because I've touched a John Lewis shirt on a man but I've never been to Africa.

The tanned BBC weather girl was wearing a navy blue jacket with gold buttons and no blouse underneath. Lou was right – even she looked like she might be fun when she wasn't pointing out incoming cold fronts. She waved an oracular claw across the British Isles to reveal a dirt-streaked whorl: wind, rain and plunging temperatures for the coming weekend. I opened a window, placed my hands over my heart and took a deep breath. It seemed hard to catch the air. The smell of frying steak sharpened the cool evening outside. Through next door's kitchen window I could see Gordon sitting at the dinner table with his back to me, enjoying someone else's cooking.

Shaking slightly, I returned to the lounge and emptied out the rubbish bin, then neatly arranged the pieces of credit cards on the table so that they looked whole once more. I don't know what I thought I was doing. The one thing on my mind was what would become of me. I only knew the house and the few streets that constituted our neighbourhood.

I could recall every inch of the view from my windows, the threadbare limes and hornbeams against low-pressure skies, the dusty box hedges, the shadows condensing with the arc of the day. Every morning, the old lady opposite would kneel on a pink rubber pad in her threadbare front garden and snip invisibly at the grass surrounding a solitary rose bush. My home, like hers, had become my fixed point on earth. As a child I had fantasised of distant travel; instead, all movement had gradually ceased until I had almost reached a full stop. I existed in a handful of routes, from the house to the shops and back again, like a chicken or a bus, or an electrical circuit for a very basic appliance.

I patiently waited for Gordon to finish his dinner, hoping that he would come and talk to me. Some awful camp comic was on television asking a woman about her most embarrassing sexual experience. He wasn't listening to a word she said, and kept repeating 'A dildo?' Mechanical laughter punctuated his lines as he greedily eyed the camera. I went to the window. In the street outside, an old man slipped on the kerb and fell over. There was no-one to help him up. I could have gone to his aid, but remained frozen on the spot. He managed to get himself onto his knees, but the contents of his grocery bag had spilled across the road.

A few minutes later, Gordon walked into the kitchen and stood at the sink surreptitiously picking his teeth. 'I can't stop,' he told me. 'I just wanted to let you know that it went very well.'

'What went well?' I asked, dreading the answer.

'The people who saw the house. A middle-aged couple, they want to make an offer. Not proper Chinese, Asians or something. I wonder if I put it on the market too low. I thought you might prefer to stay with your mother for a while.'

'I can't go all the way to Leamington Spa.' She had been living with her cantankerous sister since my father died. 'Besides, I haven't told her about us.'

'Well, it's time you did, isn't it?'

'Why can't I just stay here?'

'Well, you can...' Gordon looked doubtful. 'Only most of the furniture's going tomorrow.'

'What do you mean? Where's it going?'

'To auction. I told you, I have to act quickly. You're not the only one who's out of cash.' He made a half-hearted attempt to look apologetic. 'I have to go. Hilary's got a

stopover in Amsterdam and said I could go with her.'
He couldn't get out of the house fast enough, as excited
as a schoolboy on a date. 'I'll move the rest of my stuff
out tomorrow, and I'll leave you a couple of suitcases in
the bedroom. Don't worry about the house. I can keep
an eye on it from next door.'

'I thought perhaps we should talk about practicalities,'
I whispered.

'You mean the money. Look, I'll be fair, okay? I'll help
you out with the debt, get you into a rented flat. Don't
worry, just go to your mother's and read your books
and I'll sort it all out when I get back. You might want
to go through all your designer clothes, see what you
still need. Put the rest on one side and I'll include them
in the auction. The cash could be useful for you.'

'What else is going?'

'They'll take the furniture if we want them to. Why
don't you just leave out the things that have sentimental
value?'

'What about the things that have sentimental value
for you?'

He thought for a hasty moment. 'There's nothing I
want to keep. I'm going for a fresh start.'

He was whistling as he went out of the front door. I
had never seen him so happy, caught up in the energy of
making new plans. I wondered how we had managed to
misjudge each other to such a degree. Across the street,
I saw Lou's front door open. She emerged carrying a
Nike gym-bag with a rolled towel sticking out of it.

'Can I come with you?' I called.

'I'm well over the limit,' she warned me, throwing
open the passenger door of her silver Saab. 'If I go,
you go.'

'I just need some air.' I climbed in and unrolled the window to let the smoke out.

'Darren just came home armed with a bunch of fluorescent daisies and a box of Terry's All Gold. I have a feeling he may be after intimacy. I had to get out before I was tempted to put ground glass in his coffee. Did you reach a decision about your future?' Lou looked for a flat surface to stand her Rum Sour on and dug out her keys. At least she'd had the sense to pour her cocktail into a McDonald's shake cup.

'I guess that's up to Gordon now. I'm not going to my mother's house. She'd worm the truth out of me, and then we'd just fight.'

'You can't go on living in the house until he kicks you out. Have you no pride?' Lou started the car and lurched away from the kerb.

'I think he'll just spend his time next door. He wouldn't auction off the bed, would he?'

'So that's okay with you, is it, him flogging the furniture and moving in with the next door neighbour? You need to get away for a while, at least for the weekend.'

'How? The weather's going to be horrible and I've got no money.'

Lou flicked her cigarette end out of the window. 'Listen, there's someone I want you to meet. A girl at the pool, she works for some telecommunications firm out of town. Her name's Julie, she's off red meat, potatoes, bread and pasta because she's having an affair with Malcolm, her boss, and she doesn't want him to see her naked with the lights on until she hits target weight. They're both married. She was moaning to me about not being able to go away with him because he's paranoid about burglars. He's supposed to be in New York on business over the weekend and she wants to be with him, but he doesn't want to leave his flat unattended for some reason.'

'I'm not sure I follow you.'

'Let's see if she's there.' She crunched the gears and turned out of the street. The old man who had fallen over was sitting on a wall, trying to get his breath back. His bag had toppled over again, sending apples and peaches into the gutter.

The gym was housed on the first floor of a converted Victorian swimming baths, a grimly beautiful building banded by frescoes of cavorting maidens. Instead of repointing the graceful sworl of late-nineteenth-century plasterwork in the reception area, the council had chosen to hang sagging plastic banners for sports drinks over it. There was an expensive modern gym in Hamingwell, but Lou had been banned from there for taking a kebab into the sauna.

'Malcolm and Julie want to go away together,' explained Lou as we headed for the cafeteria, 'but the alarm system in his apartment building will be off. Malcolm wanted his wife to come up and stay there but she lives out of town and has to look after the dogs. They have this big house in the country. Malcolm's loaded, runs some kind of consultancy on the side and has always kept a city flat as a shag pad, but his wife suspected so they had to stop using it. He bought a brand-new place to fool her, but the wife found out about that too, so the only chance they've got to be together is on business trips. Julie's been on at me all week to find – hey, Julie.'

Julie was a skeleton in a leotard with the facial characteristics of a particularly bony Velasquez. The strain of having an affair obviously wasn't doing her any good. 'I've put on three pounds,' she complained without noticing that I was facing the upper end of a size twelve. 'And that's with coleslaw.'

'It's covered in mayonnaise, darling. You should try small handfuls of dried spinach on crispbread. This is June.'

I shook the offered hand. It felt like refrigerated asparagus. I wondered why nobody had told Julie she was anorexic. We had coffee, which seemed like a bad idea in Julie's case. She carefully added half a pot of soya milk while Lou and I ate doughnuts.

'June could look after your Malcolm's place for the weekend,' Lou suggested, her lips dusted with sugar. 'Water the plants, make sure nothing gets nicked.'

'Could you really?' Julie craned forward and examined me with an air of desperation. 'The flat's absolutely brand new. It's fantastic and very central, right on the south side of the river near Lambeth Bridge. All kinds of professionals are buying into the building. It's a beautiful design, some famous French architect. Jeffrey Archer's put in an offer on a penthouse.' She sipped tentatively at the coffee, but was exhausted by the effort required to lift the fat ceramic cup.

'Well, perhaps –' I began.

'Could you *really?* I don't know you from Adam, but if you're a friend of Lou's I suppose it's all right. It's just that Malcolm's –' she dropped her voice as though imparting a great secret, 'so *paranoid* about security. He owns some quite valuable paintings, horrible old watercolours. The building is having its electrics rewired this weekend so they've got to shut everything off until midnight on Sunday. Why these people can't work around the clock is beyond me. Hardly any of the other flats are occupied yet, and there's a rumour that they won't be because, well, there's the credit crisis, and the landlord is asking too much money.' Julie spoke so quickly that I had trouble understanding her. I wondered if she could get a sugar rush from Nutrasweet.

'Malcolm moved in early so that he and I could have somewhere to go. His wife wants nothing to do with the place. The paintings are in his mother's name. The mother handles the insurance premium and doesn't want the wife to get her hands on anything when they finally divorce. The wife lives in Henley and is on tranquillisers. Malcolm says they don't sleep together anymore and *she* says they're trying for another baby, so somebody's lying. Obviously I'd pay you for coming in. If we don't get away together this time, I really think it'll be over between us.'

'I'm not a hundred per cent sure,' I said uncertainly. I found the complexity of other people's relationships rather overwhelming.

'Of course you can, you said you're broke and Julie's willing to pay you,' Lou prompted, unembarrassed.

'What if I break something?' I hissed at Lou while Julie visited the toilet as a penalty for taking nourishment. 'Valuable paintings. What if I left a tap running and everything got ruined? He could sue me.'

'Oh, for God's sake, June, don't be such a wimp. What could possibly go wrong? She told me she's willing to donate her entire month's salary. He must be a fantastic shag. Think of the cash, just for flat-sitting three nights. She can easily afford it.'

But I just couldn't agree to do it. I couldn't leave my comfort zone to go and sleep in an unfamiliar bed. The thought filled me with a strange disturbance. It crossed my mind that I might be agorophobic. I felt as though I had let everyone down, my best friend, even a woman I had never met before today.

Gordon didn't come home that night. I tried to settle on my side of the bed, but my feet kept straying to the uncreased sheet beside me. Nothing was in its right place. At two o'clock a car stopped in the street and pumped bassy hip-hop against the windows. At three I abandoned the pretence of slumber and went downstairs to clean out the kitchen cupboards. Why do kitchens look so bright and bare when you turn the lights on in the middle of the night? As I jabbed at the brown figure-eights left by sauce bottles and jam jars, I called myself a pathetic useless doormat, but felt that nothing, not even this, could change me.

The next morning, innervated by a lack of sleep and vertiginous, disorienting dreams, I called Lou and asked for Julie's telephone number.

CHAPTER NINE
The Ziggurat

'MALCOLM WILL GET a bit nervous when I tell him you're staying there,' Julie warned me when we met in Starbucks on Wednesday morning.

She was dressed in a taupe designer suit that was daywear to her, anniversaries and court appearances to the housewives of Hamingwell. She had something in her cheek that rattled against her teeth as she talked. I thought it must be a gobstopper. 'He's like a wolf, he has to pee on his own territory and bare his teeth at anyone who steps across the boundary line. And he hates anyone touching his things. He was an only child. You know how they are, always have to collect things, then have to find a place to house it all.' She spat delicately into her hand and revealed a glass marble. 'It's to stop me from eating.'

A malevolent sky loomed over the town like a coming apocalypse. In the distance, four grey concrete council blocks stood guard, darkening as an iron foundry of a cloudbank settled above them. Getting away was looking more appealing by the second.

'Perhaps I shouldn't do it,' I dithered. 'I wouldn't want to upset him.' I was beginning to wish I hadn't called, but as the auctioneers had taken away most of the furniture, including our bed, there was nowhere to sleep except on the floor of the lounge in Lou's son's sleeping bag, which smelled of wasted youth and stale dope. I needed time to figure out a future for myself, and I had one long weekend in which to do it.

'No, it's fine. I'll tell him you're very responsible, but you'd better make sure everything's exactly as you found it afterwards. He's been holding back the flight tickets, threatening not to go. I was going to give this to Lou, but she's gone to a Botox party.' She produced an envelope from her bag. 'She's not trying to get rid of wrinkles, she just wants to look less annoyed. Okay, hand this to Madame Funes, the concierge, and she'll let you have the apartment key, it's just a single Yale. She won't be there when you leave, so Malcolm needs you to return it to his safety deposit box by midnight on Sunday night. It's near the flat; the address is in the letter.'

'How does that work?'

'It's like a bank deposit ATM, except that it's on a timer. You just post the envelope. You can stay until Sunday night, the power should be back on by then, and you can just pull the front door shut behind you when you leave. I don't suppose the TV or the lights will work, but there are plenty of candles, and the central heating should be on because it's gas. The fridge has already been emptied. The phone isn't connected yet and you'll find you have to go to the end of the ground floor corridor to get reception on your mobile, so it should be a peaceful, relaxing weekend.'

'I just want a place to think things through,' I assured her.

'It'll be like a retreat, but in the heart of the city. There's a very good spa nearby if you want to book yourself in for a facial.' I chose not to tell Julie that such luxuries were now beyond my pocket.

Julie pulled several squashed Post-It notes from her jacket pocket and sorted through them. She explained that she couldn't sleep at night without making lists for the next day, and that her state of hypertension was caused by consuming nothing in the past eighteen hours except a glass of lemon-juice, two Carr's water biscuits and a diet pill. She was so desperate to please Malcolm that she didn't realise how disturbing it was for other people to watch her eyes shimmering on amphetamines.

'The main thing to remember,' she said, consulting her notes, 'is to tell Madame Funes if you're going out. The keypad to the main entrance will be affected by the building works, which is why Malcolm's so reluctant to leave. He's convinced the place is being watched by every burglar in London. He'd go mad if anything went missing.'

She flicked through to another note. 'Our flight gets into Heathrow first thing on Monday morning, so he'll probably go straight to work and come by the flat in the evening.' Her mouth set itself in a lipless line. 'We're leaving first thing the day after tomorrow. That gives me three days to convince him about the divorce. I mean, if she's going around telling people they're trying for a baby, she's obviously mental. He's got a high pressure job, he can't afford to have an unstable wife.' She flicked the marble back in her mouth and rattled it against whitened teeth.

On Friday afternoon I packed the absurdly large suitcase my husband had thoughtfully left out for me, and posted my house keys back through the letter box as I left, more as gesture of independence than practicality. I stood at the end of the leaf-stickered front garden and looked up at the house in which I had spent the last ten years of my life. Bare rooms showed beyond unlit windows, just as they had on the day we'd arrived. They appeared smaller, as though they were shrinking now that life had left them, like the roots of a dying tree. Oddly, it didn't feel strange to be leaving the rest of my belongings behind. Most had been purchased in shopping blitzes, and held no meaning once the transactions had been completed.

I caught the train to Waterloo and watched the commuter towns of Kent give way to the tin-shed factory outlets of the South London suburbs. It was hard to tell where the city began, but at one point all of the green spaces I could see from the graffiti-scratched window vanished, to be replaced by angular grey streets and Victorian back-to-back houses with narrow gardens. I was entering a city I no longer knew, a jumble of disconnected office blocks and thoroughfares that no longer bore any resemblance to the city of my childhood half-memories. After this weekend I would be forced to stay with my mother in Leamington Spa until the divorce, and no matter how hard I tried, we would fight and I would be miserable. I would once more end up renting a small flat and working in a local shop, and at that grimly inevitable point my life would have turned full circle, because of an earring, because of indifference. All I had left was a brief period of transition between a reticent past and an unpromising future. I wanted something to happen.

Of course it did, and that decided my fate.

Friday morning was cold, and I knew I should have worn thicker tights. I queued to catch a taxi behind incoming passengers, tourists and business staff with laptops tucked under their arms like clipboards. The cab was a final extravagant gesture before embarking on my new frugal life, but even as I sat watching the etiolated Edwardian buildings slide by the rain-hazed window, I wondered if my husband might somehow be persuaded to come home.

I didn't understand how someone with such a thin soul could give up on me so easily unless he was forcibly bewitched. Perhaps he had never cared for me deeply in the first place, and I couldn't bear to imagine that.

The glistening cab turned off in the direction of St. Thomas's Hospital, affording me a glimpse of the London Eye's great wire wheel, its transparent capsules creeping incrementally between the buildings. The day was so dark that tourists were using camera flashes, so that each pod sparkled with sharp points of light.

Slowly shunting along the Albert Embankment between ribboned roadworks toward Lambeth Bridge, we finally entered a deserted new road that sloped away from the river. The cab came to a stop deep in the shadow of the Embankment. Above it, the sky split with a flash and rain began thundering onto the roof.

'There you go.' The driver pulled up. 'You know where you are, love?' He shouted to make himself heard.

'Not really, no,' I called back.

'You got the river in front, the railway behind you, that goes down to Queenstown Battersea and Clapham Junction, Black Prince Road on the far side, Old Paradise Street on this side and Lambeth High Street just around that corner. Tell you how I know, 'cause my old mum used to live beside the Lilian Baylis School, before that lot was all council flats. This place is brand new, used to be waste ground, bombed flat during the war. Jeffrey Archer's buying a penthouse flat, right at the top there. What a cunt.' He aimed a fat ringed finger at the roof.

I opened the taxi door and found myself faced with a splashing terrain of churned mud, bricks, waterlogged ditches and cables. 'Could you help me to the front steps?' I shouted, jamming the door open with my leg and pulling at the heavy case.

'I can't love, I did my back in watching the women's curling.' He watched from beneath his baseball cap as I struggled with the case. Rain bounced in an effervescence around my ankles as I dragged it beneath the white concrete portico of the apartment block, and stopped to look up.

Elegant chrome letters backlit with strips of azure neon read: *The Ziggurat.* Slate-edged windows finished in curvilinear mosaics rose above me. Only a few were illuminated. The wall of the building folded back on itself in an undulating shape that provided its residents with panoramic postcard-London views. The smallest apartment sat in the lowest east corner and belonged to the building's caretaker. It looked out into a dark box formed by the underside of the bridge and a mildewed stanchion of the roundabout; the views were reserved for those with purchasing power.

The paved area in front of the entrance was pitted with deep holes. Drums of yellow cable lay on their sides like giant cottonreels. Although the block was unfinished, purple and silver graffiti tags at juvenile-delinquent height had already sprouted along the white base wall. I had once seen a photograph of the City Road Police Station taken in 1900, and there was graffiti all the way along the base of the building, so it was nothing new.

In the brochure I later discovered (and presumably on the website virtual tour I didn't take) the Ziggurat was helplessly described as modern gothic. Designed by Jean-Claude Corbeau – the man himself, not one of his international teams – it boasted a steep mansard roof, but in place of a mansard's traditional attic windows were long balconies on sprung steel pivots. At the four corners stood bell turrets as grim as prison watchtowers, their peaks finished in titanium tiles to reflect the silver of the sky, lending the building a baroque, angular elegance that was described by one architectural critic as 'a hypertense anorexic's response to the Bilbao Guggenheim', presumably intended as a compliment. Although doubtless admired in the rarified circles of building academics, the Ziggurat appeared to defy the rules of *Feng Shui*; it seemed misplaced, caught uncomfortably on a dark reach of the river, forced into an angle that would benefit the residents' sight of the city but not their spiritual well-being. It was too pleased with its self-importance. I thought of Shelley's Ozymandias. What would be left of this arrogant structure in years to come? 'Look on my works, ye mighty, and despair' indeed. There's a reason why so many architects of skyscrapers are men.

I darted back to pay the cab against a timely roll of thunder. It sounded like a decelerated recording of cracking ice cubes, and shook the air.

Julie was right; the keypad wasn't working. I dragged my blue plastic valise up the steps into a wide parchment-coloured foyer containing a pair of gigantic red corduroy armchairs. The retro-future interior reminded me of the space-station in *2001*. My case left a sidewinding trail of cuprous mud slashes across the marble floor. The walls on either side were darkly mirrored, reflecting the hall in sepia infinities. A sense of intimidation overwhelmed me as the great blank space unfolded. In a city like London space is power, and only the wealthy can afford to reveal so little of themselves. I knew at once that I didn't belong in a building that smelled of fresh-sawn hardwood and laundered money.

My first task was to find the concierge's office. Cupping my hands, I peered in through tall doors and saw a small olive-skinned woman with bleached hair and bulbous eyes, shouting into a telephone. She was wedged behind a glass table and seated just around a corner, where her untidy animation would not interfere with the decor. I knocked on the window. The glass panel released a lonely twang as I opened it.

'You tell me you deliver today and you not deliver,' the woman shrieked in a manner that would cause any delivery man to tear up the receipt. Her desk was covered in penguins of different sizes. Pinned on the wall behind her were dozens of penguin postcards and several calendars featuring the formal arctic birds diving, sliding and generally falling over one another. If you make the mistake of confiding in a friend that you admire birds of any breed, you'll be given them every Christmas and birthday for the rest of your life. 'No, you no deliver. No, I say you don't.' She placed her hand over the mouthpiece and switched on an unrealistic smile. 'Can I help you?'

'Mrs. Funes?'

'Madame Funes.'

'I'm collecting keys for Malcolm Phillimore.' I dug into my purse and handed the concierge Julie's envelope.

'No, you say this but you no deliver,' Madame Funes screamed into the phone again, tearing open the letter and groping for the glasses that hung on a gold chain at her bosom. Screwing her face into a knot, she held the paper an inch from the tip of her nose and scanned it before covering the mouthpiece once more. 'You know there is no electricity this weekend from six o'clock tonight? There is hardly any people staying here because of the doorses.'

'The what?'

'The doorses! The doorses!' She waved a gold-crusted hand at the entrance.

'I know about the electricity. I'm just looking after the property for the owner.'

'Is good idea, you know, because the locks of the doorses down here is electric so they is open, and anyone, *anyone*, they can walk right in off the street. I am only going to be here since six o'clock tonight and not on the weekend. So you hand-lock the apartment on inside because anyone can walk in from outside: the rapists, the burglars, the crazy people, you know?' She wrenched out a drawer, selected the key and passed it across the desk. 'When you inside you lock yourself in because we have a man here two weeks since who kick a door in bang like this.' She made a vicious slashing gesture. 'Crazy for drugs I think, and with a knife. You will need this too for the cooker as it is electric ignition. No need to bring it back, I have many.' She handed me a plastic cigarette lighter before resuming her telephone discourse. 'YES, YOU SAY THIS BUT YOU NO DELIVER.'

I decided to vacate the office before the old lady had a heart attack, and retreated back to the hall. Dragging my suitcase to the lift, I pressed the call button and checked my watch. There were still two hours left before the rest of the electricity was due to be shut off. The apartment was on the seventh floor, one of six penthouses at the top of the building. Little natural light filtered into the corridors. Bundles of coloured wires hung from the unsecured light fittings.

The folds of the undulating corridor had been fitted with tall opaque windows, but the areas between them remained in darkness. I found myself sliding into the walls as my outstretched hand felt its way across the recessed archways to the apartments. Flicking the cigarette lighter, I searched for the number matching the taped numerals on the key. A penthouse had been constructed in each corner of the building, with two smaller apartments on the long sides between them. Malcolm's apartment was at the centre of the Ziggurat, sandwiched between the two corner penthouses on the side of the river.

The lounge I entered from the short hall was spectacular enough to freeze me in my tracks. It was a space imagined for a phantom film, boxes of glass-sided air, brushed steel panels suspended above pale oblongs of wood, three great windows opening to a balcony that overlooked a highway of chromatised water, and light everywhere even on this purblind day, the sky pushing its way in and filling my eyes with furious clouds.

Yet I had never seen a private home so devoid of personality. It clearly needed my magic touch: knick-knacks, tiebacks, dried flowers, framed photographs. There were no mantelpieces, no shelves, no flat surfaces for the arrangement of clocks and ducks. It was an idealised layout from a department store window, a theatre set for some obscure futurist entertainment, or perhaps a showflat for the world beyond. The paintings were frameless, canvases pinned back like flayed skin. They were abstracts, vast and awful, umber blocks studded with sickly turrets of yellow ochre, so ugly that they could only be worth a fortune.

Awed into removing my shoes, I made my way to the cold steel altar of the kitchen. Sabatier knives hung in decending order of lethality like razor-sharp musical notes. Everything else lived behind rolling steel shutters. It took both hands to open the refrigerator. I searched for a kettle and found an attenuated steel object that looked as though it might hold water. If Giacometti's figures were real people, this was where they would cook. The kitchen smelled faintly of the sea rather than food, and for a moment I had a fanciful image of breezes drawing the river estuary into the apartment, but then I saw the Ocean Fresh fragrance bottles plugged into the wall sockets.

A slender steel handle opened the glass walls to the balcony. Outside, atomised rain flew upwards on river winds. London lay in a globe of pale autumnal fog, the twisted, dense patchwork of the land showing through in patches of brown and olive green, stitched by the anthracite thread of roads.

I drew a deep breath and smelled the musk of Thames silt, sharpened through oxygen blooming from Embankment trees. The elements were all around, the dank wind in my hair, moisture dampening my jacket, settling in droplets on my upturned cheek. I wanted to scrub my face clean of makeup and let the passing cloudbank touch my skin. I felt like an angel looking down on the private world of the city, listening to its whispered secrets. Having arrived in a place I could not imagine, I suddenly felt like crying. The rain drifted and swirled. Sometimes the lattice of rainbow-drops rose on rogue air currents, to be flicked down again like turning schools of fish.

A decade of marriage had come to an end. In that time, what had happened in the world beyond the front garden? Celebrities and politicians had fallen from grace, riots and lifestyle revolutions had fleetingly seized the public mood, fads and follies had thrived in the lifespans of midges, failed social experiments had demanded my attention in the bitter, recriminatory pages of the tabloids. Carved into digestible two-minute slots, wars, train wrecks, floods, plagues and assassinations had flashed past me on the evening news with the vacuity of quiz show scores. The last ten years had been a firework display viewed from a safe distance. Since my marriage began, I could not recall coming to London for any reason other than to shop. Now I began to wonder how any person could have remained so disconnected from the world.

Shivering, I backed inside to explore my new surroundings, like a cat left with friends for the holidays.

The rest of the penthouse had more character. A bathroom of sun-faded Cambodian stone. A carved Thai buddha with a fat red candle melted into its lap. An undulating glass shower I could walk into without having to open a door. A textured slate floor that darkened with the first spatter from the great copper showerhead. The steaming water cascaded over my shoulders, reddening skin, scalding away the misery of the last few days. Toiletries, understated and expensive, stood in a pumice recess. I eased a snake of foam from a tube and smeared it across my fat breasts, my pale pudgy stomach, feeling the skin soften beneath my fingers. The urge to cry was stronger than ever. I saw my body twisting in the glass wall of the shower, a distant pale figure, a woman I had never seen before. *I shouldn't be here. I can't recognise myself in these surroundings.*

Heavy white towels as thick as duvets, matching bathrobes, underfloor heating, lights that faded up by the pressure of my fingertips. If the kitchen was clinical, the bathroom was decadent. No wonder Malcolm's mistress was so anxious to pin him down to a divorce. I pulled on one of the robes and raised its hood, drifting through the bare white rooms, hugging myself with excitement. It was impossible not to feel like an interloper. I did not have the right credentials to be allowed in here.

I checked the time again. In an hour and ten minutes the electricity would be cut. The implications were worrying and a little exciting. Searching the rooms, anxious to make the most of the time, I found a flat-screen plasma television recessed into a beech-panelled bedroom wall, unclipped the remote and flicked through dozens of channels. Aircraft and dolphins performed silver somersaults through the phosphorescence reflected across the windows. I surfed for American sitcoms, which I enjoyed because you never learned anything real about the characters. My heart rate decelerated to the drifting pace of my dreams. I slept in a way I had not slept for months, years.

When I awoke, I found myself in darkness.

The television screen was inert. I tried the lights. Nothing. My wristwatch read 6:25pm. The lights from the street were reflected upwards by the river, rippling across the ceiling in languid arabesques, the apartment acting in balance to the entropy of the world below.

I rose and pulled the robe tight. The air was coolbox fresh as I carefully made my way across the lounge. Six fat church candles stood on inchoate earthenware plates. Not realising that they were intended for display purposes, I lit each one in turn, illuminating my borrowed palace with wavering ellipses of light.

The refrigerator bulb failed to come on when I opened the door, but a roll of trapped chill air still brushed my bare flesh. Someone had left the clingfilm-wrapped ingredients for a cold meal in the crisper. I made myself a sandwich, bitter rye bread stuffed with ham, lettuce and mayonnaise, something I would never have prepared at home. There I would grill cheese on Mother's Pride and pour microwaved beans over it. To do so here would have been a sacrilegious act. I ate perched on a tall stool at the chromed breakfast bar, chewing oiled scraps of sun-dried tomato, savouring the flavours, then dipping into jars I had seen in food halls but never tried before.

I carefully wiped my hands before examining the ceiling-high bookcases by candlelight, working my way along the co-ordinated spines. Medical encyclopediae, volumes on skin and eyes and ears, books about burns with colour plates I didn't dare to examine. It made me wonder about the exact nature of Malcolm's consultancy. Could he be some kind of medical practitioner? Julia had failed to divulge his role outside of the company. If he was a specialist with a private practice it might explain how he managed to afford such luxury. But I thought they worked in electronic communications. Surely such diverse careers had no overlap.

I was standing in the hall, examining another excruciatingly ugly painting by the light of a candle when I heard a noise in the corridor beyond the apartment. It sounded like someone hitting the floor with the heel of a shoe.

I'm not the kind of person to investigate strange noises in dark buildings, but this one was so odd that I did it without thinking.

Of course, I shouldn't have.

CHAPTER TEN
Pasiphae

PEERING INTO THE dimness of the top floor corridor, I became aware of a tall man in a Nike T-shirt and flappy jogging shorts standing against the distant wall, and my heart-rhythm faltered. The figure remained still with his arm raised as I approached.

'I thought I heard someone outside,' I offered nervously. 'Were you banging?'

He lowered his shoe and flicked hair from his forehead. I couldn't help noticing that the pupils of his protuberant eyes diverged disconcertingly. 'I should hope so. We've got cockroaches. Bloody great brown things like they have in America. I just chased one the size of a small cat out into the hall. They must come up from the river at high tide. I thought I'd hit it, but if they're strong enough to breed after a nuclear blast I suppose they can survive a rubberised heel.'

He dropped the shoe and wriggled a bony foot back into it. 'So I'm not the only one still here. I haven't seen you before. Hang on a minute.' He produced a plastic pocket torch and shone it right in my eyes. When I waved the beam aside he ran it over my body, then flicked it to the floor.

'I suppose you know there's no power on for the next fifty-four hours. I haven't seen him lately. Is he away?'

'Who?

'The guy who lives here.'

'I'm looking after the place for the owner, just over the weekend,' I explained.

'Ah. I suppose he's off on business. They always are.'

'I'm sorry?'

'The so-called residents of this block. Our gallant captains of industry. I'm next door to you, corner penthouse of this concrete Shangri-La. North-westerly view. Not exactly Turner's vision of the river, but north-easterly had already gone. They sold most of these apartments off-plan in Singapore. Absentee owners, all of them.' He offered a long hand, with fingers that wrapped around mine like crab legs. 'My name's Dr. Elliot, by the way.'

'June.' His palm was unpleasantly moist. I could imagine his testicles sticking to his legs.

'Do you need any light?'

'I think I'll be getting through the candles rather quickly.'

'I've got a good alternative. Follow me. It's alright, I don't bite until you know me, ha ha.'

I realised I was trusting him because his voice was cultured and confident. That's the class system in a nutshell. The BBC might have Indian newsreaders now but they make damned sure they sound like Old Etonians. Dr. Elliot held open the door for me. 'Hurricane lamps,' he suggested. 'I went out and purchased a job lot from some peculiar Turkish shop in Kennington Road. They're only pressed tin but they add a touch of gothic atmosphere.'

'I wouldn't have thought this building needed any more.'

'Extraordinary, isn't it? A veritable palace of bad dreams. Makes you wonder what the architect was thinking. A Frenchman, apparently. It's their uncompromising nature that makes them so artistically adroit. And so fucking rude. He must have had a very strange idea of London in his head.'

He led the way into the darkened lounge, stopping to light a pair of the tin lamps on a sideboard. Weak light burnished maroon walls, picking up the glister of expensive gilt frames. He turned and smiled, a stern thin face framed by endearingly slept-on hair, but the eyes were bothersome because I couldn't tell where he was looking. 'At least the water's gas-heated. I hope you were given adequate warning about the electricity. You'll be undressing in the dark.'

'I'm not sure I would have come if I'd realised it would be this dark.' I followed Elliot around the room as he lit the lamps. His apartment was squarer and taller, with windows on two sides, the walls painted in deep crimsons and browns, lined with paperbacks. A gallery led to a sloping ceiling, planked like the inverted deck of a ship. I stopped before the riverside windows to check the view from a different perspective. From here, London seemed veiled in steel grey mesh. Beside the curtains, what I'd thought was a lifesized statue was revealed to be a full-sized cutaway model of the human body, its skull sectioned to expose a quarter of pink plastic brain, one bulbous eye in its socket, a bright crimson rubber heart, blue-grey lungs, maroon liver and coiled intestine the colour of a flamingo.

'Oh, that's Maurice. He's a bit startling, isn't he? 1930s. He came from a medical training college. I've grown rather attached to him.'

'You're a doctor?'

'God, no. I'm not interested in the plumbing side of things. Psychiatric research. Motivational stuff for corporate staff training. Physical and psychological effects of sudden life-change. I organise behavioural experiments on patients, poorly paid volunteers mostly, mess about with their preconditioning, change their diets and stress levels, try to work out what triggers their responses, generally fuck them about until they beg to thank me. What do you do?'

'Oh, I'm nobody at all,' I replied without thinking. No-one had ever asked what I did. Elliot confirmed my assumption that only high-powered businessmen would live in a building of such peculiarly masculine design. Women would always be less visible here.

'Come now. I rarely find that's true in my line of work. Everyone's somebody, even if they don't know it.'

'All right. I'm a housewife.'

'Is that all? I don't think I know anyone who's just a housewife. It's such a fifties word, so redolent of aprons and baking. Won't you be uncomfortable here? It's very dark. We might as well be cut off in some ghastly remote part of the country.'

There was something arrogant and suggestive in his manner that irritated me. 'I've got a friend coming over later,' I lied. 'Anyway, civilisation's just outside.'

'Do you really think so? I look out and see chimps in vans shouting at cyclists, no-one you could actually rely on. Collectively, human beings have the morality of germs.'

'I'll be fine when my friend gets here.'

'The outside buzzer's not working and the main entrance door is open. You'd better tell him to come up the stairs, and sing so as not to frighten you.'

'I won't be frightened, don't worry.'

'That is... if it's a man.' His distracting eyes reflected light like some nocturnal animal. He was studying me too intently, a hazard of his job, perhaps. 'What made you agree to stay here, I wonder?'

'The money,' I answered honestly, sensing he knew when I lied. 'A friend of the owner offered to pay me if I stayed until Monday morning.'

'So you're like one of my paid volunteers. Is this a service you provide regularly?'

'No. I'm just helping someone out.'

'If you were that much of a friend you wouldn't be taking his money, would you? Or perhaps the exchange of cash eases the social transaction for you both.' He joined me at the window, standing too close. 'Of course, I knew you weren't like the rest of them as soon as I saw you.'

'In what way?'

'My dear lady, they're the vanished rich, the overseas professionals. The kind you usually find taking leases in Hampstead and Holland Park. I've only met three other people here: a Swiss banker, a Russian electronic surveillance expert and a plastic surgeon of indeterminate and dubious origin. They're somewhat overcautious about their privacy. Not terribly interested in other people. They like to bring ladies here for a few hours, then let them out to find their way home. You could hammer on their doors screaming blue murder and they wouldn't open. Not that many apartments are occupied. The owner is asking far too much for them. Rumour has it Jeffrey Archer is buying the last remaining penthouse.'

'So I heard.'

'It has a view of the Houses of Parliament. Why would anyone want to be constantly reminded of something they can't have? Now there's a case study I'd love to conduct.'

'How did you end up here?'

'I see too much of people's emotions at work. I need a place to relax and think.'

'You could live in the country.' As he dropped onto the sofa and folded his legs, I saw that he was wearing see-through socks, pulled up too high. Not a good look.

'Oh, my practice is in town, and the building fits my needs.' He stretched out a hairy white wrist and tapped the back of the seat, as though beckoning a cat. I remained standing. 'Besides, it's rather interesting as a social experiment. I'm waiting for it all to break down, you see. That's when the real discoveries are made, when organisation collapses into chaos. Until recent times the streets around us were filled with the grandchildren of earlier residents. They shared a complex social history that informed every stage of their behaviour and allowed even the most inarticulate householder to communicate relatively sophisticated ideas. It's all gone now, of course. The homes have been tarted up into ersatz hotel suites filled with multicultural moneychurners who share no common social skills whatsoever. It's a giant leap back into a dark age, psychologically speaking. Yet there are compensations.'

'It's more cosmopolitan,' I suggested, 'more varied.'

'Yes, uneducated people always say that. It's a poor substitute for sophistication. In my opinion –'

'My friend,' I interrupted lamely, 'he might be waiting for me.'

He clapped his hands with unnerving suddenness. 'Then I mustn't keep you, must I?' He jumped up and guided me from the room. I felt relieved to be leaving, but he stopped in the doorway and turned back to me, his face so close that I could taste his breath. 'Just how well do you know the owner?'

'Not very well.'

'By which I take it you mean not at all.'

With so little experience of tangential conversation, I was unsure how to reply.

'No, I thought not. Well, of course it's your business, or rather *his* business. God knows there's enough corruption in the world without worrying about the moral grey areas of our fellow residents. Luckily for me there are no absolutes, or I'd be out of a job. And as you're just a housewife, I don't imagine many moral dilemmas present themselves.'

'I'm sorry, I have no idea what you're talking about.'

'Your friend. The owner of the apartment in which you are staying. A bit of a villain, by all accounts.' Elliot looked pleased at the idea. 'He's had a few seedy-looking visitors up here. Of course, I don't count you in that number. Here, you should take one of these with you.' He handed me one of the hurricane lamps and rested his hand lightly in the small of my back, the supercilious ushering of a doctor seeing off a disregarded patient. 'You can bring it back when the electricity returns. Now you'd better go, or I'll want to keep you here all night.'

I turned in the doorway and studied him. 'Can I ask you something about Maurice?'

Elliot glanced back at the dummy. 'Him?'

'Yes, do you hold conversations with him?'

'No, of course not. What an extraordinary thing to ask.'

'I know I would. He and I would become great friends. I used to talk to the television. You know, soap characters.'

'I fail to see the point of holding such a one-way discourse.'

'You should try it some time.' *Brush up on your conversation skills,* I thought. *It might stop you from sounding so condescending.*

That was it, my first foray into casual conversation with a total stranger. Hardly a great success. Elliot closed the door before I'd managed to find my way back to the apartment, as though he had quickly decided that I was unattractive and not worth flirting with. Unsettled by the encounter, I returned to Malcolm's flat holding the lantern high so that I could check the stark rooms.

The reflection from the river's palisade of floodlit buildings had robbed the paintings of their corrosive colour. I looked in the bedroom cupboards and found plain grey suits and white shirts, as neatly arranged as shop displays. Clearly, Julie didn't risk leaving any of her clothes here. A single pair of women's shoes, cheap and damaged, lay in the bottom of a cupboard, the only proof of deception. His wife's home would be more warmly decorated. It was where he lived. This was just for sex, any woman coming here could see that. It was why the wife avoided the place; she wouldn't want to be confronted with such obvious evidence.

I pulled back the glass doors and stepped out onto the balcony. The scene below drew attention in a way that the view outside our house in Hamingwell never had. In the far corner to the left, I could see into Elliot's penthouse. Even though the rooms were dark it was possible to discern the psychiatrist standing in his window, as motionless as his medical dummy.

I fancied a drink, but the only tonic I could find was flat, so I tipped fruit juice onto what I hoped was decanted gin, and stood proprietorially behind the bar at the rear of the lounge, sipping slowly. The room was stuffy, and the temperature control panel was not apparent in the gloom. Checking my purse I found a twenty pound note squashed into the corner, together with a few small coins. It would buy me drinks somewhere locally, but not much else. I studied the paintings by lamplight. They didn't look especially valuable, but I had only ever seen paintings in books. Seating myself beneath the largest canvas, I drank and allowed my mind to drift.

Gordon with Hilary. Lou with Darren. Malcolm with Julie. Everyone else seemed to be involved in a complicated relationship. For me there had only been Gordon. Now he had gone, and I was alone. I had hoped for a sense of elation, but felt tired and unsure of myself. Stretched out on an umber couch in the lounge, I watched the creamy flames poised in glowing wax like a line of torch-bearing monks, and tried to summon a sense of independence, but there was nothing.

The room grew warmer. No street sounds reached my ears. Up here there was only the soughing of the storm-sky. Cocooned in the huge robe, my eyelids grew heavy.

My dreams were uneasy, dislocated. First I was in Hamingwell, tree-surrounded, then looking down on a yellow room stripped bare of furnishings, bright wavering light, someone crouching naked in a corner, plangently suffering. I could sense cruel treatment of a sexual nature, the figure being painfully penetrated for the pleasure of others, and thought of a ruptured Pasiphae wilfully damaged by her beast. Before this hunched child walked a dark creature with blank eyes, rattling something rhythmically in a large steel pot. It held a ladle, clicking against the metal rim, back and forth, back and forth, the sound of a clock, or pipes quickly heating.

When I awoke and looked at my watch it was a quarter past ten, and I could still hear the clicking noise. It wasn't in my head, it was real.

CHAPTER ELEVEN
Choke

THE CANDLE CENTRED a shifting golden sphere, raising walls where there were none. The edges of the light led me to the second bedroom, where a salvaged wooden arch stood above a floor-length mirror. I studied my spectral reflection, rather pleased with it. Robed in white, candle raised, the heroine of a Victorian Gothic novel was distorted in dark machine-rolled glass.

A cool draught stippled my skin. One of the glass doors to the balcony stood ajar. I couldn't remember if I had left it like that. I wanted to close it, but was compelled to step outside.

The breeze from the river was sharper now, sour with decay. It was lighter outside than in. I looked to my right, across to the east corner balcony, nervously scanning the pastel darkness, and flinched when a torch-beam scanned the windows. Someone was in the third riverside penthouse, the one Jeffrey Archer was supposedly buying. I set the candle out of the wind and looked harder. The last apartment was set at a steeper angle than Elliot's, affording me a dim view of its interior. Its balcony door was open, a thin beam of light bouncing across the walls. I couldn't tell if the girl on the balcony was looking in my direction, but she was standing as stiffly as Elliot's mannequin, her hands raised to her throat, long black hair fluttering like flags at her arched back.

A low wave of air attacked my candle and snuffed it out. When I glanced back, the girl was outlined against the pale night like a statue, a memorial to some kind of household divinity, affixed to the building in spiritual appeasement. I could tell she was young by her slender waist, small raised breasts and flat stomach. She could have been a dancer, a model. She lifted her hands high above her tilted head, her fingers spread wide and reaching, as if waiting to be carried up into the night air. High above her, electricity flared within the clouds, like a faulty connection in heaven. For a moment I actually thought she had caused it.

Jewellery sheened the girl's long neck. The urgent whisper escaping from her throat carried on the thermals trapped between the apartments. I stepped closer to the edge of the balcony and tried to see what was happening. The crazed geometry of the Ziggurat stood against the never-night of the London sky. An unscalable drop fell to the riverside road, seven floors below. When I looked up again she had disappeared. Inside the apartment, the torchlight started to recede. I left the balcony, puzzled.

Although my own front door was closed I could hear it shifting slightly back and forth in the jamb, making a ticking sound. Freed from the grip of electricity, the latchbolt had slipped from the strike plate. Against the beating of my heart, I peered outside into the hall.

Faint luminescence pulsed where there had been none before. In the centre of the floor stood a fat black candle, obscenely leaking grease as a question mark formed around its base. Shoe prints, fresh and wet, led across the grey cord carpet tiles into the corridor from the stairs.

Then I saw them.

Beside the door of the next apartment, outlined against a panel of night sky, the torch-bearer had the girl propped against the wall with her head bowed, and had his hand locked around her throat. The girl's face was obscured by glossy black hair that fell as straight as pencils to her shoulders. The man standing before her was square-set and shaven-headed. A stitched scar ran across his crown like the join on a baseball, so deep and poorly attended that the plates had knitted badly, so that his head appeared to have been assembled from skulls of two different sizes.

The girl was barefoot and bare-breasted except for a diamond necklace, dressed only in pale baggy jeans. She fell forward, to be propped upright by her companion. She made a vague, hopeless grab at the arms of the stitch-headed man and sank drunkenly down the wall, doubling over with a high cry of frustration, or possibly laughter.

I took a pace back in alarm when she suddenly thrust out her arms toward me. The stitch-headed man turned in my direction, his features lost in darkness. His still eyes stared, daring a response.

I didn't wait to find out what he was doing, or what was going on between him and the girl. It was best not to know. In the suburbs you don't talk to your neighbours even if they're being murdered. Be it black mass, buggery or bestiality, the general opinion is that it's best to leave them enjoying themselves so long as everyone's over eighteen. The black candle suggested something more frightening than witchcraft, possibly that they were

Heavy Metal Goths. Slamming the door and running back to the bedroom, I scrabbled for matches and relit the candle, then tore open the zip of my case for jeans, a sweater, a jacket. Unable to lay hands on my trainers, I was forced into heeled shopping shoes, all the while thinking *murderers, perverts, I should never have come here*. I wondered if she was a willing participant in the kind of masochistic sex games you usually read about in the family newspapers.

Remembering my mobile, I ran back to the kitchen, found it, checked the reception meter and saw there were no bars available. End of the ground floor corridor, that was the only place you could get reception.

I realised there was someone in the apartment with me when I heard the rhythmic sound again. It was louder than before, the ticking of a cheap alarm clock, the repetition of tines on tin. And beneath it a secondary effect, a soft shuffling, like tissue paper being slowly opened.

The front door had been opened and shut, and was shifting back and forth more noisily than ever. Using the stub of candle to relight the lantern, I walked toward the sound. My feet were numb on the cold floor. Space expanded ahead, folding outward into the rooms as I raised the light. I stopped in the doorway to the guest room and shifted the lantern forward.

She was standing behind the door.

She dropped her arms over my head and I screamed, releasing the lantern. The cheap glass didn't break but oil splashed in a spray of tiny comets, setting the bed quilt alight.

I twisted in her tightening embrace, so that her stomach was against my back, and tried to tip her over, but she proved too strong. Throwing back my head I bumped against her nose and heard her yell, then bit down hard on a sweat-sour wrist. The girl pulled up her hands and I shoved as hard as I could, forcing her against the wall. I held little hope of stopping her, and yet she fell away.

Grabbing the end of the bedspread I flicked it over on itself, so that the burning patches were smothered. One crackling chunk of material floated and brushed against the wardrobe in a shower of autumn sparks. Acrid smoke hazed the air. The girl had frog-dropped to the floor and closed herself into a foetal position at the base of the wall.

I set the candle on the floor and tried to get a clear look, but she twisted from the light. Her lank black hair curtained her eyes. As my fear subsided, I heard her crying. I waited for her to look up, flinching in anticipation of some terrible sight, but her face was magazine-beautiful. She was perhaps eighteen, with empty blue eyes and the angled jawline of a photographer's model. I recognised her cheap cotton jeans from a recent sale at Uniqlo in Regent Street. The necklace was from Tiffany; I remember I'd seen it on their website and had stared at it unblinking for so long that I'd felt my eyeballs dry up.

She was trying to speak but her voice was undecipherable, a spatula-on-burnt-pan rasp that I assumed was the result of her companion trying to strangle her. But now I saw that there was a white plastic tag pulled tight around her neck, causing her veins to bulge. Her wrists were also connected by a tag, so that she looked like a product that had been delivered to an address and dumped on the floor in the owner's absence.

She tried to speak again. It sounded like; 'I need to get –'

I tried to pull the neck tag apart, but she flinched and twisted when I touched her, an eel writhing on a hook. I had no idea what to do. The look of fear on her face panicked me even more. Another flinch, more violent this time. Her legs kicked out hard as her muscles bunched. Should I go and fetch the creepy, condescending Dr. Elliot, or would that be worse?

Running and sliding to the kitchen I pulled open drawers, searching for a knife, then remembered I had seen a pair of heavy spatchcock scissors, designed for cutting chickens apart. I grabbed them and returned to the bedroom where she was lying on her back, muttering and moaning.

I tried to work the tip of the scissors under the neck tag, but as soon as I did so I cut her skin. Blood spurted out over my hands, and she gasped out.

'I'm really sorry,' I said, 'but I have to get this off.' Gritting my teeth, I pushed the scissors into another spot and more blood welled up. The tag had been pulled too tight. I knew she would die if I didn't keep going. Apologising over and over, I dug the scissor tip in again. She screamed. I kept going until it was right underneath the ratcheted plastic. But now I couldn't get the leverage I needed to close the scissors. The tip wasn't far enough in. I pushed as hard as I dared, but wondered what was killing her now, my scissors or the tag.

With one last shove I shut the scissors, but the tag wouldn't break. I let go in horror – she was writhing about with the scissors stuck to her neck, the situation made worse by my own stupid actions.

There were odd, barely healed scars on the backs of

her hands. I pulled the scissors out and was able to snip her wrists apart. Suddenly she coughed blood right into my face. I dragged her to the balcony doors. She had almost no body fat, and weighed nothing. Her body was cadaver-white and muscular. She still clutched feebly at her throat and the side of her head, but was unable to move by herself. Behind me, the light from the tipped-over lantern fanned and died to a faint blue pulse.

Perhaps I had stretched the tag just enough to let her breathe; I couldn't see because it was buried in her neck, covered in thick dark blood. I ran and brought her a beaker of water, blundering and spilling most of it in the darkened flat. She winced and allowed the water to overflow her mouth.

'I have to go for help,' I said. She fell back, and now I saw that something else was wrong.

Moving the lantern closer, I was finally able to see the side of her head. A bleeding lump rose at the base of her right ear, up toward the occipital outcrop of her skull. I had seen something similar on When Operations Go Wrong. A blood vessel had burst in her right eye. She'd been hit hard. I needed to get her into the light, so I slipped my hands under her armpits and pulled. The stinging reek of the burned coverlet made my eyes water. I lowered her against the wall and pulled the scorched duvet from the bed, wrapping the unburned part around her shivering body.

I wondered if the psychiatrist next door had any useful medical knowledge. I knew I should at least bring him here, but really didn't want to involve him if I could avoid it. I needed to think and lay down beside her, less a gesture of solidarity than an inability to act decisively. Shoving the spatchcock shears into the rear pocket of my jeans, I put my head back, listening as our respiration matched and phased.

Then it seemed that only one of us was breathing.

I had seen on television how you blow into someone's mouth and hammer on their chest but I couldn't. There wasn't any point – no air could get past the plastic tag. I could feel nothing coming from her nose or mouth. I should never have faffed around for so long. I had acted too late.

CHAPTER TWELVE
Help

WHEN I OPENED the front door again I made damn sure that the stitch-headed man had gone. Only the black candle remained, guttering in the sudden draught. My inability to help the girl was upsetting, but I have no history of being useful to strangers.

I failed to find the battery torch in the lounge, and left the lantern behind because it seemed wrong to leave the body in darkness. When I tried to unglue the black candle the wick was extinguished in splashed wax, and as the spirit of the flame departed I found myself stranded with the front door closing behind me, a truly blind panic tamping down my senses.

The bell on the lintel of Dr. Elliot's door failed to work without electricity. I slapped my hand against the wood but there was no answer. *He's out,* I thought, *he's asleep, he's refusing to help me, just like the others he told me about.* I pressed my ear on the cool maple grain and listened. Nothing. Perhaps I had only seen his dummy at the window. What kind of man kept a dissected corpse on display in his lounge? These people weren't my kind, I didn't understand them or want to be like them. The backs of my arms were sweating ice. How much time had passed since I discovered the girl:

seconds, minutes, half an hour? The absence of light seemed to rob me of other senses.

Knowing that there was nothing to be achieved by staying in the building I ran on to the stairwell, clinging to the balustrade. I needed light and space, and outside air. The London streets suddenly seemed a place of greater safety. I ran across the darkened lobby and slammed into the glass doors, banging them wide, down the steps and across the quagmire of the quadrangle to the hissing roads beyond, then struck out in the direction of the Embankment road.

Not a soul on the street, a dead stretch of riverside too bare and rainswept for anyone to be walking at night, only a distant garage and the black towers of Lambeth Palace framed in dying oaks. A boarded-up shop, a closed pub, steel shutters, some kind of warehouse, a graffiti-scabbed wall. The odd thin birds I thought I had seen hanging in the branches of a blasted plane tree turned out to be a pair of swaying yellowed condoms. Nothing was what it seemed.

A stream of cars at the roundabout, their windows closed tight, headlights on, drivers staring through their screens as if watching movies, a few people walking with lowered heads across Lambeth Bridge, one man in a luminous silver slicker. I thought he looked young enough to be a policeman, and broke into a run, my shoulder-bag bouncing against my side.

I hadn't meant to hit the man so hard in the stomach; the pavement was slick and I found myself unable to stop. I knocked the breath from him, jack-knifing him to the kerb. I told him I thought he was a policeman.

'That's what you do to policemen, is it?' He spat in the gutter and stood upright, clutching himself. A student in his early twenties, he had dropped a plastic-covered file of sheet music into the road. I helped him gather up the pages, but had heard him speak and knew he wouldn't help. He was the kind who didn't get involved, the kind who lived in Hamingwell.

'I need to find one. Someone's just been assaulted in my building.'

'I'm sorry.' Seconds ago I had knocked him over and here he was apologising.

'You don't understand.'

'I'm not a policeman. I can't do anything.'

'I really need some help.'

'And I'm really sorry,' he replied, as if it was unthinkable to help someone. 'You're covered in blood.'

He skirted carefully around me and continued across the bridge with his head down. I spotted an onion-shaped man on the other side of the road carrying a length of timber wrapped in white plastic Tesco bags. The clothes he wore couldn't have cost more than thirty pounds in total, including shoes. My habit of costing out the wardrobe of passers-by had been ingrained by years of semi-professional browsing. Accent and clothes, my only tools to judge a man; pitiful really.

'Please, could you help me? I need to find a policeman.'

'Sorry, darling, I've got problems of my own.'

'I'm in trouble.'

He looked puzzled for a moment, scratching the back of his neck until realisation dawned. 'It's a bit early in the evening, isn't it?'

'For what?'

He gave me a knowing look. 'You after business? You've got paint or something all over you.'

It took me a moment to realise what he meant. 'I'm not a *prostitute*.'

'There's no shame in it, love. It's like Toys-R-Us.'

'I'm sorry?'

'Working at Toys-R-Us. You know, a profession.'

'But I'm not. There's a young woman in my apartment building, and she's been injured. This isn't paint, it's blood. There's not supposed to be anyone else there, and now she might even be dead.' *You sound hysterical,* I thought. *Even I wouldn't trust you.*

'You want to try calling the police, love. Ain't you got no mobile?'

Thoughts flashed forward. If I called the police they would come to the block and demand to know the identity of the owner. They'd get in touch with Malcolm. He'd complain to Julie, who was already on a knife-edge, and I would be screwed. Which meant, part of me thought selfishly, I would not get paid. I needed the new start and I needed the money.

'It would only take a few minutes. Please, I don't want to go back there by myself.'

'You know what happens to blokes who have a go? Some old dear in East Street got stabbed to death for her phone last week. Seventy-something. What's the point of surviving wars to get murdered by a schoolkid? You had a fight with your boyfriend?'

'No, I have a husband. *Had* a husband. I think there was an intruder. But he may have gone. The main doors aren't shutting because the power's off.' *He can't understand,* I realised, *because I'm not making any sense.*

'I'm sorry, sweetheart. I'm due up the Welsh Centre on Gray's Inn Road in half an hour, I'm lowering their ceilings with plasterboard. I can't afford to get my head kicked in when there's a job on, I've got kids.'

I stood and watched him go, willing him to feel guilty. I'd never noticed how annoying it was to be called Sweetheart before.

The bridge led back toward the Ziggurat. The great white building was softened by the murk from the river. Rain advanced in mizzling clouds, haloing the Embankment lights and hiding the tops of buildings. In a moment like this, London reconnected to the past. I felt like the latest in a long line of distracted victims who had crossed the bridge looking for help. I had absolutely no idea what to do.

CHAPTER THIRTEEN
The Boy

THE GREEN LIGHT on my mobile returned at the centre of the bridge. I called the emergency services, something I hadn't done since my mother's pressure cooker blew up. Punched 112, selected Ambulance, and got 'You are held in a queue…' Friday night in South London. The recorded message only lasted a few seconds, and I was unprepared for the questions that followed, stumbling on the circumstantial detail.

'Are you a relation?' asked the controller, assessing the urgency of my request as he waited for the nearest callout, St. Thomas's, to answer.

'No, I've never seen her before.'

'But you say she's in your flat.'

'It's not mine. It belongs to a friend.'

'Does your friend know her?

'I don't know, he's not in the country. Can you just get someone here?'

'Is she unconscious?'

'I think she might be dead. She has a thing round her throat.'

'What kind of thing?'

'One of those plastic tags they use to do up packages. I tried to get it off but couldn't. And she's received a blow to the head.'

'Sorry, love – which is it?'

'It's both. I think she choked first.'

'She's been attacked then? You notified the police? Someone tried to strangle her?'

'Yes, and then she fell on me.'

'So she was up on her feet after she was strangled?'

'Yes, and her hands were tied.'

'Hang on, love, you're losing me. Do you know the victim's name?'

'No, she's a total stranger.'

The operator was clearly used to untangling confused stories, and calmly promised help as soon as possible. I didn't trust the ambulance to turn up, so next I called the police. This time I tried to sound more organised in my thinking, and got the promise of a constable, but it sounded as if they were very busy and weren't too likely to send someone just yet.

Looking along the bleak edge of the bridge, I spotted another passer-by and ran across to enlist his help.

That was when some old bloke backed his car over me.

It was an ancient black Wolseley with chrome bumpers and orange indicators and a steamed-over rear window, which was probably why he didn't see me. He didn't hit me hard, but it was enough to knock me off my balance. As I watched him alight from the car, I realised he was very old indeed. 'My dear lady,' he called, 'I'm so terribly sorry. I took a wrong turn and was reversing.' He was wearing a cashmere overcoat several sizes too big and an unravelling brown scarf that was so long he managed to shut it in the door.

'I wonder if you could help me,' I began, climbing to my feet.

'I don't see why not,' he replied, shaking my hand rather formally. 'I'm a retired police officer.' He flicked a wallet at me. 'Actually that's my library card, I've got some proper credentials somewhere.' He didn't look like any policeman I had ever seen. They say you know you're getting older when constables start looking young. This had to be the oldest police officer in London. If you transformed a tortoise into a human being, that was what he looked like, except he had a rim of white hair sticking out like icicles around the sides of his head.

I explained the situation and asked him to come with me, but he told me he wouldn't be able to manage the stairs with his bad legs.

'Well, is there anyone else you can call?' I asked.

'There is someone else in the area who may be able to help.'

'Thank God for that.'

He ushered me into the car and we drove around the corner to Vauxhall Bridge Road, where he pointed out a boy of no more than sixteen hunched beside a bus stop, balancing on the outside rims of his trainers, hands deep in his pockets. He was avoiding my eye, pretending I wasn't there.

'It's all right, he's one of the lads we keep in touch with around London. Our eyes and ears. Don't let him near your pockets. Shiny objects stick to him. All right, Nalin?'

The boy grunted. He looked like a million other youths, low-slung jeans with no arse, grey cotton hoodie, red curve-peaked baseball cap, an exercise in operational invisibility except when it came to looting Currys and getting caught on CCTV.

'I like your trainers, Nalin, where did you get them, somewhere in Camden? What colour would you call that, heliotrope? Listen, this lady lives nearby and all her lights have gone out – a blown fuse or something, and she's scared of the dark. It's a phobia, I've forgotten the medical term for it. Nyctophobia, that's it. I get muddled up because there are so many of them. Pogonophobia is fear of beards, did you know that? Do you think, if it's not out of your way, you would mind escorting her upstairs, only her lift's not working and my knees aren't up to it. It would be a good deed, like in the scouts, not that I suppose they do that sort of thing any more.' The old man gave me a confident smile. 'Show him where you live – I'm sorry, I didn't catch your name.'

'I'm June, like the wet month. June Cryer.' I pointed to the curved concrete wall of the apartment block, its lower levels sunk beneath the angle of the raised roundabout.

The boy watched me silently for a few moments, sucking his teeth. He had that totally bored look all teenagers have these days, as if showing an interest in anything would cause them to lose credibility. 'I'm not allowed in Finsbury,' he announced, clearing his throat. 'I have to be careful.'

'Oh.' I tried to muster an answer but failed to think of anything even vaguely appropriate.

'Or King's Cross. I got run out of King's Cross. I can't go back there. Or the Elephant.' His eyeline followed my pointing hand. 'Where d'you live then, the Ziggurat?'

'Yes,' I said in some surprise. 'You know it?'

'A mate of my dad's did the plumbing. He said he'd show me the inside but...' His thought trailed off.

'But what?' I asked, anxious to keep the conversation alight.

'He got put away. Pentonville, three years for receiving and interfering with a witness. Jeffrey Archer's buying a flat in there, isn't he? I'll take you in 'cause I don't want to stay out here. I'm not supposed to be outside.'

He was behaving very strangely, shifting back and forth on the edges of his trainers, watching the horizon. The old man didn't look at all worried. I began to have second thoughts about asking either of them for help, but had no intention of walking into a blacked-out building with a dead body and some madman possibly waiting in the dark, even if there turned out to be a logical explanation.

'It's this way.'

Mr. Officer pulled me back before I could step into the traffic hurtling across the roundabout. He gave me another reassuring smile that made him look slightly mad. I noticed he was wearing very white false teeth.

'You don't have to go right around. There's a staircase.' He pointed to a set of steps leading down from the end of the bridge. We splashed down to the ramp below, making our way past Portakabins and JCBs, across the churned mud of the square.

'The electricity's off,' I warned, brushing down the arms of my jacket.

'It's alright,' said Nalin. 'I can see in the dark. That's why I only come out at night.'

It crossed my mind that the boy might be on drugs. 'There's not supposed to be anyone else here this weekend,' I told him. 'They've only sold a few of the units and the other residents have been warned to stay away.'

'Then why are you still in your place?' he asked reasonably, stopping on the steps.

'It's this way up.' I felt too tired to explain again.

It was dark in the foyer, but blacker still in the stairwell. Somewhere far above, water drizzled from an unfinished gutter. I found Madame Funes' lighter and flicked it. 'I'm sorry about this.'

'I'll wait here, if you don't mind,' said the old man, settling himself into one of the red armchairs. 'God, these things are uncomfortable. I'd keep an eye on the place from outside, but sitting on cold stone plays havoc with my Chalfonts. Nalin, listen to the lady and see what you can make of this. I'll be here when you get back.'

'What floor d'you live on?' the boy asked.

'Right at the top, I'm afraid. I didn't know what to do.'

'What do you mean?'

'What I didn't tell you was, the girl on the next balcony looked as if she'd got into some kind of fight. It's none of my business, but she saw me looking, and I think she wanted me to help her but then she passed out and stopped breathing. The phone's off, there are no lights, it was awful.'

The stairs went on forever, as though they were expanding in the brackish gloom.

'It's through here.'

The landing door led to corridor, and the square of pale light where the half-naked girl had slumped against the wall. The footprints had dried and vanished. There was no sign of any disturbance at all.

'Which one's yours?'

'This way.'

The door to the apartment stood slightly ajar. I shoved it wider, then stepped back as cold spirits rushed me. 'I can't go in.'

'I'm not going to walk in first, am I? This could be a set-up by one of my enemies. Someone might be standing inside that door with a bit of wood.' The boy was covering his own nervousness.

'I'm not setting you up for your enemies, I promise. I'm beginning to think I'm losing my mind.' That was more honest than I'd intended. I was forced to lead the way into the corridor. 'Through here.' Extending the lighter and waving it about, I stopped at the threshold of the lounge, trying to see inside, frightened of what I might find. 'Nobody.'

'I can see that. This is lush. Must have cost you a fortune.'

'She was attacked out in the hall.'

'You got scared of the dark. I used to until I did a couple of weeks on the streets.'

'The girl is in the bedroom.' I suddenly realised what I was about to do, letting him see her in a state of undress, but it couldn't be helped.

'I thought you said she was in the hall.'

'She was but then she came into the apartment. The door was open.'

Nalin stepped out onto the balcony and peered over the wall. 'There's an ambulance going round the front of the building.'

'Oh God, I forgot about that. You go to the bedroom and stay with her.' I couldn't go back in there. I went into the corridor.

The ambulance was small and low, a white estate with yellow stripes and a discreet blue light. It looked more like a vehicle for carrying out urgent repairs to venetian blinds than a ferry for the sick. The paramedic who emerged from the passenger seat wore a white paper suit spattered with droplets of blood that gave

115

him the jaunty air of a Hoxton artist interrupted in the middle of an action painting.

'I'm sorry about this,' he said, tearing off the suit as he arrived out of breath on the seventh floor, 'we were just round the corner. Some little sod got glassed in a pub and spat teeth at me when I tried to help. I was tempted to break the Hippocratic oath by standing on his ankles. Ain't you got any lights?' He paused to try a switch in the hall.

'Everything's off. Through here.' I pushed back the front door and picked up my lamp, giving him the short version of what had happened, but I could tell from his cautious silence that he wasn't convinced. As I led him through to the bedroom, I started to think that perhaps the only thing worse than leaving a semi-naked corpse in someone else's apartment was leaving a dodgy stranger in there with it.

'You shouldn't be wandering around without lights, love, you could have an accident.' The paramedic indicated the bedroom door. 'In here?'

I walked in behind him, hardly daring to look. The bedroom was empty, the floor clean of any incriminating mark. No body, no stranger, nothing. But the air smelled acrid from the fire.

'I'm not imagining things,' I said defensively, pointing to the burned coverlet in the corner. 'That was alight but I managed to put it out.' Telling him about the blaze in the bedroom only made matters worse.

Nalin was sitting in the lounge, eating an orange.

'Well, he seems alright now,' said the paramedic.

'This isn't him,' I explained, 'it's a her, a young girl. This is just a lad the gentleman downstairs got me talking to. I don't even know him.'

'Listen, love, it's a busy night out there,' the paramedic pleaded. 'You're not pissing me about, are you?'

'No, I swear there was a girl's body here. How do you think I got blood all over me?'

'You sure you didn't cut yourself?'

'No, of course not! It came from her! I had to cut her with the scissors!' That came out wrong.

'I think you have to consider that you might have imagined it. I mean, in the dark and that. Have a cup of tea and a sit-down, love, and if you decide it was just a nightmare, you should call your GP, all right? The man downstairs is a detective, love, he'll want you to make a statement.' The paramedic was pleasant enough, calm and soft-spoken, but his seen-it-all attitude incensed me. I wished he would stop calling me Love.

'I didn't see any body either,' said Nalin unhelpfully, spitting pips into his hand.

The paramedic searched the flat before being called away to a car smash at Nine Elms. He stopped short of accusing me of wasting his time, but asked if I'd had a drink. The flat was clean. Only the smell of the smouldering duvet hung in the air like a November bonfire.

CHAPTER FOURTEEN
The Past Coming Through

ONCE HE HAD gone I searched the bedroom, desperate to find anything he might have missed that would validate what I was already starting to think of as a bad dream. One thing was odd. The floor looked too clean. There were no dust balls anywhere. It was as though the boards had been wiped. The girl was slim and light. Her attacker could have come back and carried her out. The only blood left was on me.

And I could smell her scent beneath the burnt duvet, and was pretty sure it was L'Intense by Givenchy. God knows I'd sniffed enough sticks of it.

Nalin seemed unfazed by the fact that there was no corpse in the apartment. He helped himself to a can of Coke and rooted about for chocolate biscuits, eating from the packet as he loped about the apartment, checking the view from every angle.

'I think we should go back down,' I told him.

'The old git's not coming up. He'll wait.'

I needed to construct a logical explanation for the night's events, and finally settled on one: the girl had also been staying in the building, performing a similar chore, caretaking the property for an owner. She had been visited by someone she knew, her boyfriend perhaps, and they had fought. Unable to contact anyone, she had staggered out into the corridor for help, to find the boyfriend still there.

The theory would have been fine, except for her getting strangled with a plastic tag, which suggested something a lot nastier than hasty words. So either the stitch-headed man had returned and dragged her from the building, all the way down the stairs, without passing any of us, or he had locked the penthouse door from the inside and was waiting there until the coast was clear. I suddenly realised I still had the spatchcock scissors in my back pocket, which was evidence of a sort, although it was probably evidence that I had helped to kill her.

'What have you got there?' Nalin mistrustfully watched as I brandished the kitchen implement.

'I tried to cut her tag off with them. Evidence.' I tipped the blades to catch the light.

'All the police will see is a weapon with your fingerprints all over it.'

I gave in, dropping the scissors onto the steel counter. 'You're not helping, you know.' I suddenly wanted to cry, but joined Nalin on the sofa instead. His eyes were bituminous in candlelight and oddly unfocussed, as though he was beyond reach. 'I didn't imagine it and I'm not crazy.'

'I wanna believe you,' said Nalin unreassuringly.

I took a good look at him, anxious to find something that would stop me from thinking about the girl lying on the floor. 'Surely you can't be homeless. I mean, you're so young.'

'I'm not homeless, I got places to stay. I got jobs. The plods all know me. I can't go back to King's Cross.'

'So you said. What about your parents? Where's your mother?'

'Off her head. Agoraphobic manic depressive. I was living with my dad, but now he's inside.'

'You mean in prison? Why, what did he do?'

'Kidnapping. He'd been out drinking and didn't trust himself to drive home, so he left his car in Camden High Street and came back for it the next morning. The Tube was closed for repairs and he got there five minutes after the parking laws had come back into force. Found some mouthy fucking Camden traffic Nazi clamping the car, so he and his mates stuck a few temazepams on a strip of racing tape, put it over his mouth and pushed him into a hedge. They sat on him he 'til was asleep and then stripped him, unwound the rest of the roll round his body, bagged him up, took him to King's Cross in a workman's bag and put him in the luggage rack of a train going to York. My dad got two years 'cause he was on bail at the time. My mum went back on tranks and I went to my nan's, but I didn't like it there so I fucked off. Ended up on remand for criminal damage and common assault, brandishing an imitation firearm in a shopping mall, and went to Brinsford Young Offenders. Most of the boys in my class are in Brinsford, so I was with my mates. When I got out I jumped a train to London. Then Dalston put an exclusion order on me, and I got the ISSP.' He cocked his head and listened. 'There's dead sound all the way through this place, have you noticed?'

'There was a young girl here,' I murmured, forcing the memory to life. 'She coughed up blood on me. Her attacker left muddy footprints. I don't have the confidence to make this kind of thing up.'

'I'll do one more quick check around the place, then I'd better go down and report.' The boy's identity shifted from focus; he no longer seemed the same

121

impassive teenager I'd seen lurking at the bus stop. I wondered how many other people had written him off before talking to him. Perhaps he wasn't a street-wary misfit but a fantasist, studious and lonely, less likely to be living on the street and fearing the reprisals of gangs than biding his time in an ordinary home, in a silent suburb, his family afflicted with the guilt of making him bored.

'It was real and it wasn't a mistake,' I insisted. 'I didn't imagine her. My husband says I have no imagination, so how could I?'

'One way to find out. Give me a minute.' I nodded dumbly as he collected a pair of candles from the lounge and left me on the sofa. 'Don't move from here.'

His footfalls retreated through the apartment. The front door opened and closed. For five minutes there was no further sound. Finally he returned. 'There's no-one outside. Your candles are knackered.' He reached the entrance of the lounge and set the candles back down. 'I tried the end penthouse but the door is definitely locked. I knocked but there was no answer. Didn't sound like there was no-one inside.'

'I'm out of my depth, Nalin. Maybe it's this building. There's something about these angled walls that unsettle me.'

'It's a weird shape to fit with the river, that's why. I do decorating work, but my mate's van is fucked at the moment so I'm doing nights in the burger stall by Vauxhall Bridge, earning a bit of straight. Clubbers and cabbies, gets really busy between two and five.'

'Where were you going when I talked to you?'

'Nowhere.' He gave me a guarded look.

'You were at a bus stop, that's all.'

'They're bright. Nobody can move on you without you seeing them first. Sometimes the cops drive by for a chat.' Perhaps that was it; he'd been touting for work. 'You should go down to the garage on the next corner and buy yourself a decent battery lamp, one of them emergency ones. It's safer than the lantern. You shouldn't stay here without decent lights.'

'You can stay for a while if you want.'

'Nah. You'll try it on with me, I know your type.' He smiled, and I was grateful he'd attempted to make a joke.

As we walked back down the stairs, I caught the ferrety look in his eyes that made him appear so unapproachable, although I still wouldn't have trusted him with my cutlery. His shoulders remained hunched and his hands were kept deep in his pockets, braced against sudden movement.

Outside, he glanced furtively from beneath the peak of his cap, scanning the streets left and right, never relaxing his guard. The elderly policeman was back in his car with the heater on. He wound down the window.

'All finished?' he asked, not even expecting to hear about a body. Nalin leaned in and they exchanged words.

Nalin rose and stuffed some notes into his pocket. 'He's going to take you to the petrol station,' he explained, touching the light on a fat plastic watch that turned his face blue. He wiped his nose on the back of his sleeve. 'I got to go.'

'Can I ask you something? You said you were banned from some places, and can't leave others.'

'Yeah, I told you, ISSP.'

'What's that?'

'Intensive Supervision and Surveillance Program.' He pulled up the left leg of his jeans and showed me the grey band that circled his ankle. 'Plastic. The tag beeps if I leave the area at night. I have to do therapy and re-education. And planting.'

'Is that why you can't go back to King's Cross, Finsbury Park or the Elephant?'

'No. I've got ASBOs on me in King's Cross and Finsbury for fighting and that. And Shadwell Massive keeps me out of the east.' He flicked his fingers at me in that silly gesture kids have copied from American music videos. 'There's places you can't go after you've been marked. I got into a few sites and was given a warning.'

I presumed he meant gang territories. There had been an article in the paper about a boy being pushed under a DLR train by three gang members who had forced him from the platform onto the track. An argument over a box of KFC. Dreadful.

'Is that something to do with graffiti?' I asked.

'Do I look like I'm in fucking infants' school? Online gaming. You hide code inside jpeg pixels so that when the other person opens it, their system crashes.'

'Why would you want to?'

'If they piss you off and that.'

'I wouldn't have thought you'd want to upset too many people.' I thought of Lou's son locked in his room, staring angrily into his computer screen while the street slept.

'There's people you don't,' he agreed. 'Serious gunsters and a lot of jokers. The Lock City Crew in Harlesden, the Holy Smokes and Tooti Nung in Southall, the Drummond Street Boys in Camden, Snakeheads and Wo Shing Wo in Soho, Spanglers and Fireblades in

Tottenham, Brick Lane Massive, Bengal Tigers, Cartel Crew in Brixton, maybe two dozen others. If you can convince the old git here to employ me more often, I won't be such a drain on decent law-abiding society.' He grinned at me, then lolloped off in the direction of Vauxhall Station, the ghost of a child shadowboxing as a man.

'Hop in, Mrs. Cryer. We'll get you a light,' said the old boy.

'I guess the lad told you there was nothing up there.'

'Yes, he did.' He held the car door open. 'Come on.'

The surface of the river pulsed with a sickly jaundice from the floodlit buildings. Lights strung between the lamp-posts looked mournful, not celebratory. Half the bulbs were dead or missing. The rain had calmed to a soft mist, leaving lakes in the corners of the roads. We were within sight of the Houses of Parliament, yet the area felt unsafe and poorly planned, usable only as a thoroughfare that would quickly take you somewhere else.

'There aren't many people around.'

'It's early. Never gets that busy around here because the roads don't lead anywhere.'

'All roads lead somewhere.'

'They don't go where you want them to.' He returned his attention to the blurred slush of vehicles, an elderly meerkat checking for predators. 'Quiet streets. I prefer it late, when the moon's high and the river looks like it's made of mercury.'

'You like the river?'

'Because there's more space, and there are more trees. When I was young you used to be able to walk through the tops of them.'

'That doesn't sound very likely.'

'Down in Battersea Park they had a tree-walk right beside the river, rope bridges and Chinese lanterns. It was quite magical. You could do things like that when London wasn't so crowded. Walk around empty museums, be the only person on a Tube platform.'

I smiled. 'Normally I'd be going to bed around now.'

'You're not a Londoner, are you?'

'No, I'm from somewhere you won't have heard of.'

'Where?'

'A town called Hamingwell. It's near Orpington, in Kent.'

'You're right, I don't know that. The garage is over there.' He stopped and pointed to a fierce bright area set back beside the railway arches of Vauxhall. 'It doesn't look it, but you're fine around here. It's a neutral zone. Over there, those are all gay bars. You'll get queues outside later, it keeps the area safe.' He brought the Wolseley to the kerb.

The garage was an oasis of brilliance. As I walked into it, the ferocity of the light stung my eyes. An African man in an ancient Ford Fiesta pulled forward on the forecourt near the kiosk and began shouting at the Asian cashier. Suddenly he ran back to his car, jumped in and drove it forward until the bonnet nearly ruptured the glass booth. Customer and attendant were still swearing at each other as the cashier vaulted over his counter, came out and threw a beer bottle. It looped through the air to smash across the windscreen of the car. Grains of glass scattered like a bucket of ice being emptied from a height, a fragmenting prism sparkling across the concrete, but the Fiesta's windscreen held. The African man appeared to be waving goodbye to the Asian. There was a dull snap in the air and the car lurched off, bouncing out into the oncoming traffic. It took me a moment to realise that a gun had been fired.

'Sorry about that.' The cashier was breathing hard and smoothing his hair back in place as he rang up the price of the battery light. 'Fucking Nigerians are always driving off without paying. Fucking hell. Did you see? I got a fucking bullet hole in my canopy. Fuck me. Always fucking Nigerians. You never see fucking Asian kids juking each other for drugs on the fucking street corners, do you? Asian kids know how to fucking behave. Fuck. Sorry. That'll be nine ninety nine.'

Shocked, I picked up the battery light and walked back to the Wolseley. Even Lou didn't swear that much. The old man was fiddling with the heater and appeared to have missed the entire episode. On reflection I decided it would probably have been safer to stay at the Ziggurat, with its reassuringly old-fashioned ghostly apparitions.

'Do you know anything about psychogeography?' he asked me as I climbed back in. The interior smelled of damp leather and rolling tobacco.

'The garage guy was just shot at,' I told him.

'Did you get a licence plate?'

'No.'

'Oh well.' He squinted through the window and wiped it with a length of sleeve. Presumably he was satisfied with what he saw, because he started the engine and we set off. 'The area has a history of violence. That's probably why you attracted this vision of the girl and her attacker.'

'What do you mean?'

'Ever hear of the Starling Lane murder? The road ran right through here. It's gone now. The police ended up chasing a phantom. Quite a scandal at the time. You always get ghosts near water. Specially in London.'

'Why?'

'The city's riddled with it. The canals, the underground rivers, why do you think we have so many wells? Sadler's Wells, Clerkenwell, Bridewell, Ladywell. Map the wells, connect the lines and you find that the streets of ancient London followed the hedgerows, which followed the rivers, because fields have to be watered. The lowlands were poor areas largely because they were close to the water-table and were always damp. Water and fog brought respiratory illnesses, the stagnant rivers brought cholera, and early deaths created superstitions; who wouldn't want to wish a dead child back to life? That's why ghost stories were more associated with say, the poor East End than the city's prosperous hilly north. The London of my early childhood was a city of ghosts. Despite the fact that mere proximity to the Thames was once enough to kill you, its mystical significance was once so strong that the Romans floated gods upon it.'

I unsmeared the window and looked out. The Wolseley had pulled up in front of the Ziggurat. 'Your building, it's a conversion,' he explained. 'It used to belong to a petrochemical company. Ex-Ministry of Defence property, before that slum houses, back to back all the way along the river. I'm not saying you saw dead people, but perhaps you attracted a similar event. Areas don't change. It's not a supernatural thing, just the past coming through, like a leak. Even water leaves a stain.'

'I didn't dream it.'

'You have to face the possibility that you did. Dreams are just electrostatic discharge, images from the waking day. Your subconscious forces a narrative onto them, but the story doesn't hold any logic. Don't be scared. If you see anything strange again remember, it might not even be there, so it's nothing to worry about.'

This wasn't much of a comfort, or something I ever expected to hear from a former police officer. 'You get a lot of stuff from the past coming up near the river. It's the only thing around here that never changes. It runs through the city like a dirty artery. The water, the riverbed, the shoreline, just like they always were, you're bound to get things coming through.' He made it sound like a plumbing problem.

'I didn't realise that.'

I stood on the steps, sorry to see the Wolseley leave. The old man wanted to wait until I was right inside, and only left after I assured him I would be all right. The river blotted light, creating a dark vacuum in a jaundiced sky. When I looked at the dark building above me, my nerve failed.

I couldn't bring myself to go in.

Clutching the handle of the red plastic battery light, I waited at the edge of the road and stared up at the Ziggurat. I could still hear the Wolseley retreating in the distance. For a moment I felt like running after it. The old man had apologised for not being able to do more, but I felt equally bad about being unable to provide proof of what I had seen. I felt jumpy and displaced, as though I had taken one of Lou's diet tablets. Lou believes everything operates on a basic chemical level. She says husbands are like arsenic; tolerable in very small amounts but cumulatively fatal.

The glistening angles of the Ziggurat reared up before its ancient counterpart, the only other building in the area that stood in total darkness, Lambeth Palace. I had watched a programme about the Archbishop of Canterbury's official residence only a few days earlier. It had been intended as a college for monks in the twelfth century, and its secular history was peppered with violent incident. Rioters, rebels, murderers and book-burners had trodden the grounds. One of its deceased archbishops, Matthew 'Nosey' Parker, had been dug up and reburied in a dunghill. During the time leading to the Restoration it was used as a prison, and in the second world war its ancient stones were cracked apart by German bombs.

The Ziggurat had no history, and perhaps no future, but the land on which it was built could tell a thousand tales. This was what gave it a melancholy air that no amount of glass and concrete could dispel.

So perhaps – just perhaps – I had seen a ghost. Except there had been blood. Or had I somehow cut myself, as the medic had suggested?

I couldn't go back there, not yet.

I had loaded all my change from different pockets into my purse; the total came to eighteen pounds eleven pence, and I thought there was a small amount left on my Connect card. It felt like the aftermath of the event, and I wondered what to do next.

I didn't realise how much worse things would get.

CHAPTER FIFTEEN
Cassandra

I WALKED BACK towards the river, trying to work out my next move.

You always wanted a chance to be strong, June. Well, now you have it. See the weekend through, there's nothing left for you in Hamingwell, not even a bed. I had never imagined leaving, let alone on such bad terms. A few days ago, the idea of changing surroundings had been as unthinkable as divorce or suicide. Lou always complained that Hamingwell was a prison, but it was still her home. She was full of ideas about taking revenge on her husband and son, but never got around to leaving them. I knew she had no intention of getting out because she'd just got new kitchen units. Not knowing what else to do, I decided to call her. I needed to talk to someone.

Lou always answered the phone on the second ring when she'd been drinking; instead of slowing her down, alcohol made her hypertense. Tonight she sounded as drunk as a dean.

'Darling, where the hell are you?'

I could hear Lou's TV in the background, and felt as though I had caught her out. Lou was probably sitting at home with her family, watching in an alcoholic haze, eating from a plate that was balanced on her knees, carping against a husband who was waiting for her anger to be soporifically displaced. I wanted to explain what had happened, but knew I would end up frightening myself again.

'June, I can hear you breathing but you're not saying anything. Either that, or you're speaking in a voice that goes beyond my hearing range. Lately I've developed the ability to screen out the sound of the telly. All I can see is pictures of murdered grannies and mouths moving. Darren's watching serial killer crime re-enactments, probably studying them for tips. I think it's Harold Shipman. Shame for Primrose, she must have been a size eighteen. I thought you'd have texted me fifty times by now. Hang on, let me take this in the kitchen. There's a bottle of vodka in the tumble dryer. Okay, I'm back. What's that noise?'

'Some drunk bloke is singing through a traffic cone. I'm in a South London street, near the river, just past Lambeth Palace.'

'What on earth are you doing there at this time of night?'

'I can't charge my mobile because the power's off, so I'll have to be quick. Something's happened.'

'How is the place? Julie says it's great. The perfect place to break up a married man's marriage. Darling, I've got to tell you, I had a fight with Hadrian today, the worst we've had in weeks. He's been caught trying to sell Hungarian women. You know, mail-order brides, on the bloody internet if you please. I wondered why he had so many photographs of skanky blondes on his bedroom wall. He's been acting as an agent for some dodgy company, lied about his age, running up debts and giving people this address. We had bailiffs round, how Victorian is that? Darren freaked out, seems to think it's all my fault. I had the police here, everything. Did it ever occur to you –'

'Lou, I need your advice –'

'*Did it ever occur to you* what a raw deal married women end up with? The single ones get all the empowerment and equal opportunities and beating men at their own game, and we get the last of the dinosaurs and their disgusting throwback offspring. I didn't have Victoria Beckham as a role model when I was at school. Mind you, she never smiles, does she? There's not a happy woman over thirty in our street, they're all pretending to make the best of things because they chose marriage. That's what happens when you spend your formative years flicking through bridal magazines in the hairdressers. What did you want?'

'Forget it. I'm fine. I just thought I'd see how you were.'

'Darren and Hadrian had to go down the police station to try and sort out the mess. I was out cold by the time they got back. You could always come here. I've still got your bottle of Bombay Sapphire under the sink. I can't touch it because he smells it on my breath. You sure you're fine? You don't *sound* fine.'

'There was a girl in Malcolm's flat,' I blurted out.

'What are you talking about?'

'When I went to get help she vanished and I'm not entirely sure that I'm not going mad.'

'Have you been drinking?'

'No, I... well, a bit –'

'Have you called the police?'

'I met a very old man who used to be in the police, and a strange boy.'

'Oh God, Malcolm's paintings aren't damaged, are they?'

'No, nothing like that.'

'Will he find out what's happened? There's nothing broken, is there?'

'There's nobody there now. Nobody need ever know.'

'If anyone else in the block finds out weird stuff has been going on, you'll have to call Malcolm and tell him. Oh, June.' Lou sighed wearily. 'It wasn't a complicated thing, just looking after the place. How did you let it happen?'

'I haven't let anything happen,' I replied angrily.

'I'm having trouble following you. I'd come over tonight but I've taken enough valium to drop a cow. Tell you what, I'm coming up to town tomorrow. I'll see you in the evening, around seven. I should be following whole sentences by then. Will you be all right tonight?'

'I'll be fine.' I closed the mobile and dropped it into my jacket. The street was devoid of pedestrians, lit in a sulphurous shade that leeched out any other colour. Somehow it felt safer here than back in that blacked-out rectangle of concrete. I decided to take positive action and check into the nearest hotel. I'd figure out how to pay for it later.

The Waterloo City Arms Hotel looked as if it had once been one of London's invisible Edwardian buildings, crusted in streaks of railway soot that hung like fallen shadows below the window sills. A few uplighters and vertical banners had been added, along with a basement bar called METRO and a doorman sartorially pitched between a Royal Fusilier and a guardian of the Land of Oz, and suddenly a low-end dump used by tired salesmen during conferences had been repositioned as a faux-boutique stop on tourists' tours of Europe.

The bony-faced desk clerk studied my mismatched clothes with an odd intensity. He wore a thin brass badge on his lapel, like a stationmaster, with his name, Nizwar, etched on it. He looked like he'd been working nights all his life. Unnerved, I glanced away at a fiercely ugly Chinese vase standing on a plinth in its own alcove. The hotel foyer was as over-decorated as my house in Hamingwell. Dusty swathes of marigold, lilac, primrose and lavender, colours found in the homes of old people. *Why is he taking so long?* I wondered.

When the clerk glanced up, I could see that he hated me, and couldn't imagine what I had done to upset him. 'I need to take an imprint of a major credit card,' he stated flatly. *In a place like this?* I thought.

'I'm afraid I don't have any at the moment.' I tried to sound calm.

There was an imperceptible narrowing of Nizwar's eyes. 'You have any luggage?'

'No, it was a spur-of-the-moment decision.'

The narrow eyes were now joined by smug thin lips. 'I've seen you in here before. I remember those earrings.'

I fingered my golden plastic sunflowers in some embarrassment. 'I don't see how you could have. I've never been here before.'

'No, I remember you clearly, suede skirt, knee boots, fur coat, weekend before last. Security systems convention, working the bar, I saw you. Go and sell it outside.'

'How dare you!' I managed, the breath knocked from me, but still turned and fairly ran from the foyer, horrified that someone might have overheard the clerk.

It didn't seem possible to be mistaken for a whore twice in one night. As I stumbled down the hotel steps, a female hand grabbed at my sleeve.

'He's the new manager, watches everything. I was trying to warn you but you ignored me. You're better off down the road.' The girl was no more than twenty, with the translucent yellow skin and dark eyes of a junkie. At first glance she was smartly dressed in a black sweater and skirt, but I recognised the cut of cheap clothes. I tried to ignore her and walk on, but the girl followed. 'There's a hotel behind the cut where they let us use the bar. You look like you need a drink. Come on, it's the start of the weekend and I'm flush.'

'No, really, I'm fine, thanks,' I heard myself saying, then thought *Why did I say that? I'm not fine at all. I'm nothing like fine.*

I was worse when we turned the corner and saw the back of a stitched Frankenstein head above a dirty sheepskin jacket. The bull-necked man I had seen in the Ziggurat was standing in the middle of the pavement with his hands in his pockets, looking toward the river. So, no ghosts. A real murder. In another ten seconds we would walk right by him.

The girl stopped and turned back. 'It's just over there. I've got a bar tab running, this rich Indian bloke pays when he's in town. Loaded, some of the Indians, and as nice as the Arabs if they haven't been gambling, but they're all a bit crafty when it comes to getting something for nothing.'

I looked at the girl, who smiled hopefully back. Thin face, greasy blonde hair cropped at the jawline, hardly any makeup. Fleshless legs in pale green stockings, black leather coat, worn-over shoes. 'I'm not what you think,' I said apologetically.

'At this time of night who is?' The girl tried a nervous flicker of a smile. 'I'm Cassandra. That's my working name. My real one is Saffron, I hate it.'

'I'm June.'

'That's nice. Summery. My name means yellow, but my mum called me that because she likes Indian food, you know, rice. I changed it to Cassandra 'cause someone told me it means 'helper of men,' which fits.'

'It also means disbeliever of men,' I told her.

'Oh well, that fits too. It's just over here. You can use the washroom to get some of that stuff off you.' We waited to cross the road as three police cars, one behind the other, jockeyed toward the river, sirens howling. I glanced back; Stitch-Head hadn't moved. What if he was looking for me?

The hotel was a step down from the last one. Dusty plastic panels of strip-lighting illuminated the lobby as brightly as a petrol station. Room rates were posted in italic stick-on letters, black on gold. A pot of greying plastic daffodils stood on a table covered with dog-eared leaflets for shows that had already closed. The desk-clerk ignored us as we walked through to the bar, a crimson-draped room with round formica-topped tables and brass lamps that belonged in a medium's parlour. Several of the other working girls were there with punters, forcing laughter from lame jokes or ignoring their clients completely, leaning across them to speak intimately with each other.

'If you're not a working girl, why are you dressed like one?' asked Cassandra, leading the way.

'I didn't know I was,' I replied miserably. 'I'm from the suburbs.'

'Well, you ain't a professional, you look more like you're after some extra housekeeping, and that'll get you cut if you're trying to do business around here.'

'I wasn't... I mean I'm not,' I explained. 'Would you do me a favour? See if that man is still standing on the corner?'

Cassandra pressed her face against the window. 'Big fat bloke, head like a half-sucked grapefruit? He's coming this way.'

'Oh no.' I twisted away, dropping my head. What if he came inside? Where could I hide?

'Listen, I'll be back in a minute,' said Cassandra, abandoning me. 'Washroom is in the corner. Tell the barman what you want. It's all right, he's cool. We cover for him while he does call-outs.'

I cleaned my face and neck with wet paper towels, but couldn't do anything about my top. Then I returned to climb on a stool while the barman poured gin into garage glasses. *Did she mean he's a rent boy or a drug dealer?* I wondered, studying him in terrified fascination. Hamingwell kept its vices hidden. Secretly, I liked the idea of having them on public display; it felt more honest. The evening was wearing away the last vestige of snobbishness I had brought with me, but it was difficult to pinpoint the motives of strangers when you were more concerned with staying in one piece. I dropped my head into my hands, nerves fizzing, waiting to feel a meaty fist on my shoulder. *I've been set up,* I thought, *she's told him where I am. I'm dead.*

But nothing happened. Cassandra returned, and some of the colour had come back to her face. 'That's better,' she said. 'I can't drink unless I've had a jump. Tell me something, if you're not on the game, why did you get chucked out of The Waterloo?'

'It was a misunderstanding,' I explained as Cassandra shot me what my mother would call an old-fashioned look.

'Cheers anyway.' Cassandra raised her glass. 'First of the night. I know it's always busy this time of the month but it's a bleeding joke tonight. They've all been paid. I usually work right through. Half of them have been drinking since six and are too pissed to do anything, so it's easy money. I like Christmas best, though.'

'I thought it would be quiet then.'

'You're having a laugh, incha? The thought of spending two days in front of the telly with relatives all round them brings them pouring in. I feel sorry for them, stuck at home in their little houses, all fucked off with each other.'

I tried not to cry, but couldn't stop myself. I wiped hopelessly at my face with a squashed Kleenex.

'Bloody hell.' Cassandra dug in her handbag and pressed a small white pill into my hand. 'Take this, it'll put you back on top.'

'What is it?'

'Don't worry, it won't hurt you. They're for depression. Down in one.'

'Should I take it with gin?'

'It makes no bloody difference.'

'They might be addictive.'

'Of course they're not, I read somewhere that Liza Minelli takes them, and if anyone's earned the right to be depressed it's her.' She held the glass and watched as I swallowed. 'I'd better get earning in a minute. One more drink, though, seeing as it's Friday.' Cassandra checked her pockets, then her hands. 'Actually I think that was an E, not a Valium.'

Whatever it was, Cassandra was right; it soon made things a little better. I found myself wanting to stroke the leather seats of the chairs, the wood of the table legs, even Cassandra's pale arm, to touch the bruises at the crook of her elbow, just to feel the warmth of her damaged skin. For a few minutes I became fascinated by my shoes. I told Cassandra everything that had happened in the last few hours. She didn't laugh or make fun of me. Instead, she seemed to give the problem serious consideration.

'There's no-one there now, right? Why don't you just go back?'

'I'm scared.'

'Don't be daft, stick a chair under the door and you'll be all right. No-one's tried to hurt you, have they? You just caught sight of someone else's problem.'

Cassandra's dangers were real enough: drunks who didn't know their own strength, punters who turned evangelical after sex, men who assuaged their self-loathing by being nasty after they'd come. Foreplay folded into rough stuff for no reason, she said, and all you could do was lay still, or fight them off and face a row over returning payment.

'It sounds terrible,' I told her, sniffing. 'Isn't there something else you can do?'

'Why do people always say that, as if working in a shop is better? I don't think it is. Anyway, I don't mind. If anyone hurts you, just draw on your inner child, imagine you're a kid again and you soon get over it. Kids are strong. They can survive anything. My little boy's like that – a tough little bastard.'

Behind us half a dozen women, fresh-faced and large-bodied, noisily entered the bar. They settled themselves at the circular tables, screeching with laughter, trying to order cocktails without crossing to the counter.

'Right, I've got to get earning,' said Cassandra, rising. 'I have a couple of regulars to sort out. Take your time here, and remember what I said.' She tapped her heart. 'Inner child.' She pulled the collar of her thin coat around her neck and walked out into the night.

I stayed to finish my drink. It was only when I felt in my jacket pocket that I realised my purse had been lifted.

CHAPTER SIXTEEN
Night People

I HAD TO leave. I was going to walk out and keep walking, but Stitch-Head was still standing at the entrance of the hotel. He was looking in the direction of the Ziggurat, his fists in his pockets, his scar livid beneath the light. It was simply not possible for me to slip past him. I had no idea what to do – no money, no purse – I could only turn around on my shaking legs and go back into the bar.

The raucous women who had filled the scalloped maroon seats in the corner turned out to be members of the Greenwich Baths Swimming Association Ladies Amateur Water Ballet Team. There was no escaping their conversation. Instead, I resignedly poured the remains of Cassandra's double into my own glass as the disorder of the night began to recede in the boozy brown-ale warmth.

'... the night I was born my mother had a fright and dropped me right there in the kitchen. Her brother had been in Friern Barnet for years, only he discharged himself to come and wish her happy Christmas. Walked into the house with his old keys and nearly gave her a heart attack. She broke her water still standing, and I fell out. Strong thighs, you see. She was a synchronised swimmer too, and her mother. The women in our house were always stronger than their men, but it was the men who told them what to do. Terrible, isn't it?'

It was hard for the others to get a word in edgeways when Veronica, the team leader, was in full flow. She spread over the sides of her stool in floral folds, nudging and drinking. Her friends were all of a similar bulk, friendly smiles on ruddy taut skin, their faces buffed by regular immersion in chlorine. Veronica drew me into the group as she talked. I could still see the back of that terrible scarred head through the dimpled window. Until it was possible to leave I found myself listening intently, taking in every detail.

'I didn't think it had been around that long,' said the barman, who had evidently been monitoring the conversation.

'Since 1890, only it was called Scientific Ornamental Swimming then. Esther Williams did us a lot of good, of course. We do solo, partners and teams of four and eight.' The others chorused their approval. 'Worst thing is finding music for your technical programme. That and nose-clips. We came up tonight to see Michael Ball at the Palladium, but he was off sick so we knocked it on the head and went to a vodka bar instead.'

'You should see us underwater,' added another, 'We're like gymnasts, a four hundred metre freestyle event with no time to breathe, plus the moves of a skater, the strength of a polo player and the musical expression of a dancer, all in perfect coordination. Sometimes it's a right bastard.'

'You could take part,' said Veronica, pointing to me. I didn't want to draw attention. 'You've got the hour-glass figure. We ask joiners to swim twenty-five metres, front crawl, back stroke and breast stroke, and submerge confidently. I teach everyone. My husband says I'm fat, but I feel light as a feather in the water.' She stared into her drink, silent for a moment. A friend patted her, knowing what was coming. 'My little boy. He drowned, you see. Just slipped in the bath, six years ago now and I never stop thinking about him. You have to make amends somehow.' Veronica dug in her purse and produced a card, the association details printed in azure ink on a watery background. 'Give us a call if you ever want a free starter lesson.'

Cliff Richard came on the jukebox, singing Summer Holiday. 'I love this song,' said a friend of Veronica's. 'Cliff invented the Chinese takeaway in 1958, when he ordered food on the set of *Oh Boy!* I know because my next-door neighbour's brother-in-law painted his mother's bathroom.'

Everyone immediately started discussing who else they knew by this curiously osmotic process of celebrity association. Distant connections to Shirley Bassey featured heavily, mostly in the region of house maintenance. I decided to leave before I discovered that one of the Water Ballet team had been responsible for Kurt Cobain's death.

I checked the window and found no sign of my stalker. Outside the hotel, standing on the pavement with the bulky red battery lamp in my hand, the cool night air sobered me up. My first instinct was to look for a cab until I remembered I only had small change. I couldn't bring myself to face the darkness of the Ziggurat again, but had no other destination.

It would be best to go to Lou first thing in the morning and force myself on the household, insist on staying with them and to hell with my dignity. Ahead was the illuminated entrance to St. Thomas's Hospital, and beyond that the high brick wall of Lambeth Palace. The cadmium lamp lights were filtered by the flicker of branch-tops, the moist air folding into the wake of hushing cars. It was strangely peaceful now, not at all as I imagined London at night.

I've never been this alone, I thought, loosening my coat. My parents had always been there, then schoolfriends and finally Gordon. It had been my own fault for not noticing that something was wrong. You can't see changes when they move like slow tides.

Then suddenly there were people everywhere. A queue for a club, minicabs parked by the side of the road before a burger-stall. I found myself checking the faces around me, watching for small dangers.

The smell of frying onions made me salivate. I counted the loose change in my pocket. I had never needed to count coins before.

'Oi, find any more dead bodies?' called a familiar voice. Nalin looked down at me from beneath his peaked cap as he cracked frozen hamburgers out of a plastic tube. He could joke because he hadn't held the girl as she died.

'Hello. Could I have an eggburger? I'm thirty pence short.'

Nalin slapped a frozen pink disc onto the hotplate and tossed in a handful of onion clippings. 'Sorry, I can't do it. My business partner would kill me. But you can help yourself to chipolatas.' He pointed at a plate of speared pink objects that might have been sausages, prawns or fingers, it was hard to tell. I tried one of them but it tasted tainted with petrol, so I discreetly spat it into the gutter. The burger smelled sluttily tantalising as it tanned on the hotplate. Behind me, two pissed-up lads were arguing about who was stronger, Lennox Lewis or Spiderman. Drunk men have the kind of conversations no woman can ever manage to sustain, yet they get bored when you start comparing moisturisers. I couldn't get over the fact that the street was so suddenly crowded. By this time of night I was always in bed.

'There you go, mate. Careful, it's slippy.' Nalin shovelled onions over the burger and handed the man next to me a bun wrapped in tissue. Watching the drunk attempting to eat the scalding meat, dropping most of it on the ground, I was forced to walk away, hungry, but Nalin called after me. 'I might swing by your place later, come up for a drink or something.' It annoyed me that someone with such potential should spend his nights trying to impress his mates. City life was for the confident, and those who had no faith in themselves were forced to fake it.

A series of railway arches flickered into view beneath streetlamps, like tableaux on a rundown ghost train ride. Under the first, a wide lane of young men and women formed a peculiarly downbeat queue for a nightclub. Beneath the second, a mobile soup kitchen was ladling steaming broth from aluminium pots into polystyrene cups. It was hard to tell the difference between the people queuing for the club and those in line for the soup, except that there were fewer women in the latter. *I'm on the outside now,* I thought, *just like all of them. I can't take anything for granted. This is the part I never saw. Never been in a bar alone. Never been bought drinks by strangers. Never been frightened of walking down a city street. Never been robbed or witnessed a death.*

I watched as a crowd of partygoers in cartoon Chinese garb – flowing tangerine robes and cymbal-hats – coagulated on a traffic island before darting across the road to the river, yelling with laughter. A lone rocket spiralled across the water like an early warning of Guy Fawkes' Night, before falling away in a fizzle of blue sparks. The Thames looked ugly and bare, impossible to imagine that anyone would choose to drown in it.

A van full of nurses was dropping off a night shift at St. Thomas's. A high wind in the motheaten Embankment trees pummelled branches and brushed fat ropes of lights, as if trying to steal their necklaces. An impossibly young girl handed me a club flyer: **All Unaccompanied Ladiez Free B4 1:00AM.**

I don't know what made me do it, but I joined the queue. Perhaps I thought it would be safer. I hadn't been inside a club since before I was married. A wet brick tunnel with retro-70s painted walls led to a series of steamheated railway arches shaking with bass sound, packed with dancers. Plastic glasses, fierce red lasers, scaffolding, impossible to move in any direction.

At first I kept apologising for bumping into people, but soon gave up. I was sweating hard, so I took off my jumper and stood there in my bra. Nobody seemed to notice. Two young men, both stripped to the waist, tried to get me to dance. Even I could tell they were lovers. *Oh great,* I thought, *I've already become a camp mother figure,* but I could see their point. I was standing in a deep-cleavage bra, sunflower earrings and a charm bracelet.

The dancers pushed me steadily back, until I found myself pressed against a gigantic bass speaker. The air vibrated in waves from it, lifting the fine hairs on my arms, rhythmically caressing the tops of my legs. The music changed to some kind of Indian beat that tickled the insides of my thighs. It was a long track, and as it built to a crescendo, so did I. Moving instinctively with the crowd until its mood became mine, I felt as though I had broken through some invisible barrier to join London's spiritual residents, and that whatever else happened I would always be here, a fossil stamped on the city's stone heart.

I decided that if I ever saw Cassandra again I would forgive her for stealing my purse and buy another pill.

Three quarters of an hour was enough, though. When I came out, I found that I had gone completely deaf. Someone had knocked a beer over my jumper, and it had cleaned most of the blood off, not a washing tip I'd come across before. My hand had been rubber-stamped with a picture of a teapot, which seemed an appropriate tattoo for a housewife.

I cut away from the river, passing shops that sold real things: meat, coats, hot food. The stores in Hamingwell were the opposite of those ones in Hampstead and Kensington that sold teddy bears, quilted cushions, paper lamps, tiny mosaic mirrors, objects of little use after their unwrapping. Hamingwell's few independent shops sold car parts, chicken nuggets, PCs, chipboard shelving units, prams, plastic garden furniture in green or white. They weren't as rough and glitzy as Essex, just cheap and faintly desperate.

I passed a neon-bright parlour where middle-aged West Indian men sat at formica tables silently staring at a TV mounted high in a corner, as though they were wondering how it got up there. Next door was a tattoo parlour, open and busy. Designs in the window offered a selection of Celtic symbols besides cabalistic images; a hand with an eye in it, another eye atop a pyramid. Barbed wire, angel of death, no hearts and anchors, no 'I Love Mum' here. After that a funeral arranger, bare plastic blinds in the window, a single bunch of brown dried flowers in an urn, impossibly unwelcoming. *Surely they're surrounded by fresh-cut flowers every day they're in business,* I thought. *It wouldn't hurt them to take some off a grave and put them in the window.* Perhaps they were afraid of welcoming death.

I passed a plush-carpeted gambling arcade with ornamental dragons in the window. Inside, two Asian kids were solemnly feeding coins into a machine, as if performing some form of penance.

A fortune-teller's office: '*Want To Know The Future? Ask Mrs. Phillips.*' A brave question. Did anyone, truly? I stopped before the open door and tried to see inside, wondering if they could help me with the past instead. Were the things I saw real or merely symptoms of financial withdrawal? The window contained an illuminated model of Buddha in red velveteen plastic, a painted chalk Madonna in cream and blue robes topped with a glittery wire halo, a pink Ganesh surrounded by marigolds, a plastic Shiva balanced on one side-turned foot, and a ceramic crucifixion Jesus with upturned bleeding eyes and a pity-me look. Presumably the multi-denominational approach brought in more customers.

'We're open for business, darlin',' called a woman from somewhere inside.

'I haven't got any money on me,' I warned.

'Then come back when you have. This isn't a charity.'

I paused uncertainly, no further destination in mind.

'No, wait, come in. It's a slow night.'

I took a tentative step inside. A cone of jasmine burned on a sideboard hung with paper garlands, harsh pinks and blues. The fortune teller was seated in a chair of vaguely Egyptian design, a fiftyish black woman in a navy twin-set, a Caribbean church-goer with swollen feet and a psychic sideline. The table before her was covered in a plastic cloth. 'Do you let Jesus into your life?'

'Uh, I went to church at Christmas,' I explained uneasily. I hadn't thought about religion since I was a small girl, and had only wanted to be Mary Magdelene then because she wore robes like a rock star.

'Well, it's a start. I can't be choosy. There's people wasting their money having their cards read over the internet, it's killing my business. Sit yourself down. But you'll owe me twelve pounds, you understand? You're on God's honour.' She switched on an electric crystal ball and gave it a wipe with a J-cloth. I sat and folded my hands in my lap. Hard to believe, but the place felt more normal than anything else that night. The room was an amalgam of comfortable childhood memories. 'Are you Mrs. Phillips?' I asked.

'The original Mrs. Phillips was my auntie, but she died and passed the gift to me. Give me your handbag.'

I slipped the leather strap from my shoulder and passed it across the table. I thought I was about to get my palm read, but Mrs. Phillips snapped open the bag's clasp and had a good rummage about, pulling things out at random and examining them.

'No purse?'

'I got robbed tonight.'

'No? That's terrible, so many robberies round here and the police do nothing. You see them driving past in their squad cars laughing, why is there always four of them inside? No wonder they get nothing done, going around in fours. I could tell them, split up and you'll get more done.' She upturned the bag and tipped its contents onto the table, then spread the items out before her. 'Your husband left you for another woman, you say?'

'I didn't say.'

'No, you didn't. You're a negative terminal, woman. Not many things you like to do, are there? Lucky colour green.' She waved the makeup mirror at me. 'Stay away from red. The colour of madness, bankruptcy, misery. You smell of blood. No children. Not fertile, are you? Think you would be with those hips. Your lucky mineral is plastic.'

'Plastic's not a mineral.'

'Well, no, but it's got minerals in it, like coal and stuff. Like your earrings. Who's doing this, you or me?'

'Why plastic?' I asked, because I had always liked opals.

'You don't know the value of nothing.'

'You can tell that just by looking in my handbag?'

'Anyone could. Expensive rubbish. Once you know the proper value of things, you get a better mineral.'

'I didn't know that was how it worked.'

'There's a lot you don't know. You don't get out much, do you?' This was said kindly.

'What else don't I know?'

Mrs. Phillips was studying my fingers, turning them gently in the light. 'White ladies can't bake decent bread because they got the wrong hands. Good cuticles, like moons. Full moon tomorrow night, you stand in its light and find out the truth about yourself.' She released my hands and rearranged the bag's contents about the table. 'Want to know if your man comes back? He doesn't, and you're better off for it. Leave him with his woman, she'll kill him with all her demandin'. Everybody gets one question. What's yours?'

'Am I ill?' I had no idea why I would ask such a thing. I'd meant to ask for an explanation about the violence I'd witnessed.

'No, you're not ill, just uprooted. It will pass.'

I liked Mrs. Phillips, who suited the dislocation of the night. 'When will it pass?'

'You have to have your ordeal first, darling. The feeling will go after you perform a positive action.'

'Why did you call me a negative terminal?'

'There's endings around you. Get yourself rid of them and start again.' She smiled sadly as she swept everything back into the bag. 'That's all. I've got to take a pee. Remember you owe me twelve quid.'

'You stay open late.'

'My little girlie is dead,' Mrs. Phillips explained. 'Taken by The Lord on her seventeenth birthday. I sleep in the day so I can be closer to her at night.'

I found myself walking back in the direction of the Ziggurat, but when I looked up at the black hole of the block standing against the protecting purple sky, darker now than the universe behind it, I thought of the girl with her crushed throat and the stitch-headed man who might still be stalking the building. I wanted to take Cassandra's advice and go inside, but my nerve still failed me.

The air from the Thames was brackish and sharp now that there were fewer vehicle fumes to disguise it. I cut the corner of the road, walking through the stacked timber and building supplies, then stopped and opened my mobile. There was no-one to call at this time of night. My mother would be in bed. Who else? Reluctantly, I switched it off. Tomorrow I would go back the apartment in daylight, but not tonight, while darkness removed logic and safety. I resolved to keep walking until I could find a place to sleep. It felt extraordinary to realise that I could take nothing for granted, not even the comfort of somewhere warm to sit, something to eat or drink. *I am in public,* I thought, *and everything I do can be shared by strangers*. There was no privacy to be found on the street. Cassandra knew exactly what to expect from men. I could offer a dozen different remedies for getting fruit juice out of a carpet. Which of us was better off?

I eased off my chafing shoes and walked carefully along the wet pavements. Earlier I'd seen used syringes discarded in the gutter. Tomorrow everything would be normal again. Light restored sanity. Tonight, though, I would keep moving until I could not manage another step.

At the next corner there was a fight going on, not the kind you see on television, but something real and feral between two groups of men. One kept running forward and jabbing sharply at another's head before being hauled back by his mates, only to return as his anger rose once more. The other protected his head with his arms, but refused to run away, presenting himself for punishment again and again. His nose was bleeding, and blood was soaking his T-shirt like spilled redcurrant cordial. The pair of them were less like men than different breeds of dog.

If I wasn't in Hell, it was at least Purgatory. Unable to witness any further violence tonight, I turned and ran toward the river.

CHAPTER SEVENTEEN
Stefan

I HADN'T INTENDED to end up beside an RSU soup and sandwich van under another railway arch, but I was ravenous, and the lads there had started talking to me as if I was an old friend.

They informed me that these services were dying out fast, unfashionable since Move Inside programs were the preferred method of support. The servers wanted to know why they hadn't seen me before, and thought I was joking when I told them I was going to sleep rough.

A boy in a grey woolly hat discussed me with his colleague. He recited the facts, a sermon he had delivered too many times: the homeless can't be registered by GPs, you can stand only a month of sleeping rough before long-term problems set in, forty per cent of all homeless women were victims of sexual or physical abuse. Clearly a speech was required before the doling out of food, like a Victorian lecture. Mind you, I was homeless and about to be divorced, so I guess I should have listened.

The boy in the van thought I was too old to be a dealer or a sofa surfer. He asked me if I had ever been in care. No, I explained, I'm a housewife, no longer caring how odd it sounded. They gave me a card, the address of a hostel unit offering care and support, detox advice and counselling. I tore it up as soon as I walked round the corner, and ate the sandwich. It was the kind I'd once have made at home, white bread stuffed with hard-boiled eggs. It was good, today's date on the plastic carton, donated by a chain. The soup was some kind of weird Bovril amalgam, boiled too long, gummy and bitter, but I drained the cup. Every time I moved out of the light I saw the face of the girl on the bedroom floor, skin as pale as paper, her throat a ragged crimson line, a desperate look in her too-large eyes.

I thought of the money I had thrown around in the past, not out of desire but boredom. I thought of the egg sandwich I had just eaten, someone's meal for the day, and felt sick with shame.

I found myself beneath the London Eye, the cables invisible against the sky so that the rim seemed suspended, an enemy of gravity, its glass pods shining like dinosaur eggs, then followed the Embankment until I had unconsciously returned to the site of the Ziggurat. There were benches on the Thames walk, and I gratefully slumped onto one.

I awoke a few minutes later, my limbs numb. It was colder beside the river. I was still wondering what to do when I heard a movement behind me and turned to see a young man in a fur hood noisily pissing against a wall. When he realised I was there he braked in mid-flow.

'Don't let me stop you,' I said, raising a hand and averting my eyes.

'You're the one standing in my toilet.' A French accent. The young man buttoned his flies and looked me over. He orbited slowly, then wiped his nose on the back of his hand. In any other situation I would have noticed his eyes, brown with black lashes, dirty curls over a single dark eyebrow. 'You want a glass of wine?'

'What? No, I just want to sleep.'

'You can't sleep out here.'

'I don't have to. I'm staying in there.' I pointed to the great dark building and was going to say *I just want to be left alone*, but I didn't want to be alone. I wanted to talk to strangers who weren't trying to sell me something. I wanted to touch someone.

'Actually, I do want a drink.' I nodded in what I hoped was a positive, uncrazy manner.

'In France we don't trust people who refuse a glass of wine.' Wide mouth, big grin, white teeth like peppermint pellets. He began to walk away, expecting me to follow him.

'Wait, where are you going?'

'To find a decent bottle. Come, I'll show you.'

'I don't know your name.'

'Don't do formalities, they get in the way. I am Stefan.' He turned and continued walking backwards, but held out his hand.

'I'm June.'

'*Juin.*'

He stopped before a yellow metal ship's container I had seen from the window of the apartment, then slipped into the diagonal shadow at the rear. I hesitated. 'Wait, I don't –'

'Oh come on, you must trust some people. Not everyone is out to hurt you.' He opened a padlock on a dented steel panel and shoved the door back with a ferrous scrape. 'Wait.' He disappeared inside.

Candlelight bloomed in the doorway. I entered as cautiously as a cat. The angled yellow container was filled with draped bolts of midnight blue silk and pieces of rescued furniture. Fat mismatched cushions covered a battered low bed. If the room had appeared in *Wallpaper* magazine, its look would have started a fashion.

'I have some Southern French wines to celebrate the end of the summer. A Chateau Minuty, a Bandol. Very *leger*, *le gout*, you say taste. I do people favours, they pay me in wine. I like your skin, is so pale, is it soft to touch?' He teased out the words with his hands.

'You don't look French,' I pointed out briskly.

'French Algerian, and now I am a *Nicoise*. But for a while I live here.' He pointed to the floor, then smiled again. 'I've been working on the site since they started laying foundations for the building.'

'You helped to build the Ziggurat?'

'I put in windows. You see here.' He pulled up his T-shirt to reveal a belt lined with different drill-bits, like gun cartridges. His stomach was flat and brown. The wine he finally chose was a Saumur, round and rich. I made sure I saw him pull the cork. He filled two glasses printed with gold silhouettes of Cairo. 'Like this.' He cupped his hands around the first glass. 'You have to make it warm.'

'Do they know you live here, the people you work for?'

'Yes of course. I pay a man. Nobody minds. You can't see light from outside.'

'But it's illegal to live without a toilet.'

'It's illegal to stay without a permit.' Another smile.

'If anyone catches you...' I trailed off lamely, aware that when faced with a man who found me appealing, I had raised the thorny topic of inadequate sanitation.

My pathetically English inability to accept a compliment was a habit learned from my mother, who still referred to toilet paper as 'bathroom stationery' and who complained about living in a mixed-raced neighbourhood when a family from Scotland moved into the street.

'There's nothing to be afraid of.' He raised his glass in a toast.

Perhaps not in your life, I thought, watching him. A few days ago I had been sitting at home flicking TV channels, sedated with entertainment. Now I no longer had a television.

'You're thinking too much, not drinking enough.'

We touched glasses, glinting Cairos. He was watching me with amusement. It was most disconcerting.

'Are you here on the premises the whole time?' I asked, sounding like a member of the royal family questioning someone on a walkabout. But I was determined to show a willingness to thaw.

'All day, every day. Most nights too.'

'You see the residents arriving and leaving?'

'I see everyone. I recognise them all. There are not so many of them yet.'

'You know Madame Funes?'

'Yes of course. She is a crazy woman. Parisian. *Bof.*' *That explains it.*

'Did you ever see anything weird going on?'

'Weird?'

'People coming in late at night.'

'Everyone in London comes in late at night, that is what it is for.'

'Have you ever seen a big bald man with a terrible scar right across his head, like this?' I ran my finger in an S-shape over my hair.

'No, I've never seen anyone like that. I was going to offer you some of this, but maybe it's not such a good idea.' He indicated the joint in his hand. He rolled the fat paper tighter and lit it, the leaves crackling like scalded ice.

'I've never smoked marijuana.'

'It's all right, we are in Lambeth. It's almost illegal not to.'

'I have to learn to relax. It's difficult after so many years.'

'Then this is your first lesson.' He placed the joint in my hand and lifted it to my lips, then waited with a smile of hopeful approval. I blasted him with a paroxysm of violent spattery coughing, but tried again.

'This time don't make the end wet.'

By the third hit I had started to crack it. I'd never smoked cigarettes at school because our cycle sheds backed onto the playing field and I hadn't wanted to get mud on my shoes. I told myself that a joint would help me to forget what I saw. Rough sleepers knew all about blotting out the night. I had a place to sleep, but there was a lunatic in the building. The thought made me giggle, then laugh out loud.

'I saw someone die tonight,' I explained. 'It was funny.'

'I don't understand what you mean.'

'I'm not sure I do either. Forget it. OK. I have to go. I can handle it now.' I took another hit, then handed the joint back as it whacked me.

'Where will you go?'

'Back to the apartment.'

'Why don't you stay here with me, that is if you want?'

'Thank you, Stefan, but I'm not in control right now, and I think I should go back. I have to deal with a few things.' I took his hand. 'Perhaps another time.' I thought he was going to help me up, but instead he kissed me, really pushing hard.

They're funny things, lips. Gordon's were thin and dry. Stefan's were full and moist. For a brief moment I sensed what I had been missing all this time. Perhaps it was how Gordon felt when he kissed Hilary, although with the amount of foundation she wore I imagined he would have to sprinkle sand on her face to get a good grip.

At some point – later, I couldn't remember when – Stefan's shirt came off, and I heard buttons bouncing on the floor. His dark, soft skin smelled of sandalwood and underarm sweat that lingered on my fingers. The base of his erection pressed a denim-clad post against my crotch as he unpinned my arms and guided my hands around his hard buttocks. His chest hair formed a perfect black trapezoid, a ladder of tiny curls tracing to his navel and into the low waistband of his loosened jeans. The wide, dry palm of his hand covered my pubic bone as he slipped his fingers inside my pants. The shock of a young man's cool bare hand over my sex was extraordinary; I couldn't recall the last time someone had cupped me so gently, opening me so carefully, as if he was unwrapping a tissue-wrapped buttonhole.

I sank deep into the cushions, my chocolate skirt sliding from my legs. For years I had been constricted by the curse of propriety, strapped into a sensible brassiere and expected to behave as if I was shocked and disapproving all the time, but what was all the respectability for? What had the city given me back, apart from a wider choice of fabric patterns?

I knew I wanted him inside me, and allowed him to push me deeper into musky warm darkness, the muscles in his slim brown arms lifting and widening as he raised his body over mine until I could feel his stomach tense and our raised pelvic bones grate against each other, a cauterising molten centre to our bodies that could light up the little cabin and provide enough electrical power for most of the shops in Oxford Street, plus a few going down toward Marble Arch.

Stefan's right hand slipped smoothly across my stomach and up to my breast, tapping my nipple as if nudging a fruit machine. The left supported me in the small of my back. It seemed a good idea to move further down the divan, especially as his mouth was still glued to mine and was gently forcing me in that direction. He was so light that I could hardly feel him straddled on top of me. Instead, there was the heated V of his thighs where they touched my hips, his forearms against the sides of my ribcage, and that wide outrageous tongue, coming to rest in the back of my mouth. I felt an unfamiliar warmth settling across my pelvic floor. He was everywhere at once, rolling up fabric, unsnapping elastic, and I was drowning in the divan. My rucked skirt was a suburban absurdity against the elegance of silken Arabic cloth. I was enveloped in perfumed heat, pinned through the lower, hotter heart between my legs, burning with the secret smiles of the night. Dark, flickering flames held me in place. I was somewhere I had never been, but had always desired to be.

It was a seduction conducted backwards, starting with the fierce, hard culmination, his eyes never leaving mine, his body pulling back and pushing in with decreasing connection, penetrate and withdraw, gentler and gentler, resolving to a faint and tender kiss.

Some minutes later, I realised he was sitting beside me smoking. 'You know where I am,' he said over his shoulder. 'Come and visit. I will be here.'

Rising carefully to my feet and testing the ground to stop it from rolling, I tried not to lose my balance. I clawed my hair back in an attempt to look sensible and in control, and pulled the container door open a crack as Stefan refastened his jeans and took a slug of wine. I drew in dank river air, trying to work out exactly what had just happened. 'Thank you,' I said.

'You are welcome, *Juin*.' That smile, so wide and neon-white and dangerous. I didn't care how much he had practised it on other women, I liked the idea of being one of the other women. It made me feel normal somehow, part of something. Strangely, I felt more in control than I ever had with Gordon.

It was still the heart of night, but a soft yellow light profiled the skyline of the Thames. Only the Ziggurat stood in sinister blackout. As I made my way across the churned-up quadrangle, the cool night air cut through the light-headed power of the joint. I pushed open the lobby door and tiptoed across the marble space, my pulse lifting as I reached the stairs. It was necessary to feel for the edges of the steps with my bare feet.

With a sobering sense of unease I climbed toward the apartment, scared to think about what I might find, but a little more prepared.

The stairs were laced with ladders of shadow. In darkness the building was a Caligari's cabinet of disorienting angles. As I paced steadily along the corridor, a fear threshold gently nudged at my stomach wall. The joint had left me hungry and agitated. Winds fluted and scraped across the acute edges of the building, rain tapping like showers of gravel against the far windows.

Armed with the battery light, I examined the corded corridor floor once more. No blood, no marks, no sign of an anguished victim collapsing against the parchment walls.

I tore the events down into minutes and seconds. I had stepped onto the balcony and watched as the bare-breasted girl raised her arms to the sky. I had seen her in the hallway with Stitch-Head. I had entered the bedroom and found her within the strangling collar. She was less a figure of flesh and blood now than a missing frame from a film, an opaque, silvery tableau from a forgotten Victorian ghost story. If there was no body and no-one to come looking for her, how long would it be before she ceased to exist at all?

She would survive so long as I did, which was why her attacker had come looking for me. He'd been watching the building for most of the night, but had given up before I returned. All I had to do now was leave and never come back.

The remaining candles in the apartment had burned out. Propping the battery lamp against the wall, I searched among the jars, packets and tins in the warm refrigerator. There was nothing to eat at the stripped house in Hamingwell, and I couldn't go begging to Gordon, who was on his way to Amsterdam with his pumpkin-coloured mistress. Saffron had been right, I decided. The door had a lock. All I had to do was stay the night and go the next morning.

The flat was silent, only the whispering of rain against the glass, the bluster outside tearing like riptides at the corners of the building. I tried to sit calmly with my eyes shut, but my heart was too noisy. In the bathroom I found cabinets stocked with pain-killers and – Lord be praised – Temazepam, good for at least four hours of slumber. Taking one of the small white pills and making my way to the bedroom, I doused the light to conserve its power and sank into the softest gooseneck-down duvet I had ever felt against my skin. I thought about Stefan, slender and tanned, lying in his casbah container, and my limbs grew heavy.

I was no longer someone's wife but a woman, sinking into sleep, to be reborn in a giant storybook bed.

CHAPTER EIGHTEEN
City Life

DREAMLESS DARK WAS lapped by light and the sound of distant morning traffic. Drifting yellow blooms swam across my vision, shrinking to pinholes of dust as I opened my eyes. The rain had stopped, the sun so bright that I was forced to shade my face. The curtains had been left open. The pitiless brown paintings refused love even in sunshine.

I rose and checked my watch – nearly eight. No more pills from now on. I was glad I'd forgotten to empty the contents of the bathroom cabinet into my handbag before leaving Hamingwell. The bathroom water was still scalding hot, powered by the basement gas boilers. I scrubbed out the fuddle of sleep and felt the cool of the morning on my skin. I could no longer smell Stefan on my body.

My first instinct was to cook a breakfast of fried bread, bacon and eggs, but the cupboards had been cleared of perishable food. After years of guilt about my eating habits I wondered if it was possible to change, even though there was something pleasurably obscene about eating a fry-up in such smart surroundings. Searching the shelves I found vacuum-packed fruit, mangoes and peaches.

I slivered soft ripe flesh apart and ate, sad at the thought of leaving all this behind. My case was filled with expensive flower-print clothes that now looked naïve in such a stripped-back setting, so I settled for a grey sweatshirt and jeans before taking a final look around the apartment. I binned the items with bloodstains. I would pack and be gone within the half-hour.

It was almost possible to dismiss the previous night, but for the shears and the man with the stitched head. The world was sharp and bright, strangeness dispelled, rationality returned to its rightful position at the head of my mind's army. Standing on the balcony nursing a ceramic tub of milky coffee, my unknotted brown hair drifting around my face, I felt a sense of sophistication for the first time in my life, not the bogus sophistication of gold-card credit but something placid inside. Apart from anything else, I had been propositioned by a very attractive young man several years my junior. The thought filled me with new confidence.

Below, matchbox traffic shunted and braked at road junctions. River launches were puttering up the Thames like battered bathtoys. A distant haze presented the London Eye in low resonance, its glinting glass pods imperceptably rotating. The futuristic ferris wheel gave London the air of a half-constructed funfair. I tried to recall Phillip Larkin's comment about London in the sun – something about 'its postal districts packed like squares of wheat'. I'd been wasted on the residents of Hamingwell.

A few minutes later, packed and ready, I stood in the hall and took a last look around the apartment. Everything had been returned to its rightful place. I would lose the money I so badly needed, but at least I'd be safe. I ventured back out into the top floor hall with my case and nearly had a heart attack.

'Jesus, you made me jump!' The young West Indian woman had a white plastic toilet brush raised in her right hand like a club. 'I didn't think there was anyone else here today.'

'Neither did I.'

The young woman lowered her lavatorial mace. 'Sorry, I'm cleaning the flat next door. I'm Fragrance.' She snapped off a glove and shook hands with stiff-armed formality, a member of staff meeting an employer. I noticed we were dressed in almost identical clothes.

'There's no-one staying in there at the moment, is there?'

'No, I don't think anyone lives here full-time. It's a contract job. I've only been doing the place a month. There's not much to do, ash-trays, dusting, some washing up, and they've got their own linen service. I was told it's for corporate hospitality.'

'There's not a girl staying there, very attractive, slim, about eighteen?'

'I don't see anyone, I'm always gone before they return. I'm supposed to do the place on Fridays but I had to take my little boy to St. Thomas's for his ears. Did Mr. Ashe find you?'

'Who?'

'The man from the gas company. I told him I thought someone else was up here. You're supposed to be out tomorrow night some time.'

'It's okay, I'm not going to be here anyway.'

'It's just for a couple of hours. He's shutting down the system, but he's not allowed to let anyone remain in the building while he's doing it. I'm sure he'll be more than happy to explain. It took me ages to get away from him. He's in the basement, a big bald man in a red hat. You must have heard that weird clanking sound.'

'No, I'm afraid I've been dead to the world.'

'I told him if I saw anyone I'd tell them. Save him coming up. I've got to go back to the hospital, so I'll finish here tomorrow. Don't worry if you hear someone moving around, it'll just be me.'

'I'll bear that in mind.' Perhaps it was better for someone to think I was still in the building. Fragrance's description of the gas-fitter in the basement sounded close to that of Stitch-Head. The best thing, I decided, would be to take a look from a distance. I slipped my case back into the apartment and went downstairs.

I found Ashe up an aluminium ladder hammering on a steel cylinder with the end of a spanner. Ashe was bigger. The fat at the base of his neck formed a crease beneath his shaved head, and his stomach stretched a vast oily vest over the belt of his jeans. On top of his toolbox were six pairs of pliers with different coloured handles. Gordon used to lay out his drill-bits like that. Men are genetically programmed to display tools in obscure groupings. Then they draw lines around them on peg boards. Go figure.

'You're not supposed to be down here,' he called, attacking the pipe more violently. 'You the lady in one of the penthouses?'

'I'm just staying for the weekend,' I lied.

'Can't be here tomorrow night between ten and eleven. We're shutting the system down to install new valves, and we can only do it while the electricity is turned off otherwise it'll trigger automatic ignition while the pipes are full of gas, and you don't want that. Look at this.' He pulled out a yard of paperwork covered in spidery diagrams. 'There's lads out there with degrees who can't tell you what this lot means, and I've only got an hour to sort it out.' I was already losing interest. 'The power's back on at midnight, and I don't want to leave unignited gas building up. Health and Safety.'

'Does that mean it's dangerous?'

'No, love, this electronic stuff's state-of-the-art, which means I can't thrash it with my spanner to get it working. I've never seen a place like this, everything's arse-backwards. The workmanship's slick but it's all too complicated. I tell you, I wouldn't want to live here.'

'Why not?'

'Microchips. Nothing's built to a standard gauge, so you can't fix anything yourself. Couldn't have kids here, either, because of the low balconies, the unsupervised pool and gym, the easy-access garbage chutes to the incinerator. Doesn't conform to Health and Safety if you ask me, but there's ways of getting round these things. They don't want families here, just rich singles who'll pay the service charges and be happy to live alone with a lot of high-tech gadgets. I tried to talk to that mad French woman about it but she didn't seem to understand, just screamed her head off at me.' He shrugged and returned to hammering his pipe.

I was going to leave, but the day outside looked so inviting that I decided to take a walk around the neighbourhood first. I didn't want to have to carry my case with me, so I slipped it behind a table in the foyer. As I left the Ziggurat and walked from Lambeth towards Waterloo, the morning felt freer, lighter, a gold mirror-image to those rare days before pleasure relied on spending. The city looked different at pedestrian height. You saw another London when you walked it. The atmosphere changed from one road to the next. In the most derelict areas of London perfectly preserved

173

terraces were tucked from the view of cars and buses, so that there was hardly a part of the metropolis that didn't hide secret streets, parks, tunnels or gardens.

I watched and listened. And I talked to a cab driver as he leaned against his cab, drinking tea on his break.

'Oh yeah, College Place N1, Fournier Street E1, Markham Street SW3, Kelly Street NW5, parts of Commercial Road, the backstreets of Whitechapel, behind St. Bart's, off Hatton Garden, bits of New Cross, Southwark, Tooting, there's what I call nice roads all over, but I'll tell you what.' He stuck a Kit-Kat into his tea and noisily sucked the chocolate off. 'The posher the area gets, the more crap it becomes. Chelsea, Barnsbury, Hampstead, Highgate, they all full of bankers pretending they're living in little villages with their organic fucking bakeries and craft fairs, and it's bollocks. They scream blue murder if McDonalds opens in their high street, but drive through a shit part of town and you'll see KFC bunging up takeaways that look like clown's houses. Go to any rough area and have a look around, you soon find canals and alleys, parks, footbridges, tunnels, all kinds of hidden stuff.' He drained his tea and smacked his lips, chucking the cup into the gutter. 'This was a right trouble area, and now all of a sudden it's professional. There's people paying six million quid for a luxury flat, and they find themselves living next door to a hostel full of alkies. I'm not sure who it's worse for. Then there's your immigrants scratching about to make a living, just like the old lurks and sewer-hunters. We don't have any cats-meat men no more, but we got every other bugger. Right, I'm back on duty. But I'll tell you, anyone who says London is like everywhere else now has never done The Knowledge.'

I thought about what he'd said as I passed a bow-windowed Victorian house with a stucco façade and an overgrown front garden, standing in melancholy isolation behind lanes of stalled traffic.

I started to notice other people, and watched where they were going. A group of Asian women were heading for the gates of a small factory, their grey raincoats, headscarves and jumpers pulled on the top of bright embroidered sarees, British clothes smothering rich colours with dull common sense. They stepped into the road to pass around some teenaged girls in short-sleeved T-shirts and microskirts on their way home. A night shelter was discharging a line of homeless men wrapped in identical tartan travel blankets. A private development had two new silver-blue Ferraris on a chained-off forecourt.

I walked, I watched.

Strange run-down shops of a kind I had never seen before: a pet store selling snakes and iguanas, its overheated interior causing its filmy windows to run with condensation, a shop that only sold gargantuan trophies and plaques 'For All Occasions'. Motorcycle Repair & Bespoke Leather Goods, Jamaican Patties, Jerk Chicken, Shawarmas, Violin-makers, Knives & Luggage, Nightclub Lighting & Deck Rental, Curry In A Hurry, The Kite Shop, Halal Butchers, a barbershop with a yellowed photograph of George Michael in the window. It was virgin territory for me, the stores filled with alien items, most still shut at ten in the morning, the pavements plastered with chicken boxes, the dirt washed into beach-patterns by the night's rain. Flats above shops, Indian beats wafting down from rows of opened windows, music to accompany the slow stretching of limbs, like the opening of flowers.

I saw bad things, too. A yellow plastic police cordon around a pub, officers interviewing kids on the street, plastic-wrapped flowers stacked against the bar doors in an impromptu tribute to a fatally stabbed boy. A phonebox covered by adverts for luxury chocolate desserts that afforded its junkie occupant the perfect spot to shoot up. A row of dirty blue nylon sleeping bags laid end to end like giant caterpillars waiting to pupate, silted up with windblown trash. Blood smeared on the spiderwebbed glass door of a fried chicken outlet. Two desolate, shabby men drinking at the road edge who could have stepped from the pages of Henry Mayhew's journals.

I counted the loose change left in my shoulder-bag, not even enough for a sandwich, so I drank a mug of fierce orange tea in a supermarket café. It scalded, tasting better than any I'd had in the restaurants of expensive department stores. I made a mental note of my change. It was odd to feel so many small coins in my hand.

The supermarket was hemmed in by a twenty-foot chicken-wire fence that wouldn't have appeared on its original design. If you had to come up with a picture of a really frightening place, it's what you would have drawn, a cross between a concentration camp and a slaughterhouse. It made my skin crawl, but I didn't have enough money to go somewhere nicer.

My attention was distracted by a woman in the high street who had just called me a cunt. Before I could wonder how I had offended her the woman had lost interest and was now calling the derelict phone box next to her a cunt.

Does Nigella Lawson have this problem when she goes to shop? I wondered. *When she's striding sturdily along a country lane with a wicker basket on her arm, do people call her a cunt? Presumably her nearest village is typical of those all around the country, with a one-way system and a Post Office that is now a Chinese restaurant, or does it have a wool shop and a chemist with a weighing machine and tall glass bottles filled with coloured water and a newsagent who stocks sherbet dabs, jars of boiled winter mixture twists, practical jokes and postcards on a revolving stand? In Nigella-land it's always 1962, which means that the lucky bitch can still have live eels from MacFisheries dropped straight into her shopping bag and doesn't have to take cover every time an engine backfires in case it's the start of a gang war.*

I rang Lou's house from my mobile but got Lou's monosyllabic son. Hadrian seemed to have trouble recalling that he lived with his parents, and could not volunteer information as to their whereabouts. His mother had gone to the gym early, perhaps she was shopping, perhaps she had run off to join a Balkan circus.

I tried Lou's mobile, no answer, and resisted the impulse to call Gordon. He certainly hadn't tried calling me. One bar left on the Nokia. I'd forgotten to bring the charger with me, not that it would have done much good, given the number of friends I had managed to accumulate in a decade of marriage.

There was my mother, but Ruth always sounded disappointed when I called, as though she wished she was talking to someone else. I got on better with Gordon's grandmother, Rose, an opinionated former actress who played to the gallery when she wanted sympathy, but was kind enough. Apart from a nicotine-stained uncle in Surrey and an agoraphobic schoolfriend at the edge of town, there was no-one else to try. The reality of my isolation came as a shock.

I passed the riverside aquarium, and would have gone in but the ticket was expensive. For the first time in years I was forced to deny myself something; a strange new feeling. I thought of the house in Wetherby Road, empty and ready for selling. What did Gordon expect me to do, conveniently vanish into the mist? He said he would make arrangements for me, but we hadn't discussed divorce. I leaned on the black metal balustrade and watched patches of mist brush the surface of the brown river. Two boys on the foreshore were throwing stones into the water. I imagined bringing a child here, walking hand in hand into the city, seeing the world through amazed young eyes.

I realised I hadn't thought about shopping since I arrived. Once, early in the disillusionment of my marriage, there had been an episode. I could no longer recall what had sparked it off. Walking out of John Lewis with something, a jacket that I'd forgotten to pay for, I hadn't been concentrating but wasn't entirely innocent, certainly not enough to convince the detective who stopped me. The store hadn't prosecuted, but Gordon had been angry and for a while I just stayed in bed, leaving the washing until the bathroom basket was overflowing, forgetting the housework, not interested in anything much. We had never resolved the matter, but I knew Gordon suspected a delayed reaction to what he called 'the motherhood issue'.

Waterloo Bridge Road yielded a Barclays bank. The area was quieter than it had been the night before, the wealthier residents presumably having traipsed off to the country for the weekend. Clutching my Connect card to my chest, fearful of losing my only remaining link to the world of financial independence, I waited in the queue. Money was freedom, I wondered why I hadn't thought of that before. Ready cash was not something to be taken for granted.

The sky was clouding over fast, and the terrace of buildings had fallen into shadow. As I punched in my number and selected a withdrawal of sixty, knowing that there was a total £72.50 in credit, I was vaguely annoyed by the graffiti-scarred, cola-stained screen showing a calm blue lake. *We are dealing with your transaction.* I squeezed my eyes shut, unable to watch, waiting to hear the sound of the mechanism counting notes. I opened one eye. Nothing had happened.

'It keeps doing that,' said a girl behind me. Pierced lip, pierced nose, shaved-off eyebrows, startling vermillion tufts of hair. She was underdressed and hanging onto her boyfriend's arm as though it was a Tube carriage pole, unable to prevent herself from shivering. 'I use this cashpoint all the time. It's them kids from the estate, they stick their gum down the slot. You wanna punch the number in again.'

I took the advice, but this time the machine swallowed my card. Surely the balance couldn't have been wrong? But as there was no arguing with the bank, that was the end of it. My lifeline had been cut. A brief stab at independence had been pathetically cut short. I dreaded working out how much was left in my jacket pocket.

Without money there was nothing I could do. A walk in the park – except that I had never been for a walk by myself, and had no idea where the nearest park was located. I wondered if Julie and Malcolm were having a good time in New York, at it like knives in a rumpled bedroom far above the steaming streets, while back in England their respective partners showered gifts on their knowing offspring.

At the corner of the stairs leading to Waterloo station a young black man was playing a saxophone. The thick, clear notes cut melancholy shafts through the space above the concourse. Timetable board codes speckled out and regrouped, sending passengers off like flung-apart atoms. Everyone had a destination. There were greetings, hugs, leave-takings. Children were lifted from their feet like puppies, partners gripped each other tightly, each waiting for the other to break away. The longer I looked, the more I felt as if I was moving deeper within the city, growing toward the people who inhabited it.

Wandering among the book stalls beneath Waterloo Bridge, I watched an obscure East-European music troupe playing carved wooden instruments well or badly, I couldn't tell. I stood beneath a railway arch and felt the rumble of trains through my bones; London breathing.

Carefully turning out my shoulderbag on a bench, I was excited by the discovery of a squashed five pound note in one of the corners. I ate lunch in a café that had no rocket salads or seared tuna, just liver, bacon, egg and chips, overcooked to perfection. There were plenty of other places, steel stools in bare stripped-pine rooms, dishes chalked on high blackboards, but the Cappanina

Café felt like an endangered species, realer than the rest. Pensioners sat alone, absently stirring tea – no fancy coffees here – scanning the pages of the *Daily Mirror*, the memories of lost ones tucked far back in their minds but always present somewhere. I overheard two electricians arguing about gin, of all things.

'If it says *London Gin* on the label, it don't mean it's distilled here, just that it's from a continuous still and made with juniper berries.' In stained overalls they sipped their teas, seated together like a pair of Toby jugs.

I bought a packet of chewing gum and shoplifted a pocket A-Z, as I didn't want to lose the last bar on my mobile using the streetfinder. As I studied the neighbourhood names, the A-Z gave me the power of an angel, looking down on the city from above with everything neatly labelled. Leathermarket Street, Tanner Street, Morocco Street – it was easy to see what kind of industry used to be here. There were still retail outlets selling belts and bags. On the other side of the river and spread further about, dock streets named Tobacco, Lime, Vinegar, Pearl, Clove, Cork, Mace, Juniper, Oyster, Lavender, Timber, Mutton. I found myself committing them to memory in the same way that I remembered dress materials. The reaches of the city beyond Chelsea, Albert and Battersea Bridges interested me less. These were the residential areas of the ingenious rich, their crescents and closes once peppered with coteries of artists, now filled with stockbrokers and the lost children of industrious parents.

So much life in such a small, dark stretch of water. A life founded by strong, enterprising men so that women could only look and buy what they produced. It had always been the way of the world.

It was a new world now; I had caught a glimpse of it on this bright day, and wanted to be part of it. The sealed, stiff city of the guidebooks had changed, and something unbordered was taking its place. With the closure of the map-book, my own resolve strengthened. I would return to the Ziggurat, not to collect my bag but to stay there and see it through. I would survive on air if I had to, last out long enough to be paid for my trouble, and start to build a streamlined new life. I would no longer require the safety of freshly-purchased objects. And as for the horror of last night, well, it would have to remain unexplained, as so many things were in the world.

The map-book had provided an extra dimension to the city, one of time instead of place. How many others like me had come here filled with hope for the future? How many of them had survived?

However many it was, I thought, make it Plus One.

CHAPTER NINETEEN
Hallucination

I HAD TO search fast for my mobile before the voicemail kicked in.

I hadn't expected to hear from Gordon, but the sound of his voice was a reassuring connection to home – even if, technically speaking, neither of us had one any more. Despite my new resolve I still half-hoped that he was calling to announce the end of his affair. Perhaps Hilary had fallen under her trolley, or had succumbed to makeup poisoning. Perhaps falling cabin pressure had caused her breast implants to detonate.

'How are you getting on, June? How's your mother?' I hadn't told him about deciding to stay in London.

'I'm not in Leamington, I'm looking after a flat for a friend of Lou's.'

'That explains it. I was hoping you'd at least be able to stay out of trouble.'

'What are you talking about?'

'I thought you'd be more considerate. You know I'm in Amsterdam. I'm trying to make a go of it with Hilary. She's in the next room, having forty winks before dinner. Have the police been in touch with you?'

For one disorienting second I thought he must know about the boy in Malcolm's apartment. 'The police?'

'You lost your Connect card.' He sounded as if he was talking to a child.

'Oh, that. The cash machine ate it.'

'Was there anyone standing near you?'

'A couple behind me, why?'

'And they suggested you re-enter your number. Christ, June, you fell for the oldest trick in the book. They're con artists. They jam the machine, you insert your card and get it stuck, they watch you re-enter your PIN number and keep a note of it, then after you've gone they get the card back and use it. How could you be so stupid?'

'How do you know what happened?'

'There's a security check still in place on your plastic. The fraud people couldn't get hold of you, so they called me.' A police siren whooped behind me, drowning Gordon's voice.

'I'm sorry, Gordon, what did you say?'

'I said have you got any money on you?'

'Nothing. I had my purse stolen.'

'I don't believe this. The first time you're left to your own devices and everything falls apart. Listen, I'm back on Monday, I'll let you have some money, can you at least manage until then?'

I resented his knowledge of my failing independence, his easy offer of a cash bail-out. I was determined not to accept it. 'I might as well get used to sorting out my own problems.'

'I don't know what you're going to live on. Perhaps it'll do you good to have a little responsibility. You know, June, for ten years I earned the money, I balanced the books, I did everything for you. You're nearly thirty now and you haven't much to fall back on. It's time you learned a few hard facts about life. Men won't carry you forever. Hilary's waking up, I have to go.'

The fierce sun was turning the sky Wedgwood blue, throwing shadows into sharp relief and igniting the vitreous panes of deserted office buildings. The extravagant new apartment blocks ranged on either side of the Ziggurat stood guard over the river like wealthy watchtowers.

Stefan was standing in the doorway of his portable casbah sharpening a kitchen knife, the container warmed by its shade of evening primrose. 'I've been keeping an eye on the place for you,' he said, smiling. I saw now that there was gold in the brown of his eyes. 'No-one's been in or out of the building, so you are safe. I'm cooking a Moroccan fish tagine for lunch, want some?' A smell of frying lemons and cardamon drifted over the site.

'I'd love to, but I have some things to do,' I told him.

'Come and see me this evening if you like.' His smile grew craftier. 'We could have a little fun. Here.' He beckoned me, pulling a bamboo skewer of oily fish chunks from the frying pan.

I bit a hot, pungent flake from the stick with the edges of my teeth. 'It's delicious. What is it?'

'River fish.'

'Surely not this river.' I coughed and must have looked horrified, because he started laughing.

'Yes, but further up, not from this part of the Thames. The fishes are small, and you must cook them thoroughly, the water has bad flavour. I have a cousin who catches them. It's a very strange river, you know?'

I knew about the power of the Thames. It has tides that move twelve miles in either direction and vary

185

by up to forty feet, a current running five times faster than the strongest swimmer, water filled with bacterial diseases, colder and less buoyant than the sea because there's no salt, seventy bodies fished out each year, some never identified. A person has less chance of surviving a fall into it than slipping under a Tube train.

'I'll pass on the fish,' I told him.

'Okay, but I'll be watching out for you, funny English lady.' He tilted his head to one side. 'You look different today. You look – I don't know – it's good.'

Everything in Malcolm's flat was as I had left it. The acrid smell of smoke in the bedroom had dissipated. Sunlight was magnified by the river and flooded the bedroom, enlarging it by bleaching out the shadows.

I made camomile tea and watched the sluggish ebb of the tide, listening to the distant muffled roar of traffic, a power station of a city, its residents operating like the components of some arcane perpetual motion engine. It could have been a view from any hotel window; I couldn't smell the bitter Thames water now, or feel the wind race up the estuary to be dissipated in the city's tower blocks, but I could sense its energy resonating through cold glass.

Somewhere out there in an alley or a park, in the river or on a piece of waste ground, that girl's body was waiting to be found. Where had her boyfriend taken her? What had she done to be attacked like that? How had he come and gone without Stefan seeing him? I wanted to know, less out of concern for her than to satisfy my own curiosity.

Figuring I was about to spend the rest of the weekend alone, I searched the flat again. No matter how much I tried to dismiss it, the image of the girl refused to leave my mind. I remembered thinking how clean the bedroom had been when I returned, and decided to take another look. If I hadn't checked under the bed – old habits die hard – I would have missed the tiny shard of metal that lay there. I supposed it might have been there for days or weeks, but the position, behind where she had fallen, made me wonder if it had come from her.

I was forced to lay flat on my stomach and stretch, but the object remained beyond my grasp. The frame was steel and difficult to budge, but I succeeded in moving it a foot or so, enough to slip my arm between the bedhead and the wall. What I found in my unfolded fingers was a sliver of tin, one side smooth, the other slightly serrated. At first it was impossible to see the thing clearly, but as I tipped it to the sunlight I saw it was a key, one of those baby keys you find in the tiny locks of jewellery caskets. Had she been wearing a lockable chain or bracelet, something holding the secret of her identity?

I pocketed it and was changing my sweatshirt when I heard something fall in the kitchen, a metal spoon on tiles. It rocked to a stop and I held my breath as I stepped into the hall. Someone was standing in the kitchen.

'June?'

'God, Lou, I completely forgot you were coming.'

'I couldn't find you. I've been wandering around upstairs for the last half hour. I left your address at home.'

Lou had pinned her hair up with chopsticks, something she only did when she was very hungover. Sometimes she couldn't find them and used a pair of forks she'd stolen from the Bollywood Nights Curry

House. It was the furthest she'd ventured with ethnic fashion. 'I caught a train to Waterloo. I was too wasted to drive. You phoned me last night making no sense whatsoever, then I come round and find all the doors wide open. I've been ringing doorbells but they don't work. I thought you'd been murdered.'

'Not me,' I replied. 'I don't know who. After all that, didn't I lock the door? Actually, I'm not sure the keys fully work by themselves. I warned you, the electricity's off, nothing seems to work properly.'

'You really didn't dream this whole thing?'

'The girl collapsed in the bedroom. I tried to help her, but for all I know I might have killed her.'

'What on earth did you do? Dear God, don't tell me someone pegged out in here.'

'When I came back with some help, she'd disappeared.'

Lou breathed a sigh of relief. 'So she couldn't have been dead, that's something.'

'No, I think she was dead.'

'How do you know?'

'She'd stopped breathing, Lou.'

'Shit. Would you recognise her again? How did she look?'

'Like a model. Very slim and beautiful, weirdly so, almost too perfect.'

'The way men like them, you mean, idealised. I think about guys like that all the time, especially when I look at Darren slumped on the sofa picking his feet. I don't know what I'm going to do about my family. We're not like any family you see on TV, neighbours popping around to sort each other's problems out, everyone bonding and *relating*. We're just alone together.' She sighed and studied me anxiously. 'You're *absolutely* sure you didn't imagine this episode of yours? How much did you drink?'

'Not a lot. But later I had a joint and some kind of pill.'

'I don't believe you. You used to moan if I gave you caffeinated coffee.'

'And I took that diet pill you gave me.'

'I gave you that over a year ago. God, this is too weird.'

I opened the balcony doors and we sat outside at the steel breakfast table. The air was warm but laden with moisture. Gulls spiralled above us, flying ahead of distant stormclouds, working their way inland. I sat with my hands against my forehead, fighting a headache.

'You said there were no lights, so how could you remember what she looked like?'

'I'd borrowed a lamp from a neighbour.' I thought about skipping the part where I nearly burned the place down, but decided to come clean. 'I promise you, she was dead. Somebody took the body away while I was out and quickly cleaned the place up. The man who killed her.'

'How long were you gone?'

'I'm not sure. Forty minutes, three quarters of an hour.'

'And this policeman who wasn't a policeman…'

'Retired. Very old but kind.'

'Your mind could be playing tricks. Think about it. It's the first time you've been away from home in years.' Lou looked back at the lounge, still set about with the white emergency candles I had found bundled in a drawer beneath the sink. 'I knew Malcolm was making a packet but I didn't think he was this rich. He has better taste that I'd imagined.'

'How much do you know about him?'

'Let's see.' Lou thought for a minute. 'He's around forty-seven, looks good for his age, a workaholic, a serial womaniser, takes tablets for his cholesterol and has got Julie on a string. He has these things – what do you call them.' She waggled her fingers at the sides of her head and made a face.

'Hearing aids.'

'Sideburns.'

'There aren't any photographs of him, or anyone else.'

'There wouldn't be. I think his wife uses the place occasionally. He doesn't like to leave any incriminating evidence.'

'He's not involved in anything illegal, is he?'

'Not as far as I know. He's a bit murky about his sidelines, though.'

'What sort of sidelines?'

'He runs another company. Medical products, I think.'

'It must be successful if he can afford to collect abstract art.'

'Oh, they're inherited. That's why they're in the mother's name. They had to be registered in order to maintain provenance, and that means taxes.' She looked back at the lounge. 'Speaking of which, where are these famous watercolours?'

I had assumed they were stored away. The pictures on the walls were oils. 'He wouldn't keep them out in the open, would he?' I thought of the Da Vinci cartoon cocooned in its gloomy home at the National Portrait Gallery. 'Don't watercolours fade in bright light?'

'So where are they? That's the whole point of you looking after the place, June. Please don't tell me someone just walked in here and took them. The lobby door downstairs was ajar and you left the front door open, Jesus.'

'They must be here somewhere.'

'You mean you haven't seen them the whole time you've been here?'

'No, there are only these great ugly canvases. He must have the rest locked away.'

'Just how much did you drink last night?'

'Before it happened? A couple of gins. I can't really remember..'

'Before you saw this dead girl.'

'Yes but I know how much I have to drink before I start seeing things.'

'Unless there was something wrong with the drinks. Men are capable of anything when it comes to sex.'

'I thought Julie said he was a nice guy.'

'She's desperate. Right now she'd date Hannibal Lecter.' Lou returned to the lounge and began pulling bottles out of the cocktail cabinet, opening them and sniffing their contents. 'If you're sure you didn't imagine it, that's a different matter. But this is not gin, I promise you. Is this what you drank from?' She held up an empty decanter.

'Yes, that's the one.'

'Couldn't you smell the difference? How will I ever make a decent alcoholic of you? This is too sweet, it smells like nail polish. Didn't you notice it was too dark when you poured it out?'

'I told you, there's no electricity. I had to mix them by candlelight. What is it?'

'You've been drinking absinthe, baby, favoured tipple of the French decadents. If you used it in the amounts I mix your gins in, you probably suffered psychoactive hallucinations. This stuff contains wormwood, it's the speedball of liquor, messes with your nervous system.'

'But I haven't felt hungover.'

'That's because there's very little alcohol in the good brands. There's this stuff called thujone that stays in your system and accumulates, causing all sorts of weird shit.'

'How come you know so much about it?'

She stuck her hands on her hips and looked at me. 'What do you think I do at home, cooking and cleaning?'

'But the fire I caused was real.'

'Yeah, so you set the bed alight when you dropped the lamp. You're in a different environment, away from home, everything's new and strange. What other explanation could there be? You honestly think some half-naked supermodel walked in off the street and was tied up before choosing to drop dead in your presence, only to disappear without a trace?'

'I know the difference between what's real and what's imagined, Lou.'

'You've obviously never been on a dating site.' Lou studied me appraisingly. 'Where the hell are the paintings?'

'He must have put them away somewhere. When I arrived at the building the concierge was still on duty. There's no way anyone would have got past her.'

'All right, if you're sure. But remember, you're the one who went out and spent £4,000 on everything from abdomenizers to angle-grinders and then didn't remember what she'd done.'

'That was different.'

'I don't see how. You've never exactly been in touch with reality.'

'What do you mean by that?' I demanded indignantly.

'I mean, darling, that everyone in the neighbourhood knew your husband was plugging the transit-tramp next door, even you, only you 'forgot' it, just like you forgot your little shopping sprees.' Lou reached out a consoling hand. 'I came here today because I was worried about you. I brought you some cash.'

I bristled. 'I don't want to be reminded of what I used to do. And I don't want a handout from you.'

'Come on, June, I'm your best friend, I can say things no-one else is allowed to. It's only fifty quid, that's all I have on me but it should keep you going. Don't do a number on me. Unless you really want to bite the bullet and come back. I could put up Hadrian's old bed in the box-room. You have to tell me now, though, because we're taking a ball-hedge up to Darren's deranged parents in Aldershot tomorrow and we'll be staying over because he doesn't like driving on motorways at night and I'll be too spazzed to see straight.'

'No, it's okay, I'm going to stay here. I have to get everything sorted out in my head. I'll go to my mother's on Monday morning, after I've returned the key.'

'Okay, you're sure as hell not missing anything in Hamingwell. But don't drink anything else you find in the cupboards. And call me if you have any more trouble. Promise?'

I forced a smile. 'I promise.' I told Lou not to leave the money, but she did anyway, slipping the notes onto the table in the hall, and I was secretly grateful. After she had gone, I edged a chair-back under the front door handle.

Back on the balcony, I studied the brick face carefully. There were no handholds, no cables, nothing connecting the apartments. They were large and separate, isolated from each other in the sky; it was their key selling point. If the people I saw were really there, they must have come in through the front entrance, and I had failed to hear them moving about because of the absinthe.

I leaned as far as I dared and tried to see into the corner penthouse, but grey blinds were drawn across the double doors of its balcony. Had they been drawn this morning? Perhaps Fragrance had closed them.

As I absently watched, the far blind twitched slightly, as if an observer had seen me and quickly withdrawn.

It's no good, I told myself finally. *I have to do it. There's someone still in there. Maybe he's waiting to get rid of the body. I'm partly responsible, I have to know.* It couldn't be Stitch-Head, because I'd seen him prowling the streets, and Stefan had seen no-one come in. That meant there was a third person involved.

The hall was in permanent gloom, and required some fortitude to traverse. The building was so silent that even a low breeze could be heard mumbling around its corners. Unable to find a bell, I knocked hard on the corner penthouse door. The sound was sharp and shocking. I waited, fidgeting, for a full minute, but nobody came. A faint noise came from inside, a clearing of the throat, the scrape of a chair.

'Hello?' I knocked again.

A deeper silence descended. I pressed the side of my head flat against the wood and discerned a regular movement of air, soft shallow breathing. There was someone in the flat, a man on the other side of the door, but he wasn't planning to reveal himself.

He was inside, inches away, I could almost feel him. My fingers spread across the warm wood, sensing the presence of another human being alone in the shadows.

CHAPTER TWENTY
The Balcony

ELLIOT ANSWERED THE door of his apartment in a creepily short blue towelling robe. He looked liverish and guilty. His skin as slick and breath as shallow as if he'd been running or having a marathon bout of afternoon sex, and his hair was sticking up on one side like a duck wing. For a moment he didn't seem to remember me.

'Oh, it's you.'

'I need to talk to you. Can I come in?' I had changed into a skirt and high-heeled shoes in order to make myself feel more normal, but it was normal for Hamingwell, not here, and with Elliot in a state of undress, exposing my legs no longer seemed such a good idea.

He seemed reluctant to admit me, not quite standing far enough aside to allow me by. 'All right,' he decided, smoothing his hair into place, 'but I'm expecting someone very shortly.'

'This will only take a minute.' Something in his attitude stopped me from telling him too much. 'You said you know the man whose apartment I'm looking after.'

'That's right, and you don't, do you?'

As I passed his bedroom door I caught a glimpse of several leather straps attached with rings and buckles, laid out on the duvet in a fetishistic order that reminded me of Mr. Ashe and his pairs of pliers. He led the way into the kitchen, scratching, and poured himself orange juice. *Big evening ahead?* I wondered.

'No. I lied to you. I didn't want you to think... the truth is, I'm here because I have no choice.'

'Everyone has a choice, June.' He seemed bored by me and walked away, so that I was forced to follow him.

'How much do you know about Malcolm Phillimore?'

'Oh, is that his name?'

'You haven't spoken to him?'

'I thought I told you, nobody knows anyone here. I saw him in the hall a couple of times. Actually, I had an argument with him.'

'What kind of argument?'

Elliot dropped onto the sofa opposite, his robe falling open at an uncomfortably high level. Either he hadn't noticed or was unalarmed by the notion of displaying his genitals to virtual strangers. 'I really don't remember. Something... wait.' He glanced over at the eviscerated dummy standing against the bare wall. 'He was complaining about a delivery, something that went astray in the mail room. He thought I'd taken it. The Funes woman, she gets everything wrong. She told him I'd signed for his package but I'd done no such thing. It was just an embarrassing confusion. He was apologetic afterwards. Seemed pleasant enough. Isn't he something to do with plastic surgery?'

'What about the neighbour in the corner penthouse, on Malcolm's far side?'

'What is this? Are you conducting some kind of survey? I'm not going to find my comments turning up on Facebook, am I?'

'I just wondered.'

'I think he's Eastern European, doesn't speak, doesn't smile, hardly ever at home. But there's someone else in his apartment, his wife or girlfriend maybe, young and rather sexy. She never goes out. I think there's something wrong with her.'

'How do you know that?'

'Dr. Marac told me. He has the flat directly below this one. The Eastern European heard he was a doctor and called him up one night in a frightful panic. The girl was apparently having some kind of seizure, ranting on in a language he didn't recognise. Marac couldn't do anything because it turns out he's a doctor of philosophy. I asked him what happened but he wouldn't tell me. She sounded a bit messed up, you know... ' He pointed back at Maurice's sectioned face and single staring eye. '... in the head.'

'How do you mean?'

'Apparently there'd been a lot of screaming and shouting from her, then later she was fine, came to the door as if nothing had happened, couldn't understand why people were complaining. Maybe she suffers from Tourette's. It's nothing to do with me, of course. I told you, we keep to ourselves. You pay this much for privacy.'

'But Malcolm's right next door, he must have heard things, seen things.'

'Ah, yes.' Elliot looked at me shiftily. 'Well, maybe they're all involved together, in and out of each other's flats.'

I couldn't tell if he was making a point or being sarcastic. His robe had opened further, exposing a testicular sac like a fortnight-old peach. I wondered if he did this with all his female guests, in the same way that baboons exposed their backsides to mates. He lazily flicked the robe back in place.

'Only captains of industry can afford to live here, and it's never a good idea to put them all in a group. Do you know what the rates of mental abnormality are in this country? One in five among the general populace, one in three among senior corporate executives. The higher you go the screwier it gets, psychologically speaking.' He began to clean his nails, demonstrably bored. 'These people aren't for you. Especially while the lights are out. I think you'd be better off away from here, back in your little terraced house.'

'Why are you staying here?'

'My dear lady, I've nowhere else to go. I spent every penny I have on this place. Home for me was Zimbabwe, and I'm not about to go back there. You ask an awful lot of questions. Is there any particular reason?'

I wasn't about to explain myself. It was time to leave before Elliot's entertainment arrived. I wondered if the girl could have been kept prisoner in the corner penthouse. And the whereabouts of Malcolm's valuable watercolours was still preying on my mind. Julie had given me her number in case of an emergency. I hated to consider the option, but it seemed best to call New York, just to make sure they had been safely hidden.

I left the building and waited until I was clear of the Ziggurat's deadening shadow, then used the last bar of my phone's life. The line was faint, not helped by the traffic churning past outside.

'Room 1727 please.'

After a few moments, a woman answered.

'Julie?'

'Yeah. Who is this?'

'June, Lou's friend. I'm really sorry, but I had to ring.'

'Wait, let me take this in another room.'

I held, listening to the rustle and snap of distant connections. 'Malcolm's working in the lounge. It's supposed to be a soundproofed suite. We're twenty floors above the traffic but I can still hear it. I thought we weren't going to talk. Is there anything wrong?'

'No, the apartment's fine, I just needed to check something with you. It's been preying on my mind. About the paintings.'

'What about them?' Caution crept into Julie's voice.

'Where are they?'

'What do you mean? They're where they always are, on the lounge walls.'

'Yes, I know the big pictures are there, the oils, but where are the watercolours, the valuable ones? I wanted to check that you'd stored them away somewhere.'

'I don't know what you're talking about, they're on the walls right beside the others. You must be able to see them.' The tone had notched up to one of panic now.

'What am I looking for, exactly?'

'This is what you called me for? Wait, let me think. Six 'Don Quixote' lithographs by Salvador Dali, four French watercolours from around 1850, I forget the artist but they're all blues and greens, a Matisse sketch, a study for Orpen's 'The Absinthe Drinker' and two small ink drawings by Millais.'

My stomach turned. 'I didn't know –'

'Wait, I haven't finished. There are two Delauneys, a Chaim Soutine, a pair of small drawings by Villon I think, four Hockney sketches, a Wesselman and a matching set of eight Warhol prints.'

There were no such pictures anywhere in the apartment. I had checked every cupboard after returning from Elliot's. Nothing was locked away.

'I think I'd better to talk to Malcolm,' I said faintly.

'Why? Don't tell me there's one missing.'

'No. That is… there aren't any at all. No lithographs, no watercolours, no sketches.'

'What are you talking about? Jesus, the place is stuffed full of them, why do you think he was so paranoid about leaving the apartment this weekend?'

'You don't understand, there were none when I arrived, not a single one. There are just four big ugly oil paintings.'

Julie wasn't listening; she'd gone into some kind of fear spin-cycle. 'I don't know anything about the other pictures. It's the small ones you're there to look after. You're telling me they've gone? Oh Christ. Oh Christ.'

'You're sure he didn't put them in storage?'

'Of course I'm sure. He didn't want to draw any kind of attention to them, they're not –' I suspected she was going to say *legitimate*.

'Listen, Julie, someone came into the apartment last night, two people actually, three if you count the paramedic, but they didn't steal anything.' Unable to hold back any longer, I found myself telling her the full story, piecing it together in the wrong order of events, knowing that this was absolutely the worst thing you could do when someone was far from home.

'This is crazy, you're telling me some tart dropped dead in the flat? A complete stranger?' Julie all but shrieked.

'I think she came to me for help, but it was too late by then.'

'How did you meet this person?'

'I was out on the balcony and looked across to the next penthouse, and there she was.'

'Wait, back up, what the hell are you talking about?'

'What do you mean?'

'The apartment has no balcony.'

'What?'

'Malcolm's apartment hasn't got a balcony. You're talking about the penthouses on the top floor, do you know how expensive they are? He couldn't afford one of those. It costs him a fortune to insure all the art he inherited from his family.'

'Well, what could he afford?'

'The next floor down. The sixth.'

'I'm on the seventh.'

'Then you're in the wrong apartment.'

'Oh my lord.'

CHAPTER TWENTY-ONE
The Move

I THOUGHT BACK to my meeting with Madame Funes. The old woman had handed me the key while arguing on the phone. This was the same person who had confused Elliot's mail. For all I knew I could be living in the apartment Jeffrey Archer had earmarked. 'That means your paintings are still in the flat below,' I told Julie. 'I thought I was seeing things.'

'You'd better get down there quickly and check to make sure that everything's intact. He'll kill me if anything's missing. God, that means you have the wrong key. Malcolm wanted to get a better lock fitted, it wouldn't hold if someone put their shoulder against it.'

I apologised profusely and rang off, breaking into a run as I crossed into the lee of the bridge. *Go back to the suburbs before you make things worse,* the city was saying, but I was determined not to obey.

A heavyset woman with strong Slavic features was disconsolately sliding a broom around the atrium. I examined the latch holding the glass doors of the concierge's office shut. The one thing I had in my pocket that would fit between the panels was my World Of Wood discount card, but the steel latch was held in place by a hand-turned ratchet. There had to be another way in. At the rear of the office was a narrow wooden back door, new and still unpainted but barred shut. The unsealed lobby entrance meant that any passer-by could get this far into the building. If I broke into the office and simply switched the keys, nobody would ever have to know.

I had seen people kick doors open on TV. Half-heartedly booting the lock, I nearly broke my foot. *What am I doing?* I thought, *I've never broken a law in my life, unless you count Barclaycard repayment terms and the odd Winona Ryder incident in department stores.*

Hobbling over to the cleaning woman, I eyed the roll of keys at her waist. 'I'm sorry,' I lied, growing a touch more glib with each attempt, 'I've left my key in the concierge's office. Could you let me in?'

'I'm not supposed to.' The woman leaned on her broom. If she was waiting for a tip, she was out of luck.

'But surely if someone's locked out of their own apartment.'

'Building's empty. Nobody here this weekend.'

'You're wrong, I'm staying here and there's at least one other person. Please, I can call Madame Funes if you want to check on me.'

The cleaner thought for a moment, then made her way to the office with a weary sigh. She stood watching me muddling at the telephone. 'Do you have her number?' I asked, stalling for time.

The cleaner pointed to a printout stuck on the wall. I punched the numerals but kept my finger on the cut-off.

'You've not got a line,' said the cleaner. 'Press nine first.'

To Hell with it, I thought. *I'll have to call her.*

'Madame Funes? June Cryer, we met yesterday afternoon.'

'No, I met no-one yesterday afternoon, I was busy.'

'Yes, we did meet. You meant to give me the key to Malcolm Phillimore's apartment but gave me someone else's by mistake.'

'Yes, maybe I remember you but I no make mistake,' shouted Madame Funes.

'Yes, I'm afraid you did.'

'I never make no mistake,' she yelled. 'They always say I make mistake but they lie, they all lie.'

I wondered how long this was going to go on. 'The key you gave me is to apartment 701.'

'IS IMPOSSIBLE,' Madame Funes explained loudly in a tone reserved for times when she could not imagine being wrong. '701 is Dr. Azymuth and he is away in China. He tells me if anyone stay with him.'

'He's a doctor?'

'That's right, he does the plastic for the faces. A-Z-Y-M-U-T-H. A plastic surgeon,' Madame Funes explained.

'And you're sure he's away at the moment?'

'Yes, I tell you already, he is in China, he call me to ask if the electric is fix this weekend. Who is this?'

'She said it's okay to get the key,' I smiled at the cleaner as I replaced the receiver. I unhooked Malcolm's set and was going to replace the others, but the headline of the Ziggurat's brochure caught my eye.

DREAMING OF LONDON LIFE?
The Ziggurat is a city dream come true.
State of the art construction that combines classic architectural elements with cutting-edge design in the heart of London.

I picked up the sales leaflet and studied the computer-rendered illustrations. Beneath a fierce cyanic sky more suited to Luxor than London, an impossibly sleek computer-rendered building rose beside the Thames, unencumbered by scaffolding, transit vans, plastic rubbish sacks, yelling drunks, sleeping-bag-people or abandoned washing machines. Other colour photos showed Harrods, Hyde Park, a guardsman's busby and Buckingham Palace. Leafing through the glossy pages, I realised I had yet to discover the sauna, swimming pool and basement gym that would be used by these royalty-obsessed Harrods-shopping high flyers. A car park on the great flat roof was operated by a hydraulic lift; this was presumably out of action, as was the 'eco-unit', whatever that might be. I studied the map on the back of the brochure. Apparently the basement housed the eco-unit, an automatic electronically-fired incinerator capable of flash-burning the building's rubbish within minutes and compacting biodegradable ashes for collection, with vents accessible from the end of every corridor.

Suddenly I was sure I knew what had happened to the girl who had been tagged outside Dr. Azymuth's apartment. I slipped the correct Yale, 603, into my pocket along with a brochure and the key to 701. The cleaner relocked the office behind me.

Back upstairs, I unlocked Dr. Azymuth's door as quietly as possible and checked that the flat was still empty. My clothes took just a moment to repack. I remade the bed and hung the doctor's dressing gown in his wardrobe. I had intended to leave immediately, but when I sat on the end of the bed, the girl's face returned to prevent me. If 701's occupant was out of the country I could afford to take my time, but his call to the Funes woman meant he could be planning to return home at any moment.

I carried my bag down to Malcolm's apartment. The Yale unlatched the door, but I could see why Malcolm had been worried; it would have been easy to break in. The rooms on the sixth floor were smaller, darker and yes, filled with little pictures. Dali's etchings of Don Quixote, scratched scars in copper and black, lined the lounge, a beautifully simple Matisse, the sumptuous Delauneys, some innocuous Hockneys. No balcony, no separate kitchen, just a steel counter in a corner, but the same vast windows dominating the lounge.

The storm was moving in fast across the river. The water of the Thames now had a brownish pummelled look, like flooded flagstones. I paced the apartment, unsettled and unsure of my next move, knowing I must do something. I felt stranded between two worlds, belonging in neither the vacuum-sealed lifestyle of my past or the shifting shadows of the present.

Two courses of action suggested themselves. I could get Mr. Ashe to check out the eco-unit facility, but fear of what he might find lying there dampened my enthusiasm. Or I could go back up to the flat. Thinking that it belonged to Malcolm, I had assumed that its owner was innocent of any involvement, and had respected his privacy by not looking in any of the private drawers. Now I wanted to see what kind of man could live here.

As I headed up to 701, each step unsettled me further. I had failed someone who had turned to me for help, and the fact that she was a total stranger only made it worse.

I admit I was being nosy. I didn't think it was going to get me killed.

CHAPTER TWENTY-TWO
The Flesh

701 LOOKED DIFFERENT to me now. The bedroom walls were shades of discoloured flesh. The great cubes of light I had admired by morning light seemed glacial and bruised with shadows. There was no longer any sense of normal life lived within these walls. The kitchen pots glistened because they had never been used. The medical textbooks no longer appeared to be articles of scientific reference but catalogues of a disarranged mind.

I began in the kitchen, sorting through drawer after drawer, finding only steel utensils, unopened instruction booklets for the new cooker and freezer, mats, cutlery. No item except foodstuffs to betray a hint of personality. One thing hadn't changed; it was still a single man's home, barely inhabited. The lounge yielded no more items of hospitality than a hotel room.

One high cupboard turned out to be sealed, but a small key left on the shelf below opened it. Here a dozen further medical volumes were concealed, probably because their colour plates were livid horrors; illustrations from the Firefighters Burn Center in Florida, operational procedures for the Heal the Children foundation, volumes from the European Society of Plastic and Reconstructive Surgery, the

Injection Therapy Unit, the Lipoplasty Society, the Anglo-French Burns Association, the American Cleft Palate Association.

The images would have made Dr. Frankenstein blanch; torn lips, burst eyes, leaking aqueous humour, sliced gums, rolls of yellow fat dripping from liposuction tools, spikes through skulls, flayed faces, shredded muscles in every shade of scarlet, pink, brown and purple like close-up porn shots. I wished I hadn't looked.

On the topmost shelf was a booklet outlining services offered by the Azymuth Harley Street Cosmetic Surgery Clinic. Dr. A. L. Azymuth specialised in facial reconstruction, but his clinic could handle 'thighs, bums and tums', as the brochure coyly put it. Azymuth was pictured on the back, slim-jawed, bony, fortyish, Indian or possibly Egyptian, a trustworthy face for any insecure patient.

I searched his wardrobe. White shirts and bland navy suits, several pairs of identical black-toed Oxford shoes, nothing to mark out a man as a lunatic or an accessory to murder.

I dragged over a chair and climbed up, searching the tops of the built-in wardrobes. The cardboard box was not concealed, merely awkward to reach.

It contained over thirty pages of barely legible eight-point print from internet sites in Hungary, Siberia, Romania and the Ukraine. The names and addresses were occasionally accompanied by webcam pictures of young faces fast growing old with lousy diet and the stress of poverty.

A file followed every name, each page carrying the personal details of men and women: nationality, address, height, birthdate, weight, colour of eyes. The names appeared exotic to me: Omar, Valya, Jaspinder, Sergei, Lata, Anuradha. Medical histories followed, half-filled forms and pages frequently marked INCOMPLETE. Diabetes, HIV status, history of heart disease. It didn't seem likely that they were overseas patients coming to England for treatment. For a start, the few photos that yielded any detail showed cheap clothes, self-inflicted haircuts, bad skin, poor posture. I'd seen enough footage of asylum seekers running across government land to recognise the signs of long-term hardship.

Perhaps it was some public-clinic sideline of Azymuth's private practice. I knew that many private doctors worked in them one or two days a week. I was preparing to give up when I came across the photograph of the young girl whose bloodstained head I had cradled the previous night. Her hair was shorter and tucked under a white scarf, but I could tell it was her. The name on the file was Petra, but there was a second name beneath her photograph – 'Cleo'. Some of the other files bore pairs of names.

Petra, too, had undergone a medical examination, but the handwritten notes accompanying her form suggested that surgery had been carried out on her face, specifically rhinoplasty, mole-removal and an eye-lift. Her form had been stamped: FOR PLASTIC.

It made no sense for impoverished Eastern Europeans to come to Azymuth for expensive cosmetic surgery. For a moment my mind filled with gangsters switching identities, changing their faces to escape conviction, the curse of watching too much TV. Then I thought, you know, white slavery. People trafficking. Perhaps it was just difficult to accept the fact that the doctor might simply be keen to help others.

Disappointed, I replaced the box. Or at least I tried to, but something was blocking the space at the back of the shelf. Standing on tiptoe, I reached in and closed my fingers around a waxed-cotton sack, pulling so that it fell into my upturned hands.

With the sack on the floor I stepped down and tugged open its drawstring. It took me a moment to realise that the currency bore the bridge symbols of euros. Even by my own poor calculation, I could tell there was about forty thousand pounds at my feet. The varying condition of the notes suggested they came from a number of sources. What kind of man kept so much money loose in his bedroom?

They come from Eastern Europe, I thought, *they pay him cash for cosmetic surgery operations, cash because they can't transfer savings from bank accounts. He takes their money, promising to help, then murders them, stuffing their bodies into the Eco-Unit.*

This theory, I had to admit, was even more absurd than the last. The internet photographs featured men and women who were already attractive in their own ways. They just needed the glow of wellbeing that a few months of good diet, some sun and better dentistry would bring. They required a little grooming, not new faces. It made no sense. I studied the pages again. Not one of the featured patients was over twenty-five. Azymuth was doing something to them, why else would he be hiding their details in the back of a cupboard? Why else would one of them turn up in the building on the very weekend that no-one would be there to see her die?

I set out the pages in rows across the bedroom floor, looking for links as the first spatters of rain hit the windows. Distant thunder rolled across the heathlands of North London. The room grew darker as the battery on the garage torch began to dim. I was about to look for more candles when I heard a key in the front door. I'd known that Azymuth could come back at any time, but this was more than inconvenient. It looked like burglary. The money was spread all over the bed and the floor.

I caught the flash of a torch in the hall, heading away to the lounge. I couldn't trust myself to explain my presence in the apartment, but where to hide? Getting under the bed would trap me in the room. Besides, he would only have to glance at the chaos to see that someone had been rifling through his personal belongings. I slipped into the shadowed L-bend of the corridor and ran lightly toward the kitchen, pulling open a tall broom closet and shutting myself inside.

It was worse than I'd thought. First, I have a dust allergy. Second, Azymuth wasn't alone; I could hear two men talking. One voice was public school, the other had the sealed-throat glottal stops of Essex English. I peered out through the door grille, but it was possible to recognise Dr. Azymuth from his photograph, even in the half-light of his upturned torch. Dressed in a rain-spattered anorak, tall and angular, he was as awkward as an ostrich. His companion wore a blue nylon jacket, his face muddled in darkness. One of them was wearing Vanilla Tobacco by Tom Ford, at a hundred quid a bottle. I watched them stop in the shadows of the kitchen entrance and held my breath, praying that the dust wouldn't make me sneeze.

'Can I offer you a drink?' asked Azymuth.

'Nah, I got to get back.' The companion had his back to me, walking toward the door. 'He's cancelled your last two appointments.'

'But I've already booked them in. They only need to be ten days apart.'

'You'll have to take it up with Mr. Rennie. I'm just telling you what he told me.'

As soon as they had moved from my sightline I placed my ear against the door and listened, then stepped out into the kitchen.

Silence.

A scuff in the hall, past the closed door of the main bedroom.

Now they seemed to be standing outside the flat. I looked and saw their backs through the gap in the front door. *It's other people's business,* I told myself, *nothing to do with me.* My fear had been overcome by my determination to see the matter through. Even my mother grudgingly admitted that tenacity was one of my few virtues.

With the closing of the front door, I crept out into the hall.

Azymuth was standing inside with his arms folded over his torch, watching me. 'Would you mind telling me what on earth you're doing in my apartment?'

'This is so embarrassing,' I began, attempting to brazen out the situation by adopting the voice I used for returning clothes. 'I'm in the wrong place. There was a mix-up with my key. Madame Funes gave me yours by mistake.'

'You were hiding in a cupboard. Anyway, the concierge isn't here today.'

'I know that. I only just found out it was the wrong key.'

'Surely you could tell you weren't in the right flat. Or even the right cupboard.'

'That's just it, I'm minding a place for a friend –'

'What friend?'

The last thing I wanted was to get Malcolm into trouble. 'More a friend of a friend. I agreed to flatsit for him. Here's your key and I'm really awfully sorry.' My subservience to professional men could be nothing short of pathetic. I'm surprised I didn't offer to do his ironing. I extracted the 701 Yale and dropped it onto the hall console. Azymuth was walking from room to room, prissily checking everything. Any second now I knew he would see the mess in the bedroom.

I kept talking, trying to distract him, but the doctor would not be turned from his purpose. When he pushed open the door to the master bedroom, he stopped dead in his shiny Oxford-shod tracks. 'Come here. Did you do this?'

My confidence flatlined. 'No... uh, I just –' I shifted away from him, aiming toward the front door. 'Some other people were... listen, what goes on here is your business, I'm nothing –'

'Have you been going through the confidential files of my patients?' He lowered the torch so that it flared in my eyes.

'I have to go,' I insisted.

'I don't think so. Not until I get some kind of an explanation.'

Looking into his angry brown eyes, I felt for a moment that he didn't have any idea what had been going on. But the girl had been a patient of his, left to die in his apartment. Surely Azymuth shared some guilt of her death? There was no point in trying to lie my way out;

I just wanted to know if he was somehow responsible. I needed something to make sense in this impregnable, pristine world, even if it was something unbearably cruel. I mean, for years I'd believed Jeffrey Archer was honest, but it all made sense when he went to jail. It was embarrassing for him, but closure for me.

'I saw a girl attacked here. Right where we're standing.'

'Attacked? What on earth are you talking about?'

'She was strangled with a plastic parcel tag, and she was one of your patients. I can show you.' Before he had a chance to answer, I dropped to my knees and scrabbled through the sheets on the floor, finding the girl's photograph. 'This one, Petra Valenski.'

He barely glanced at the picture. He didn't need to. It was obvious that he recognised the name. 'What would she be doing here?'

'I don't know. What did you do to her?'

'It's no business of yours. You have no right to ask anything, you're in my apartment with some cock-and-bull story about mixed-up keys, threatening me, who the hell do you think you are? I'm the one who should be calling the police.'

'The girl was on your property. Any forensic team would find evidence in seconds.' I had no way of knowing if this was true, but it sounded good.

'You're mad. Who *are* you?'

'Nobody, just a housewife.'

'I can see that,' he said, rather insultingly I thought.

'But I'm the type who makes a convincing witness.'

Perhaps he decided to humour me then, because he suddenly changed his tone. 'I don't understand. What exactly do you expect me to do?'

'It would help if you could explain who she was.' I was pushing my luck, but couldn't seem to stop myself. 'These files all belong to your patients?'

'No, they're... well, I have a client. He sends them to me.'

'You mean like a broker.'

'I suppose so,' he said irritably.

'And they're all for surgery.'

'Yes, it's just minor stuff, enhancements mostly, noses, lips, eyes, wrinkles, spot and mole removal, nothing structural beyond the odd bit of jaw realignment.'

'What did you do to her, Petra Valenski?'

'Hardly anything, as it happens. She was almost perfect. I made her a little fuller in the face, nothing that a few months of good eating wouldn't have done. Just a couple of local injections in her cheeks. Oh, and I pinned back her ears.' Professional pride crept into his voice. 'It's was a very neat piece of work.'

'That's all you did?'

'In my opinion she didn't need any cosmetic work at all, and she had no opinions of her own that I could understand because she spoke no English. She'd only been in the country a few weeks. When I took the booking I was told how much to spend, but I decide how much surgery to perform, and in this case I chose to keep it minimal.'

'And the broker paid you?'

'You really saw the girl in here?' he asked.

'As clearly as I see you now. She was rolling about on your rather attractive hardwood floor, choking to death.'

'All right, I'll deal with this.' He waved at me dismissively. 'You have nothing to worry about. Just go back to your own apartment.'

'What about the police?'

'It's not a matter for them. I can easily find out what's been going on. I promise you, I'll take the appropriate steps.'

'All right. I'm in apartment 603 But I won't go anywhere until you tell me what happened.' I warned.

'Don't worry, you'll be the first to know.'

I returned to Malcolm's flat shaken but relieved, happy to have passed the buck so easily. I suppose I thought I was providing Petra with some kind of closure. In hindsight it seems absurd that I had expected to be told the truth and allowed to leave, but you have to put it down to my misplaced faith in authority figures.

I honestly didn't imagine that my life was at risk too.

CHAPTER TWENTY-THREE
Dirty Hands

I TRIED READING for a while, but descending black clouds had turned the room dark, and after attempting to follow the same sentence a dozen times by candlelight, I gave up. Never read Dickens when you're in a state of alarm, it doesn't go in.

Having glimpsed something of a city I'd ignored for so long, I now felt restless indoors and wanted to see more, but I could tell by the unnatural flatness of the river that it had started to rain. From the window at the end of the sixth floor corridor, the car park and the dug-up green in front of the lobby were visible. The reduced height meant that I could now see through the plane trees to the roads facing away from the river. Stefan's yellow steel container was the brightest thing on the ground, but his door was closed.

While I waited for Azymuth to report back, I tried to imagine what everyone else was doing on a wet Saturday afternoon in September.

No-one was simply out for a walk; they all had destinations and looked as if they were running late. I thought of the taxi driver on his break; London seemed to be filled with pockets of the past, crossroads and alleyways truncated by postwar road layouts that had sealed them into history. You could still see where the bombs had fallen. Planners had left their territorial marks by wedging predatory offices into sedate terraces, superseding the unfashionable comfort of Christian conformity with something more devious and aggressive. These replacement buildings were locked into specific eras; brutal seventies concrete, plastic eighties toy-boxes, anonymous nineties towers that revealed their interiors like dolls' houses.

From this height the Victorian and Edwardian redbricks still carried an identity of understatement and scruffy utility. Looking down on the grey mess of railway lines, torn-up arterials and dingy backwaters, I wondered if the area could offer someone like me a fresh start.

As I made a sandwich, I began to wonder if the doctor really intended to visit me with news. I had no plans for the evening, but the cash Lou had left would provide me with anything I needed. I was listening to the rain hitting the lounge windows when there was a knock at the door. Pushing my plate back from the edge of the kitchen counter, I wriggled down from one of Malcolm's awkward swivel-stools and called into the darkened hall.

'It's me, Mrs... I don't remember your name.' It took me a moment to recognise Azymuth's voice. I opened the door six inches, keeping my foot against the base, then relented when I saw the distraught look on his face.

'What's the matter?'

'Can you let me in for a moment?' He looked over his shoulder. 'I don't think I should stay out here. Just let me in, will you?'

I opened the door a fraction wider, and he barged inside.

'Listen, I think I may have done something rather impetuous. I telephoned my client. I'm not supposed to contact him directly, we usually use e-mail, or a colleague of his comes around.'

'The man who came to your apartment with you?'

'Oh, I forgot you heard us. I just wanted to get this business about you seeing the girl sorted out.'

'Did you tell someone I was a witness?'

Azymuth looked flummoxed and embarrassed. 'Not in so many words. I wanted to find out what's been going on. Mr. Rennie – my client – thought I was still away. He asked how I was sure the girl had been in my flat, and I had to explain about the mix-up with your key.'

I shifted uncomfortably. 'You've not been doing anything illegal, so why are you worried?' *Tell me you're not involved in something bad,* I thought.

'It's not quite as simple as that,' he said, confirming my fears. 'Technically I've broken the law. I'm required to practice according to BMA guidelines, there are all sorts of rules. I'll be honest with you. May I have a drink?'

I led him to the lounge and borrowed his torch to hunt through Malcolm's cabinet. He accepted the tumbler of warm vodka from me and downed it in one swallow.

'I'm in the middle of a rather messy divorce, and it's proving expensive. This is a good sideline, just a few minor cosmetic procedures a month and I get a healthy retainer paid up-front in cash. It's not hurting anyone, you understand, quite the reverse. Do you have any idea how many professionals accept work on the side in this city, picking up a few tax-free dividends? Councillors, dentists, lawyers, it's part of the invisible economy.

If you're in banking, you're contributing to the third world debt. If you're working in insurance, you might as well go and join the Mafia. Everyone's hands are soiled to some extent.'

'Yes, I get it,' I said, a little dismissively. 'I'm not criticising you.' I began to get a very bad feeling about the doctor's contact. 'What's this broker of yours like?'

'We've only met face to face a couple of times. I was introduced to Mr. Rennie through a mutual friend at Henley Regatta. To be honest, he made me feel rather uncomfortable. I'm not being snobbish, you understand, but he's one of those school-of-life opportunists, given to the most frightful cod-philosophising, and the other people in his office, well, they all look like taxi drivers.'

'Why is Mr. Rennie helping your patients to get treatment?'

'I have no idea. Obviously he's making a profit somewhere in the transaction, but it's none of my business. He says they're all personal friends, which is patent nonsense, and pays me to improve their looks. Says he wants to do something to help them, to make them feel good about themselves, but he isn't the sort to display an altruistic temperament.'

'Petra wasn't feeling very good about herself when I tried to save her life.' Azymuth's keenness to distance himself from anything sordid annoyed me.

'I can only think that she got into some kind of trouble. Before I operate I always ask patients if they're on medication. Just an aspirin can interfere with the healing process. Petra looked to me as if she might be on drugs, and that meant the possibility of compromised immunity. I didn't want to carry out surgery on someone who might not heal. Luckily, I only had to perform very minor work.'

I thought of what Elliot had told me, and things started fitting together. 'She stayed in the flat next door to you while her surgery was healing, didn't she?'

'How did you know that?' asked Azymuth.

'That's why she came to your apartment when she needed help. You had operated on her, and you were her neighbour, someone she trusted.' *Or she came because she saw me, and wanted my help*, I realised.

'Listen, I think you ought to get out of here, just in case there are any problems.'

'What kind of problems?'

'I don't know. Mr. Rennie doesn't work alone. If his partners know what happened to her, maybe they won't want anyone else to find out. I would go home if I were you. There are some unsavoury deals going around – nothing involving me, you understand – but the less you know, the better. You shouldn't have got involved, and you don't have to be any more. Just forget it ever happened.'

I wanted to explain that I had never been scared of anything until this weekend. That something had awoken inside me, and would not easily be settled again.

'Someone hung around to remove her from the apartment. Someone who might still have been in your flat while I was there.'

Azymuth glanced nervously from the window before turning back to me and clapping his hands. 'Look, pack your bags and I'll see you out of the front door and into a taxi. Then that's the end of your involvement.'

I had no option. I went to the bedroom and stuffed my toiletry bag back into my case. An overwhelming sense of failure settled on me as I lifted it from the bed and headed toward the front door. Azymuth peered nervously out into the corridor. 'I think I'm going to head back to the country for a few days, you know? Just until things sort themselves out. I've got a nice little place in Norfolk. A bit on the damp side, but a change of pace from London. I just came from there.'

'I thought you were in China.'

'No, just outside Norwich. Who told you that – Mrs. Funes? She gets everything wrong.'

We reached the gloom of the stairwell. In the distance an ambulance siren whooped and faded. Better to hear it, I remembered reading somewhere; they were turned off when the patient was dead. 'You really don't have to come down with me,' I told him, 'I'm fine.' The doctor's discomfort was starting to infect me. Clearly, he wasn't telling me everything. Azymuth might not have known the girl well, but I began to suspect that he knew what she had done.

'I didn't mean to alarm you,' said Azymuth nervously. 'Mr. Rennie has absolutely no idea who you are. I just explained that someone was staying with me, I didn't tell him your name.'

'Fine, but perhaps you should let me know a bit more about him. Just so I know who to avoid.'

'I can't tell you anything. You know how these people are, they're so secretive. He's some kind of entrepreneur. He said the girl was supposed to pay back some money he'd lent her, only she didn't bring it.'

'So he saw her?'

'Sorry, didn't I mention that? He told me they had a drink in Soho and the girl went home to get the money. She didn't return. She must have come here.'

'And that's all? Where does this Mr. Rennie live?'

'I've really no idea, and if I had I wouldn't tell you, for everyone's sake. I don't even know if that's his real name.'

It was then that I recalled the little key. At the time it had looked too small to be important. I made a mental search of my clothes, trying to remember where it was. On Azymuth's bedside table, along with some old bills I had weeded out of my shoulder-bag.

'I'm sorry, I have to go back up to your apartment. I've forgotten something.'

'I'm really not sure that's such a good idea.' Azymuth was sweating. We'd reached the corner of the stairwell. 'Tell me what it is and I'll get it for you.'

'No, it's okay.' For some reason I found myself wanting to hide knowledge from the doctor. If he had informed this Mr. Rennie about me so easily, he couldn't be trusted to stay silent with anyone else. I reached the seventh floor with the doctor coming up fast behind me. Azymuth darted ahead and pushed open the unlocked door.

'I'll just be a moment,' I told him, quickly heading for the bedroom.

It was there on the night stand, a slender metal pick less than two inches in length. It looked as if it might unlock a child's toy. I hoped I hadn't ruined the chance of finding fingerprints on it. Carefully turning it over in Azymuth's torch beam, I could make out the word MOM on one side. An American abbreviation for mother? It looked as though it belonged to something that would be owned by a woman. Suddenly the torchlight went away as Azymuth headed out into the hall. A moment later he called to me.

'I'm sorry, I didn't catch that.' But he was talking to someone else. I moved closer to the door.

'–hanging around here.'

'–with your lady friend.'

'And I already told you, I don't think she –'

'–care what you think. He wants to talk to her.'

'I don't know where she is, she's just –'

'–name and address. All you have to do is tell me who she is.'

As the conversation's implications hit home, I peered over at the mirror reflecting the scene in the hall. Azymuth was talking to a man in a blue nylon Nintendo jacket who had a meniscus of stitches running across his shaved head like the seam in a baseball. Stitch-Head was back, and he knew the doctor. My hand slipped across my mouth, wedging between teeth.

'I can speak to Mr. Rennie myself and straighten this out,' Azymuth offered.

'There's nothing to straighten out. He doesn't want to talk to you. Your services are no longer required. Didn't you get the message? We're not doing the top end of the market anymore, so we don't need the plastics.'

'He still owes me a considerable amount of money.'

'You know how to get paid, doc.'

'I told you, I have no idea where she lives.' A series of beeps sounded. Stitch-Head was making a call. He dropped his voice for the phone conversation. I heard single words, a low mumble, a phlegmy arc of dark laughter. Silence. Then a scuffle, a slither of nylon, a light thump against a wall.

I looked in the mirror once more. Azymuth had tried to make a run for it, and Stitch-Head was holding him with an arm across the throat. I gave a yelp, but he appeared not to hear. He was digging into his pocket, pulling out another of the plastic parcel tags. He locked it in place and tightened it sufficiently to drop Azymuth to his knees. The doctor was bent double, gagging and coughing on the pale beech boards, his veins bulging.

'Just tell me who she is.'

I edged toward the balcony doors and eased open the lock.

'Tell me who she is, doc.'

I knew that the doors would grind in their tracks, but had no choice. Pushing the heavy glass wall back inch by inch, I strained to hear.

'I know when you're lying, doc. Tell me and I'll take it off.'

Seven floors down, no other exit.

'Say the words or I'll fucking kick you to death.'

The wind was blowing hard and nearly toppled me as I stepped onto the balcony. The sour river air carried the doctor's rising screams into my head, whether I wanted to bear witness or not. I was penned into poisoned ground, and nothing would let me leave it.

I watched in horror, and saw.

CHAPTER TWENTY-FOUR
Escape

I STOOD BESIDE the lounge window, in the shadow of its tall curtains, hardly daring to look as Stitch-Head kicked Azymuth again and again, his movements exactly repeated like some arcane automaton.

The doctor, curled tighter than a question mark, absorbed the kicks without flinching or making a sound. The scene unfolded in silence, a dumb show playing to an audience of seagulls. Reflected clouds shifted across his attacker's face as he concentrated on the job at hand, as earnest as any craftsman tackling a task where it was important to be thorough. I heard what I thought was the sound of breaking ribs.

Unable to bear it any longer, I edged my way along the balcony and climbed back into the bedroom, carefully avoiding the step. The journey to the front door was a distance of no more than ten feet. It might as well have been five miles.

I could hear the sounds in the flat once more. Azymuth was finally whimpering, a high thin sound like a dog wanting to be walked. I had no thought of helping him. These people were not in my world. The most important thing was to get out without being seen. It didn't help that I was wearing heels, but I was loathe to remove them in case I dropped one. Every step I took across the floor sounded like someone tapping in a nail. Even as a little girl, you could always hear me coming. My bracelet rattled as I slowly opened the door. I felt sure even my sunflower earrings were making some kind of noise.

Nevertheless, I decided I would have to manage three and a bit yards of total silence before legging it out of the building. What I had not accounted for was my reaction to the pool of blood shaped vaguely like an elongated map of Italy, shockingly red against the creamy polished wood. It stemmed from Azymuth's head, starting in a satanic halo. I bit my hand harder, but a sound like a trodden puppy escaped my lips. It was just enough to distract Stitch-Head from his occupation and grant me his attention.

I could not get past him, and was forced to return to my position beyond the bedroom doors as he strolled toward me. Searching for a way out, I looked across the vertiginous wall of balconies to the roof, where something was being constructed around the lift machinery housing. A yellow rubble pipe extended from the site to the ground, jointed like a series of plastic dustbins with their bases cut out. The mouth of the tube began at least six feet beyond the end of the balcony.

There was no way back and no way out. As Stitch-Head stepped through the doors I reached a decision, clambering onto an aluminium terrace chair set against the balcony wall, then up onto the wall itself.

The wind from the river was much stronger away from the lee of the building. In my high, very pointed heels, I knew I would only be able to keep my balance for a few seconds at the most. My stomach was flopping over with fear, but I was also aware that the rough concrete top of the wall was ruining the knees of my tights.

'Come on love, don't be daft, get down,' Stitch-Head instructed. He didn't want me falling into the traffic-filled street, although from my own experience it was debatable whether anyone below would notice.

His hands reached up to haul me down, and at the very moment he touched me my stomach churned and kicked, and I threw up on him. He was studying his soaked shirt in horror as I swung around to face the plastic pipe and the wind took away my balance.

I half-fell, half-leapt toward the chute, and managed to miss it by a good four feet, tumbling head-first into the cold night sky.

A net of springy green nylon mesh had been fastened around the pipe in a shallow funnel to catch stray debris. I fell into it like a trapeze artiste missing a cue. Screaming as I bounced up and down with the net between my knees and nothing but the ground yo-yo-ing far beneath me, I now found myself lower than the balcony edge, and could see nothing above it but the sky.

Stitch-Head stuck his surprised face over the parapet, then reluctantly attempted to climb down after me. He was a big man, and the mesh started to pull free with his added weight, tearing loose along the wall edge. I scrambled away, trying to leave the net, but every action caused a reaction that pulled me back. It was all very undignified. As I reached the mouth of the pipe, I knew I would have to climb inside. The drop, I felt sure, would kill me. Poised across the top with one leg in the hole, I hung indecisively until Stitch-Head had closed in, the mesh tearing around him.

Then I pulled in my other leg and removed my hands from the sides.

All I could do to break my fall was thrust my limbs out against the walls of the tube. I managed to keep braking my descent as the yellow pipe twisted and revolved under my weight, threatening to pull itself apart. It was like being in a waterchute without lubrication. The joined sections slowed me down, and at one point I stopped altogether. I tried to imagine how a dancer or gymnast would cope with the shifting plastic pipe, but doubted any of them had ever fallen off the top of a high building.

The skin tore on my hands and elbows, and one of my heels snapped off as I fought to keep from dropping too fast. Finally I could support the weight of my body no longer, and fell the remaining way.

I landed on a sheet of plasterboard placed across a skip, which softly shattered. It wasn't as bad as I'd thought, but it must have looked pretty bizarre. I imagined builders watching from the other side of the road: 'Look, someone's thrown out a perfectly good housewife.'

At least that's the last I've seen of this building, I thought, *Jeffrey Archer's welcome to it.*

I raised myself up from sore knees and checked for damage. Then I climbed out and ran on shaking legs; what else could I do? Certainly, I was surprised by my own energy – I felt nothing until I had distanced myself from the place and reached the main road. Numbness was replaced by a wall of pain. Everything hurt at once.

I missed the pedestrian signal and I was nearly killed running across the Albert Embankment against the lights. A van screamed to a halt in a shower of obscenities, and a Nissan Sunny ran straight into the back of it. As I cut away from the river, anxiously looking for light and the safety of other people, my remaining heel snapped. *I'll have to take those back,* I thought, gasping for breath. *I hope I've still got the receipt.* I slowed to a walk and looked behind me. Stitch-Head was right there, but not running, just talking into the phone. How the hell did he do that? Then I realised that in my panic I had come the long way around the building.

He was clearly expecting me to stay on the main road, so he was taken by surprise when I broke away toward Lower Marsh, where the ancient street market was still crowded with customers. I stole a glance at my watch, puzzled; the stalls should have packed up by now. What was going on?

In seconds I was in the thick of them, shoppers ambling past stalls of fruit and clothes, a scene that had hardly changed in centuries. But there was something odd: no sound came from anyone.

It was then I realised that they were examining the merchandise too carefully, as though they were working on their motivation, and knew they were television extras. At the next corner I faced a battery of lights covered by sheets of opaque plastic, and saw that they were filming some TV soap because there were no actual celebrities, only actors who were vaguely recognisable for playing nurses and policemen all their lives. *This is it,* I thought, *it's just as I imagined, I've finally become a walk-on in my own life. Mrs. Bloke has found a place to live where she can wander around all day gormlessly examining grapefruit and squeezing loaves of bread.*

I could see Stitch-Head a fair way back in the crowd, steadily ploughing toward me, easing startled extras aside. The kids who had been employed to keep civilians away from the wide-shot had pulled out walkie-talkies and were looking ineffectively puzzled. Ahead, the road was closed off with a portable steel barrier, forcing me to the side of the stalls. Any second now I would be beyond the crowd and back in danger. My broken heels were killing me. I suddenly had no idea what I was doing or where I was going.

It never crossed my mind to ask someone for help because I knew that they were actors, not real people. Besides, part of me was still a housewife. I longed to stop and fondle produce. Asking for help was not in my daily lexicon. Mind you, being chased across town by a highly motivated gargoyle was not a normal part of my weekly schedule either.

All I could think to do was drag the barrier aside, allowing the extras to spill out into the road ahead. Someone was shouting at me. Another white van – surely not the same one that nearly ran me down – pulled into the part of the road not covered by the shoot. Presumably he was as puzzled as I had been by the appearance of the night-market.

The confusion got worse. Having been instructed to cut the scene, the stall-holders started calling out for instructions, the fake customers refused to move aside, and there, right at my side, was Stitch-Head, lunging forward with something metal in his hand, a knife or perhaps even a gun.

An African man was selling kitchenware from a decorating table, hundreds of identical apple corers with yellow plastic handles, but he didn't appear to be part of the crew, just some chancer who had pitched his stall alongside the actors. I grabbed one of the corers as I dropped beneath the table in panic, stabbing out at the skinhead's chubby leg as he passed.

I promise you, this isn't natural behaviour for me. I have never intentionally attempted to injure anyone in my life, even though my mother-in-law gave me enough encouragement. The blade, an item sold on its extreme sharpness, passed so smoothly into the muscle of his right calf that for a moment I thought I'd missed. He bellowed, I stood up in fright, the table went over scattering knives everywhere and he slammed into me.

In the seconds that followed I thought he must have suddenly developed a stomach ache, then saw that his left hand had a crimson seam. He had hurt himself on something that had fallen from the table, an absurd accident, could I be that lucky? Then I saw the yellow plastic corer in my right hand, and realised that I had stabbed him a second time, in the side.

Now that the ferocity had left his eyes he looked pale and rather smaller than he had on the balcony. The actors around me were pulling faces at each other, more concerned about being upstaged than witnessing a real-life drama. The African was ranting and waving his arms furiously, but no-one was pointing the finger of blame or trying to stop me.

Stitch-Head was lying drunkenly on the pavement, twisting about like a worm on a hook. Me, I still looked more like a housewife than someone who would snatch your mobile. At the edge of the set, kids in hoodies were standing by with their hands thrust deep in their pockets, trying to be identical and feeling nothing but embarrassment.

Shocked by my own lack of remorse, I turned and fled. I knew I would have to break my own promise and return home. I needed to hide in familiar surroundings before I succumbed to the madness of the streets. I told myself that my resolve had not failed, that I had simply been pushed out of my depth. My holdall was back in the Ziggurat, but nothing on earth would ever get me back there. Besides, I had Lou's money, and that was enough to take me away.

A pair of luminous yellow jackets were pushing in my direction. Someone had actually called the police. It was time to get out of town. My one remaining advantage was that I could blend in with any group of ordinary passers-by, so I headed for the station as fast as my shattered heels could carry me.

CHAPTER TWENTY-FIVE
Ransacked

THE FACE IN the mirror came as a shock.

I thought I looked normal, but in the train's toilet, my dirt-streaked cheeks, upthrust hair and torn clothes – hardly noticeable in London – were a little too deranged for suburbia. I looked like a bag lady who had been encouraged to dress normally by welfare officers in order to get her through a court examination. Washing my hands and attempting to repair the damage to my clothes with handfuls of cold water only worsened my appearance.

Hamingwell had never seemed strange to me before this evening. Now it looked less like a place to live than one of final repose. I had expected there to be ghosts in London. Instead, I saw them here. Perhaps ghosts need deserted places to find a voice. They couldn't make themselves heard above the din of so much living in the city.

I walked from the station on broken heels. My skirt was torn, a vertical spatter of blood at the crotch. I looked like Jack the Ripper's blind date. I was wearing my torn puffer-jacket pulled over a T-shirt; you could have found better dressed crack-whores. But there was no-one around to see. The wives had done their weekly Tesco run. Their kids were sealed in their bedrooms hammering the hell out of their consoles. Their husbands were 50-hour-a-week career men picnicking *al desko* in their offices or sleeping their home-hours away on couches, unwatched cable channels flickering in every lounge.

I turned into my street and discerned movement. A familiar silver Saab slewed to a stop beside me. The passenger window disappeared and Lou leaned over.

'June, did the police call? I've been try to get hold of you but your mobile's off.'

'I'm sorry, it's dead. Police?'

'You've been broken into. Only a short while ago. Isn't that why you're here?'

Lou was my keyholder. 'Did the alarm go off?' I asked.

'No, that's the funny thing. The constable reckons it was a professional job. He's quite cute.'

'I don't understand, why is he talking to you?'

'I see everything that happens around here, don't I? Jesus, it's bad enough having Hadrian under arrest without –'

'They're keeping him in?'

'They reprioritised the mail-order bride thing when they found out he was dealing ecstasy on the net. One of the junior officers fancied himself as a codebreaker and figured out that Hade was selling drugs under the local patrol car call-signs. They've bagged up the entire contents of his bedroom and taken it away as evidence. At least it will save me vacuuming. I'm joking but I'm upset, okay? It's how I cope.'

'I know that,' I said gently.

'The neighbours' shutters have been twitching like semaphores. But what happened to you? It looks like you've been in some kind of explosion. If this is the latest London fashion I'm not keen. Don't tell me you've had a vajazzle. Wait, let me park, don't go into the house without me.' Lou slid the car into a handicapped drivers' space and jumped out, cuckooing it shut. 'Nobody knew how to get hold of you. The police tried you at the Ziggurat. Oh shit, there he is.'

Inside the wrought iron front gate, letters, receipts and documents were scattered across the lawn. In fact, the bill for the lawn was on the lawn. The constable found a set of crumpled school swimming certificates sticking out from under a bush. 'Penelope June Cryer, Upper 4B,' he read out. 'Thirty Yards Bronze.' A jewelled brooch, a gift from my grandmother, was hanging in the roses like a crystallised flower. Other pieces of unworn costume jewellery lay sparkling in the grass like frosted shards from a rainbow.

I dug for my house keys, trying not to panic. If the police were here, perhaps they already knew about Azymuth's body and would think I was involved, which, when I came to think of it, was close to the truth. In fact, I seemed to be leaving a trail of bodies in my wake. How the hell did anyone get my home address?

Stitch-Head couldn't have found out where I lived unless I'd left something in the apartment with my name written down. My last credit card bill, which I'd taken along out of sentimental value, had been lying on the bedside table since my arrival at the Ziggurat. My plastic; first it had failed me, and now it was betraying me. He had taken my address when he had returned to remove the body on Friday night.

'You won't need these, honey,' Lou indicated the spare keys she kept for me. 'They kicked your front door right in. That nosy old bitch from number five came by and complained about the state of your garden, then tried to make off with your watering can, can you believe it? Some people.' Lou pushed open the gate for me.

We trooped inside, me, the constable, and Lou following more from a ghoulish desire for adventure than sympathy. The lounge had been torn apart, mud and broken glass trampled into the carpet, a sole unwanted sofa gorily eviscerated, the few last pictures splintered. Upstairs, the mess was even worse. The desk Gordon had left behind had been emptied drawer by upturned drawer. Metal shelves fixed to the wall containing work files – mostly purchase orders for shoes – had been torn out of the plaster. It looked as though the house had been pitched on its side, then uprighted.

'They've made quite a mess,' said the constable, who was obviously a college major in the Bleeding Obvious. 'I know this is a distressing time for you, but I was wondering if you knew who did this?'

'Absolutely not.' It nearly killed me to withhold evidence. I'm crap at keeping secrets. Also, there was something unencouraging about the police officer. He had a dyspeptic look on his face, as if he was still trying to digest a particularly starchy pub sausage. He seemed to be waiting for me to make a slip. When he suddenly thrust his hand in his pocket I thought he was going to pull out a pair of handcuffs, but it turned out to be a tube of fruit gums. He explained that he ate them to stop himself from smoking, and tried to offer me one, but they were all stuck together.

For a moment I thought of trusting him enough to tell him the complete truth, but then I remembered that he was the law, and came to my senses. He might look like an awkward, big-eared youth in a too-large helmet, but you could bet there were operatives at his station involved in monitoring calls and electronic conversations, probably with some kind of attachment to GCHQ or Interpol or something. They would find out what I had done if I gave them cause to suspect anything.

'The fingerprint man's already been. He wondered where all the furniture was,' said Lou, 'so I had to explain that you and Gordon were selling the house.'

'It was a good job your furniture had already gone,' the constable pointed out. 'I know it's a mess, but will it be possible to know what's missing?'

I had no idea what to say or where to start. Clearly, I couldn't tell him about Azymuth without implicating myself in the events that had followed. Playing dumb would be the only way I stood any chance of avoiding arrest.

'I saw two men leaving the house,' Lou told me. 'One looked liked a caveman, heavy-set, bald, young I think – I only saw their backs – the other was slim and smartly dressed. They got into a new model Mercedes saloon with blacked out windows. That's when I called the plods.'

'What made you do that?' asked the constable, clearly used to being referred to as a plod.

'Oh, come on. June never has visitors, she doesn't know anybody. Nobody comes sightseeing in this neighbourhood. You can come and stay with me, June,' she offered. 'I'll kick Darren out into the shed. He'd be happy there. He's reconditioning a motorbike. It's a mid-life thing.'

'No, Lou, I'll be fine. No-one's going to come back here.'

'Don't be stupid, you don't know what goes through the minds of these kids.'

'They weren't kids, and they were looking for me,' I whispered, pulling her to one side. 'This was a warning.'

'A warning? You've only been up in London for two days, what on earth do you need warning about?' she whispered back. 'I thought we agreed you'd suffered an hallucination.'

'You wouldn't believe what's happened since I saw you.'

'The way you're looking, I probably would. You can't stay here. Look at the place.'

'I want to be in my old house, Lou, even like this. I need time to think.'

Lou looked uncertain. 'All right, but if the house creeps you out, ring me and come over. Our plans have changed because of Hadrian's skirmish with the law. I've got Darren's mother staying with us now, but I can always chuck a sleepie into her dragon food.'

The constable came around the corner. I couldn't be certain he hadn't overheard us. 'It might be advisable to stay with a friend tonight,' he suggested.

'Really, I'll be fine.' I made a show of walking around the lounge. 'There doesn't appear to be anything missing,' I told him, 'but it's hard to be sure.'

'Perhaps you could just have a look through the rest of the house for us, if it's not too upsetting for you.' I made my way up the stairs, avoiding him.

I had clothes in plastic sacks in the wardrobe. They had been knifed open and emptied, but there were things I could still wear. If Rennie's men were looking for some clue to my present whereabouts, they would have drawn a blank. Clearly, they hadn't expected me to return to the Ziggurat, and even if they had, there was no way for them to know that I had switched apartments. The building was large enough to get lost in, and no sound carried from floor to floor. Unless they were posted at the main entrance night and day, they would have missed me.

But why were they putting in so much effort to find me? There are witnesses who are dangerous, and others who just want to run away and hide. Surely they'd have pegged me for the latter.

'Burglary can leave you feeling very uncomfortable,' said PC Big Ears, 'you'll be given a support number you can call,' but I looked around the wrecked room and felt nothing. There was a casual insolence in the way they had passed through the house, confident and amoral, as though it was just something they would normally do, like eating or sleeping. The lights in the bedroom were pointlessly smashed, a couple of unsold bedside tables full of inhalers and used tissues upended and kicked in.

'No,' I assured the constable, 'I really don't think anything's been taken. There's a lot of vandalism around here. Kids. I've had trouble before.'

'So you've made previous reports to the local police?'

'No,' I admitted, but I was running on adrenaline now. I could handle these two.

'Well, if you're sure you'll be all right.' He looked uncertain.

'I'll take care of her,' Lou told him, placing a protective arm around me. Before he left, the constable gave me a card with the number of a support line on it, and I gave him the number of my defunct mobile. I assured Lou I would be fine and sent her home.

There were stalagmites of glass everywhere, so I wrapped myself in the slashed innards of a quilt and settled in a corner of the lounge. Odd bits and pieces had been left behind in the rush to clear the house, but I couldn't find a phone charger.

I slept without sleeping pills for the second night in four years. Muddy dawn light woke me through unclosed curtains. The carpet appeared to be covered in diamonds. Realising how hungry I was, I looked for something to eat, but the refrigerator had been unplugged and cleaned out. I washed in cold water, dressed in a black sweater and black jeans and tidied myself as best as I could. Then I went off in search of a transport café.

I was becoming addicted to such places. It was pleasant to sit at a plastic-topped table in a steamy overlit room while the sky was still deep grey, listening to electricians and plasterers swearing and laughing about each other, their jobs, their birds, the government and anything else that crossed their minds. They looked at me with curiosity, but smiled when I caught them looking. I wondered why I hadn't come here before.

An odd side-effect of everything that had happened was being comfortable in the company of strangers, and becoming less mindful of my own behaviour. I ate a plateful of eggs, bacon, fried bread, beans and tomatoes that would have had Nigella throwing up in horror, and read a copy of the *Daily Mirror* that someone had left on the next table.

I thought about Azymuth operating on a penniless immigrant's face and tried to imagine how much it had changed Petra. She was young and hungry. She had wanted a new life. What had she traded to get it? Her face? What had it looked like before? The pre-plastic photograph in Azymuth's files appeared to be not much different from how she looked when she died. In the picture she was a little thinner, less tanned, free of makeup, her hair brushed back behind her ears. If the changes were so minor, as the doctor insisted, what was the point of making them at all?

I thought about the private patient files. The age range and physical types were very close. They all had the same look, as though they'd been singled out for some kind of service industry. Perhaps they all had a particular disease prevalent in their age group.

I turned the mug of orange tea in my hands, trying to make sense of someone else's world. What could Azymuth possibly have known that was dangerous enough to cause his death? Why was it necessary for his associates to trace my address and turn my life upside down?

I remembered the conversation I'd had with Lou on the day it had all began, and suddenly knew the answer. I paid the café bill and ran all the way back to the house.

CHAPTER TWENTY-SIX
Identities

I THOUGHT OF it because Gordon's mother kept a pair of pugs called Antony and Cleopatra. On that first day, I had been sitting in the kitchen matching beers with Lou's Rum Sours when we'd had a conversation about how to work out your porn star name. That was what Petra's other name, Cleo, sounded like: a porn name. I wondered if it could be an alias to disguise her real identity. Then I remembered the secondary names beneath the other girls' pictures; 'Honey', 'Brandy', 'Suki', the nomenclature of pets. It sounded as though they had all been rechristened. It seemed a long shot, but it sort of made sense.

I knew nothing about pornography except that there was a lot of it on the web, and I only knew that because Lou was downloading it all the time, printing out screen-grabs and leaving them in the bottom of Darren's briefcase for him to find at work. These little acts of terrorism seemed to make her life easier.

'I need to use Hadrian's laptop,' I told Lou when she opened the door. She was still in her dressing gown, her night one as opposed to her daytime schlepping-around-the-house one.

'He's taken it to a friend's house,' she explained. 'It's not a real friend, just someone with faster broadband.

Darren's knowledge of Crimewatch paid off and he managed to call a decent lawyer, but his mother is starting to think I'm related to the Krays. Are you going to file an insurance claim?'

'No, I have to find... do you think the police will press charges against Hadrian?'

'God, I hope so.'

'What are you going to do?'

'Don't worry about us, we always find the appropriate level of dysfunction we need in order to survive. Darren's reading Deepak Chopra and wants to discuss my anger issues. There's nothing left in Hadrian's bedroom. Funny, they stripped it bare and it still smells like Tutankhamen's tomb. Darren has a computer in his shed.' Lou led me through to the garden and unlocked an overgrown door. Inside, I manoeuvred around various bits of motorbike to some planks that had been arranged on top of a Workmate to form a makeshift desk for a PC and speakers. 'The police don't know about this one because I forgot to tell them about it. What are you looking for?'

I seated myself on a yellow fibre-glass engine housing. 'A porn star.'

'What?'

'I'm looking for a girl called Cleo.'

'I won't ask why. The best place to start would be under my husband's bookmarks. He uses his office phone number as a password. No imagination.' She ran the cursor down a list of pages.

'Not an American site, an English one.'

'Okay.' We scanned the lists together. 'There are zillions, so it's hard to know where to go. Wait, there should be an A-Z of names.' I was surprised by her dexterity with a keyboard until I remembered how much time she spent alone. 'Here, links to personal websites.'

'You don't mind Darren looking at this stuff?' I asked.

'Why not? It stops him from pestering me. I wish he'd take up some of these penis enlargement offers, though. Don't look so self-righteous. He got most of the dirtiest links from Gordon.'

'My Gordon?'

'That's how all the husbands in this whole neighbourhood spend their evenings, duh. They don't have the technology to build robot women so this is the next best thing. No 'Cleo' here. You sure it's an English site? Wait, there's a search engine for hardcore stars here somewhere. I used it when I was planning my hen night cake thing.' Lou had once tried to set up a company specialising in novelty iced genitals, but before the company registration came through she had been sent a lawyer's letter by Greggs bakery, who had discovered that she was using their sponge bases.

Lou typed and waited. 'My God, there are thousands.'

There was no way of refining the search by country. The people who used the service clearly weren't interested in demographics. I only ever went online to buy from discount designer outlets. I had given up after realising that even the most sophisticated technology was ultimately reliant on a relief postman hammering a package through a letterbox that was clearly too small for it.

There were seven girls listed by the name of Cleo. 'There are two registered to the UK, but only one represented by a London company, SlavStar. They specialise in Russian, Ukrainian and Hungarian performers. There's a web address for them.'

'Can you go to it?'

The page scrolled down. 'It's not a free site,' warned Lou. 'You'll have to enter credit card details.'

'I can't, you know that.'

'Let's put Darren's in, then. I know the number and expiry date of his VISA gold card by heart.' Her fingers flew across the keyboard. 'We're in. We enter his name, like so. He'll be getting Viagra ads for the rest of his life, big deal. If you want to see what Cleo looks like, there's a picture of her further down, look.' She moved aside to show me. 'Don't tell me you've become a lesbian and fallen in love.'

I found myself looking at the girl who had collapsed on the floor of Azymuth's flat.

'Jesus, listen to this. 'Cleo is a reincarnation of an ancient Egyptian queen, and treats all men as her sex slaves. Demanding and passionate, her commands must always be obeyed. In her spare time, Cleo loves to reveal her private kingdom on the internet. "Just like my horny ancestor, I have met some very wild men," Cleo tells us. "To me, every man is my Mark Antony. If you want to see the pleasure I give them, you'll have to enter my sacred site." Oh, this is good. "Mark Antony, adult actor". I love the way they call them that.' She tilted the screen toward me. The image showed a burly, tanned teen leaning on a Greek pillar in a laurel wreath.

'What on earth's that sticking out of his toga?'

'Whatever it is, he conquered Gaul with it. Adult entertainment is no longer technically illegal in the UK. We're following European guidelines now. Legitimise the business and you eliminate the criminal, that's the thinking. Obviously they hadn't met my son.'

'The real Cleopatra was Macedonian, not Egyptian, and she had a huge hooter,' I pointed out. The present-day Cleo could have had that fixed. Azymuth hadn't mentioned rhinoplasty. 'Has she got an email address?'

'You're joking. Of course she doesn't list her address, imagine the nutters she'd get. Look, you can buy her film *Cleopatra's Pyramids,* and she has a fan club. You want to try her chatroom? You won't talk to her, just some employee in Djakarta, but you might find out something more.'

'Show me how.'

Early on Sunday morning turned out to be the perfect time to chat online about pornography. No wonder the local church was empty. Twenty minutes later we had an address. Not where she lived, and no location for SlavStars, but one forlorn-sounding online stalker going by the hotmail name of kooldude352 knew the central London address of the minicab company Petra used, and confessed to having waited outside for a glimpse of her on numerous occasions. I made a note, Argosy Street, then ran it through Google maps.

'Are you sure you want to do this?' asked Lou. 'It's kind of deep water, especially for a housewife who's been getting out less than Stephen Hawking.'

'Harsh, Lou.'

'There's an Argos House in London SE8 and loads of Argos Roads, but no Argosy Street, Road, Crescent or anything else. It's just a stupid name made up by some creepy fan. I don't know why I'm even listening to you. The whole idea is idiotic.'

'But the girl exists,' I assured her. 'Maybe there's another way to trace her.'

'Okay, that's it.' Lou was tired and in need of a drink. 'I demand to know what this is all about.'

So I told her everything, including my part in Azymuth's death and the kitchen-gadget-stabbing of Stitch-Head.

'Christ, June, how could you have become involved in something like this? You mean this was why your house got smashed up, they were looking for you? Why didn't you go to the police?'

'It's easy for you to say that, you're on familiar terms with them, but I'd never spoken to a policeman in my life before this weekend. You always told me they were nothing but trouble, and look at the mess you're in with Hadrian.'

'Well, you have to give yourself up. They're bound to have got your fingerprints on the... what was it...'

'An apple corer, although it may have been a combi-potato peeler.'

'Even muggers have rights now. He'll probably want to sue you if he's still alive. It'll be easy enough to trace you.'

'But not to find me,' I insisted. 'There's one safe place I can go.'

'Where's that?'

'Malcolm's apartment. They have no reason to look there, why would they when it's the wrong flat to begin with? Azymuth was attacked back in his own flat. I'll find out where Petra was living somehow. Maybe the street is just spelled wrong.'

'And then what? What are you going to do, walk in there and make tea for them, ask them to cough up the address of a strangled porn star? And suppose they did, would you then go around there alone and walk in on a bunch of gangsters? I don't know this side of you, June. You got yourself into a panic when one of your salad servers got stuck in the dishwasher, and now you're planning to do a Travis Bickle. I'm sorry, but this is where I bail out. I have to mix a drink and take it back to bed with me. I can't be part of this paranoid fantasy.'

'I thought you were a friend.'

'I am also a wife and mother, and as a family we're pretty screwed up at the moment, something I'd quite like to sort out.'

'I never heard you say that before. You told me you hated your life.'

'Yeah, well.' Lou lit a cigarette, embarrassed. 'I talk a good game,' she said. 'You'd better leave before Darren wakes up.'

I hated losing my only real friend, but I had to see the weekend through. As I was leaving Lou's kitchen I saw her mobile and purse lying on the counter, and slipped them into my pocket. I had left my shoulderbag at the Ziggurat. With only loose cash and a handful of cut-up credit cards left, I needed money to get back to town. Besides, Lou would always be able to borrow from Darren. It was a good job he hadn't left his wallet; I'm not sure I would have been able to resist his credit cards.

I was walking back to the house when I thought of Stefan. He would at least be able to warn me if anyone had come back to the Ziggurat. I decided to head into town and ask him for help.

When I put my hand in my jacket pocket, I realised I still had the tiny key from the floor of Azymuth's apartment. Now I took it out and examined the faint engraved letters. The word MOM made no sense, so I turned it upside down. WOW.

I'd seen the logo dozens of times before.

World Of Wood.

The name on the only card I still possessed. We'd bought our dining room furniture there. The World Of Wood was a discount megastore that people like Azymuth would never have heard of. I felt sure that the key was Petra's, and that it would unlock something purchased from there. The good thing about megastores is that they're open on Sundays.

I admit it now, I got distracted.

I should have been heading for Stefan's container, but somehow I was sidetracked into a shopping trip. This is what comes of not having a properly thought-out plan. The bus stopped right outside the outlet, one of a series of depressing corrugated-steel boxes built on the outskirts of Hamingwell next to a vast ugly mall. The place was empty; the credit crunch had cleared out browsers.

I made my way through arrangements of *Thanet* leatherette swivel-chairs in search of someone who could help. I suddenly realised how long I'd been deprived of shopping. A baggy brown velvet sofa the colour of elephant dung looked positively inviting. I dropped into it and eased off my shoes.

'Can I help you at all?' asked a beautifully spoken young black man who looked like he'd recently been polished. Beneath his gaze, I became aware that in my all-black action-figure outfit I no longer resembled other housewives from the Hamingwell area. I produced the key and handed it to him.

'I wonder, can you tell me what this opens?'

The young man, whose badge identified him as Sholto, presented me with a fabulous helpful smile before accepting the key. *Sholto,* I thought, *your mother must have had high hopes for you, and look where you've ended up. You should be angry, not cheerful.*

'This could belong to any number of products,' he explained. 'Do you have a record of your purchases?'

'If I did, do you think I'd be asking you what it's for?'

'If you'd like to come with me.' He led the way to the rear wall of the store, which was lined with fake dining rooms and lounges, like little theatre sets. 'I'd say it's from one of our older models. These keys are pretty much interchangeable. They're not security keys. They're more for decoration.'

'What do they fit?' I asked, looking at the rows of dark cherrywood shelves.

'Bookcases,' he shrugged. 'This is a bookcase key.' He stopped before a glass-panelled case with double doors and fitted the key in the lock. One twist and the front of the case opened. 'See?'

'That wouldn't keep anyone out, though, would it? I mean, they could just break the glass and put their hand through, or pull at the door until the lock smashed.'

'Er... I suppose so, yes.'

I'm behaving abnormally, I thought, *I sound like a B-movie detective.* The salesman left my side and leaned into a cupboard to flick a rack of switches.

Every lamp in the store came on, an illuminated mirror-maze of gilded soft furnishings. I stared about myself in a state of retail hypnosis. The World Of Wood card in my pocket glowed with an inner warmth, as though it was responding to the life of the store.

'Is there anything else I can help you with?' asked the salesman.

I tried to fight the feeling, I really did. I took a long, deep breath and held it. Then I released a carefully controlled smile.

'I'd like to see your standard lamps,' I told him.

CHAPTER TWENTY-SEVEN
Relapse

THE NEXT TWO hours were, frankly, a blur.

All I knew was that I had done it again, after I had sworn not to. Worse, I had betrayed a friend. It turned out that Lou kept a plastic wallet of credit cards in her purse along with – foolish woman – her pin number.

I bought a fat-legged *Georgiana* table, four burgundy velour cushions with piped gold stitching, the *Alicante* foldaway dinette unit with built-in carriage clock, a dozen double-Damask dinner napkins hand-stitched by Sardinian nuns and a limited-edition ceramic sad-faced clown. At that point I hit my limit in the wonderful World Of Wood.

Fatally, the slip that came with my receipt offered me discount credit at Fabulous Fitness, which happened to be next door. Lou's VISA came out for the Electro-Stim Facial Spa, a pair of invisible shoe infill height maximizers and a flesh-coloured back brace.

This was my old stamping ground. The mall was crowded with angry-faced girls bulging out of tight shocking-pink tops, the kind of premature mothers who looked feral and cornered by life. Everything was within easy walking distance, and you were encouraged to keep walking; guards kept moving teenagers from benches.

Despite my recent conversion to minimalist understatement in the Ziggurat apartments, I slipped back into my former cluttery lifestyle as though I had never left it. With eyes wide and tubes unblocked by so many glittering retail opportunities, I set off to smack up Lou's American Express card.

Before I went spending, I always liked to case the joint online, like a burglar. That way I could work out how long it would take me to get from mixed separates to designer eveningwear, just in case they decided to evacuate the building suddenly and I hadn't finished shopping. Department stores try to distract you with perfumes and cutesy gold fiddlebobs, but it never works with us professionals. I can cover most malls in under an hour without a bathroom break. You have to be able to do these things properly. The staff smell bonuses and follow me like starving wolves. Most can be lured into performing the function of human clothes-rails with a pleasant smile and a teasing hint of retail frailty.

Two doors along from the designer clothing outlet I discovered PC World, Toys 'R' Us and Adventure, where I bought a tent and several scuba accessories. By the time I reached Spangles, the discount jewellery outlet, I was being trailed by two store detectives and a suspicious security guard. The assistant refused to let me open an account there because I became confused about my home address and foolishly presented her with three options, my old Hamingwell home, Lou's billing address and for good measure, Malcolm's apartment in the Ziggurat.

When I eyed an Emeralique necklace with a centre pendant big enough to choke a walrus, the store detective pinned me over a display case and rummaged through my pockets. When the cops showed up I was convinced they would somehow connect me with the murderous path I had blazed across London, but they seemed more interested in discussing the previous night's football with each other.

Mr. Barjatya, the manager of the World Of Wood, was a hefty Asian man who looked as if he had recently been dipped in chip fat. He swept into the store and spoke with the guards, and when he saw that I was their captive, his expression became even more surprised.

'Mrs. Cryer, I didn't know it was you. This is one of my best customers,' he told the policeman. 'Please let her sit down.' I collapsed on a divan as Mr. Barjatya explained that it was probably just an unfortunate mistake and that he would speak with the other managers about not pressing charges. I felt sure he knew I was guilty, but incredibly, he let me go. Presumably he and the other managers were familiar with the spending habits of lonely housewives and preferred to protect someone whom they considered to be a long-term investment. I would return, he hoped, to gratefully spend a fortune in his store the next time I was afflicted with a shopping brain-cloud.

I needed to clear my head and start thinking straight, so I shared a mug of coffee with Mr. Barjatya, who politely suggested that after I'd had a chance to rest I might like to arrange 24-month payment plans with him. I agreed so enthusiastically that I felt guilty about climbing out of the window of the ladies' toilet and legging it across the car park, but I was determined not to stay in Hamingwell any longer than was necessary.

I clung to the knowledge that nobody knew about Malcolm's flat. I would be able to stay there, at least until I could return the keys. On my way back into London, I ignored the five messages on Lou's mobile and decided to check in with Stefan. When I arrived outside the yellow container I found him cooking Toulouse sausages on his Calor Gas stove. He handed me one without thinking, as though it had already become a habit to let me check his cuisine.

'One day you'll have to come to dinner properly,' he suggested. 'There are some policemen looking for you.'

'Who?' I asked, alarmed. 'When was this?'

'I've just been talking to them. They said to call them if I saw you, then they took half my sausages and some napkins. They were in a white Rover in the corner of the car park. You just missed them.'

I wasn't sure whether to feel comforted. 'What did you tell them?'

'That I didn't think you'd come back.'

'I had to, Stefan. People can't be allowed to disappear without a trace.' I thought it best not to explain why both sides of the law were looking for me.

'Why can't they? It happens all the time. This is nothing to do with you. Everyone is on the move, you can't expect to keep track. Look at me, I am paid in cash. There is no paperwork. I am invisible. You can always get lost in the crowd.' Stefan slipped his hand from my waist in order to give his saucepan of fried onions a stir. 'The police find the body of a teenaged girl in a park, and to me the question is not who killed her, but why have her parents not reported her missing? No-one knows how to behave anymore. Why should you risk yourself for someone you didn't even know?'

'I don't see that I have a choice.'

'You mean you feel responsible for what happened.'

'I've contributed to the injuries and possible deaths of three people, Stefan. It seems unlikely that my path could cross with people like this, but the two worlds have bisected somehow, and the result has been some kind of... misinterpretation. Getting to the truth is the least I can do. It's the decent thing.'

'I always hear this word in England, and I don't know what it means. Something selfish, I think. These people who got hurt are living in a world you should not pretend to be part of.'

'So they can just go around behaving however they like and we're all supposed not to notice?'

'They're just not very fucking nice, okay? I don't like to think of a lady like you staying in that building with those animals. They pretend they're respectable, just because they have professional careers. Just because they're doctors.'

'Wait, what do you mean?'

'Many of the big apartments have been bought by doctors. Not good ones, I think, not honest ones, the other kind.'

'You're sure about this? They're all doctors?'

'That's what we heard, and they're all friends, many Russians I think.'

'How do you know?'

'Come with me, I can show you the cars.'

'But the car park is empty,' I said, pointing to the bare tarmac spaces beside the building.

'That is only for visitors. Residents have their own floor.'

I followed Stefan to the grille at the base of the building, and we peered down into the underground car park. Six identical dark blue Mercedes 350 saloons were parked beside each other. Even in the shadows their chrome and enamel gleamed with lascivious opulence. All six shared the same three-letter combinations on their plates. It looked like a shadowy megastore called 'World Of Wealth'.

Stefan rose and began walking back toward the container.

'Wait,' I begged, running after him, 'Stefan, tell me, what else do you know about them?'

'Nothing. Maybe they all work together. Who knows what goes on? The city is filled with these groups, they keep their secrets and cover their tracks. I'm just a manual worker, I have nothing to do with them, and nor should you. I'll tell you this. Last month one of them ran over the foreman's bull terrier and broke its leg. I was the only one who saw him do it. I also saw him check his rear-view mirror and back the car over it again rather than take it to a vet. I see it all, but I say nothing.' He broke into a gallop. 'I think my dinner is burning,' he called back. 'You can join me if you want.'

'Save me some,' I shouted as I headed up into the Ziggurat, pausing briefly to look back.

'What are you going to do?'

'I don't know. Find out enough to call the police when I get away from here.'

'They'll think you're crazy.'

Stefan was at the door of his container with a saucepan in one hand, wrapped in the breeze-blown purple beads that hung across the entrance. For a moment I wondered if he was as crazy as the rest of them.

I looked around for the police, but there was no-one in sight. Anyway, what more could I have dared to tell them? That I had witnessed more violence or that I had stabbed someone in the street before being caught shoplifting?

By now I was getting used to a six-flight run up the building's central staircase. Dr. Elliot answered my knock. He had no choice, as I was hammering hard and would happily have battered the door down. I'd seen his silly fetishwear laid out on the bed and wasn't scared of him. He could have answered the door dressed as Lady Gaga and I'd have breezed right past.

'You lied to me,' I said breathlessly, pushing into the hall when he answered. 'You know Dr. Azymuth and the others. You know what's been going on around here. You might as well tell me, just to get me out of your hair.'

CHAPTER TWENTY-EIGHT
Responsibility

'YOU SHOULDN'T HAVE come back, Mrs. – I keep forgetting your damned name. They're looking all over for you. We've had the police up here, knocking on all the apartment doors. I didn't answer. You know, you're making life very difficult for everybody.'

Elliot appeared even more sickly than he had at our last meeting. This time I could tell that he had ingested some kind of drug. His skin was the colour of tracing paper and the shoulders of his undignified shortie dressing gown were dark with sweat. I explained what I now knew to be the truth, but he seemed inattentive, his eye diverted by the ominous dark clouds building beyond the lounge windows.

'You know I'm not going to go away,' I warned him, 'not until you tell me the truth about what they did to that poor girl.'

Elliot grimaced and batted me away, as if he could no longer be bothered with lies. 'There's nothing much to tell. If I do, you must promise that you'll leave immediately. You've gone beyond just being a nuisance, you know.' He waved his hand drowsily at the door. 'I really don't want you here. I can't afford to be involved.' Behind him, the dissected figure of Maurice was outlined against a golden sliver of sun.

'I just want to understand for my own peace of mind.'

'Well, I certainly can't give you that.'

'Fine. Tell me something and I'll go away, I promise.'

'All right, come and sit beside me.' I sat at a safe distance from his bare upper thighs. 'Here.' He tugged one of the Ziggurat brochures from the back of the sofa and laid it out. 'Floor plans of the building. Corridors, exits, stairwells. The land is a royal estate, leased to a private international consortium and subleased to preferred suppliers. The biggest supplier has several hundred companies registered in the city, one of which is a very profitable international outfit called Slavista, one subsection of which is a company called Slavstars. Are you managing to follow me so far?'

My God, I thought, *the home of Mark Antony, he of the protruding toga.* From princes to porn stars in a few degrees of separation.

'Slavstars employs a great number of illegals who work for cash in hand, so no-one reports them if they suddenly go missing. Which means that your 'victim' probably doesn't even have an identity. The good doctor Azymuth does, of course. He has a criminal record. You know what companies like Slavstars actually do?

'Don't talk to me as if I were a child. You're going to tell me they're linked to organised crime.'

'That's rather an old school idea, gangsters keeping their stars strung out on drugs and making snuff films – which incidentally don't exist and never did, except in the minds of rabid politicians – but the public loves a good horror story.' He settled wearily back into his sofa, and seemed in danger of falling asleep. 'Actually, they give kids the chance of a better life, teenagers who grow old fast in the decaying cities of the Eastern Bloc. They help stupid little girls and boys who have nothing to trade except their looks. Most of them work for a few years and retire with more money than they ever dreamed of. A small handful screw up and ruin it for the rest. Recently one of the girls made a mess of things and was punished. Even you must agree that it's only fair to penalise the ones who try to cheat the system.'

'So you allowed someone to choke her to death as a punishment.'

'Good God, it's nothing to do with me,' he complained indignantly. 'Now, if you want to make a point, go to the police and tell them what you know. They'll file your report with all the others. You'll have done your duty, they'll have done theirs and everyone can forget about it.'

'The police wouldn't believe me.'

'Why not? You look so terribly respectable.' He made the word sound dirty.

'Perhaps I was. I don't think I am now that I've been seen stabbing someone in public. Besides, I got myself arrested this morning. A very young police officer told me to stay out of trouble.'

'You might want to take his advice.'

Elliot wouldn't get rid of me that easily. I remembered that his bedroom contained more leatherwear than the average MTV set, and gambled on him having much darker secrets he wouldn't want exposed.

'If I did go to the police I'd have to give them the names of people I've talked to, and I don't suppose you'd want to be involved.'

'Absolutely not.'

'But I would give them your name.'

He reached a decision. 'If I explain something to you, will you just disappear and leave me in peace?'

'You've got yourself a deal.'

He peered at me from half-shut eyes. 'These new adult stars, Russian, Romanian, Lithuanian, asylum seekers, economic immigrants – they arrive along the south-east coast of England homeless and broke. How would you feel, coming here for a better life, only to find yourself stuck in Margate on £50 a week? The young ones are met by industry reps, or they answer ads offering auditions in adult magazines. The top companies give them cash in hand and a little plastic.'

'They get credit cards?'

'Cosmetic surgery. Simple stuff: chemical peels, blemishes removed, breast augmentation, pectoral implants, features tidied up to make them more photogenic. They're used in movies, supplied with money and places to stay, then dropped when they can't perform or when they start looking too used. Azymuth did the facial nip-and-tucks.'

'And what's your part in all of this?'

'Oh, barely nothing at all. I just do the psychological evaluations, see if the new employees can be trusted, check that they're up to the work. It's simply a bit of freelance, entirely above board. Although, of course, none of us would be needed if the public didn't require its fantasy figures to look like comic book characters.'

'So you and Azymuth are employed by the same company. And I suppose the girls get passed around amongst you?'

'Don't be disgusting. It's a professional business, no different from any other. Workers don't handle the merchandise. Everything was fine until the directors realised that this building was still half-empty. You know, it's difficult finding somewhere suitably attractive to film. Nobody wants to watch their fantasies being played out in council houses. Well, some do but that's a niche market.'

And after they started filming here, in a property they already leased, the next logical step was to start using the building to dump their troublesome trash. Every corruption escalates unless it's stopped. But why here? I wondered. Why would they kill a girl in a new building when you could dump her out on the streets? Bodies are found in parks and canals with depressing regularity.

'It's interesting to consider the psychological implications within a society that requires constant stimulus to continue functioning. But perhaps that's for another time. I think we should draw this little chat to a close.'

'You can't cloak this in fancy psychology,' I said. 'You've taken money from people who destroy lives.'

'Oh come on, one has to end the burden of responsibility somewhere. You buy products manufactured in sweatshops that impoverish and shorten the lives of millions. There's no point in beating your breast about it if you're powerless to initiate change. Pour me a bloody drink, for God's sake. Don't just stand there like some kind of sitcom charlady.'

I spilled Courvoisier into the largest glasses I could find. 'I have nowhere to go,' I told Elliot. 'Dr. Azymuth is dead because he wouldn't tell anyone where I was. I owe him something.' I passed the glass and watched him drink.

'Don't be so naïve. How do you think the doctor found his beautiful apartment? They gave it to him as payment. He knew there would always be an element of risk.'

'What do you mean?'

'Were you even listening to me? The doctors have consultancies on the board of the estate corporation, who lease the land from the MOD, who are pals with the ministers who smooth the way for new legislation. The estate owns the entertainment company, and indirectly owns the clinic, and the men from the ministry, the board members, the corporation directors and the company managers probably all drink together at the bloody Garrick for all I know. While you're on your little crusade, why don't you check out the corner penthouse? That's where they do all their filming. Ask your little friend down there, the one in the yellow container who watches us all the time.'

'What's Stefan got to do with it?'

Elliot was leaning alarmingly to one side. He made an attempt to perk up, opening his eyes wide. The effect was pretty scary. 'He used to help sign up the talent. Hanging around the pubs in Dover and Folkestone, chatting up the ones he thought had a bit of potential. He'd give them a contact number, tell them how they could make good money in London and get a cheap place to stay. Where do you think your little friend Stefan comes from?'

'He told me he's French.'

'That's probably the first place he remembers, arriving across the border in his mother's arms. He's Moroccan. His sister's still out there peddling her fanny on the streets of Marrakech. And as for Azymuth, he could bore for bloody England, going on about how he and Stefan saved poor little Petra from the clutches of the police.' Elliot took a swig of brandy and closed his eyes. For the first time, I realised that he was as scared as Azymuth had been. He seemed relieved to have someone to talk to.

'What do you mean?' I prompted.

'Oh, the doctor went down to meet Stefan from the train at Waterloo. He used to follow the boy around like a love-sick puppy, it was all rather disgusting. So, Stefan arrived from the coast with Petra, who was travelling without a ticket, and there'd been a row with the inspector. She was pretty feisty, used to looking after herself. Before anyone could call the police, Azymuth paid the fine and smoothed everything over. Petra said she had come via Afghanistan, although how she got through the Pakistan border I've no idea, given that the Americans are crawling all over the place accidentally shooting children. She said she had nothing except the clothes she stood up in and a dusty old book she kept clutched to her bosom, probably some volume of religious claptrap passed down by her grandparents – they all have those.'

'Stefan and Dr. Azymuth brought her here?'

'Not at first. First they settled her in a bed and breakfast place over in Victoria, where they keep all the boys and girls, so if their charges got into trouble there wouldn't be any connection with the company. No-one is ever forced to do it. They choose for themselves, and most of them are thrilled to bits.'

'So what went wrong with Petra?'

'I imagine she decided to leave but Mr. Rennie wasn't ready to let her go. After all, she was an investment.

Azymuth had been paid well for the work he'd done on her, making her more photogenic.'

I recalled her body lying on the floor. She had perfectly rounded, high breasts. 'Did he give her breast implants as well?'

'Not that I know of. She was a star earner, but difficult, moody. Rennie's accountant set most of her money aside in a deposit account so that she couldn't suddenly take off.' Elliot was half asleep and starting to spill his brandy onto the couch.

'Then Petra must have had some money hidden away,' I pushed, trying to keep him awake for a few moments more.

'Well, that's what Rennie thought. The girl wouldn't own up, and from what I understand the whole thing turned nasty. That's why you've got to go now. The next time they come back, they'll come for you.'

'You and Stefan are the only ones who know where I am.'

'And I'd have to tell them in order to protect myself. You can see that, can't you? It's nothing personal, strictly business.'

A thought had been nagging at me. Why had Petra gone to Azymuth's flat at all? Why had she jumped me? Because she needed help or because she thought I was someone else? Had she expected to find the front door locked and the doctor away?

Then I remembered that she had spoken. Even with the collar around her neck she had tried to tell me. 'I need to get –'

I could only come up with one answer; despite being terrified and in pain, there was something in Azymuth's flat she needed before leaving.

I realised that I'd been wrong about the key. It belonged not to Petra but to Azymuth, and it fitted something in the bedroom. Petra hadn't arrived with it – it was already in the flat and she couldn't find it because it had fallen behind the bed. Perhaps she had searched for it before, but this time had been caught, questioned, tortured. Somehow she'd got away and tried to find it again.

The bookcase key. Whatever Petra had come by to collect was in the bookcase in Azymuth's bedroom.

I had to go back there.

But I also wanted to see inside the penthouse, where Petra had made her films. I could take pictures on Lou's phone. Elliot was losing his battle to stay awake. He had begun to slide off the leather sofa. I sat beside him, waiting for his eyelids to fall and stay shut.

I'd given up taking Temazepam to sleep, but it had proven worthwhile crushing up a whole blister-pack of them and keeping the fine white dust inside the gold teddy bear on my charm bracelet. I'd come up with this idea on the train, watching other passengers dozing. The powder had settled on top of the brandy like chalk dust, refusing to mix, but in the half-light and his anxiety for a drink, Elliot hadn't noticed a thing. I could see the white rime left on his glass.

I lifted one of the oil lamps from the floor and tiptoed away from the snoring form sprawled half on the floor. On the hall table I found a large bunch of numbered keys. One, I felt sure, would belong to the penthouse.

I raised them as quietly as possible and left, pulling the front door shut behind me. As I wearily returned to the hallway, rainclouds snuffed out the last vestiges of afternoon sunlight. It felt as if I was surrounded by those everlasting staircases by MC Escher, ones which would never allow me to reach my destination, and never entirely escape the determined grip of the Ziggurat.

CHAPTER TWENTY-NINE
The Set

I SHOULDN'T HAVE had the brandy. I hadn't eaten, and the drink went straight to my head. I meant to go directly to Azymuth's flat and find out what the key fitted, but I wanted to see where they did it – where they made the films. If I hadn't gone there I'd have been back sooner, and everything would have turned out differently.

The dark clouds were shrouds that slowly enfolded the settling red sun. Moving through the deepening shadows, I felt like a housebound sister of Van Helsing, mistakenly venturing into a nest of urban vampires. My stomach hadn't stopped churning since I returned, but there was a part of me that deliberately drove on into the darkness.

Sunday was surely the best time to take a look around. I wanted to enter forbidden territory, to see what had been kept hidden, so I headed for the penthouse. According to Madame Funes' plans, the corners of the seventh floor were occupied by the four largest penthouses, all supposedly unfinished and unsold. The two at the far end had no front doors. Dustsheets lay over unpolished marble floors. The third was the Ziggurat's main show flat. Its view across the river swept from St. Pauls to the Savoy and the Houses of Parliament, with the misty blue-green of Hampstead Heath rising in the distance.

The door of the fourth corner penthouse was still locked, but as I had expected, one of Elliot's keys opened it. Opaque plastic sheets covered a hideously glitzy black-and-gold lounge suite that looked like a cross between a lingerie box and a Russian brothel. Globe lamps hung on steel-whip arms in nudging retro-eighties irony.

Fascinated, I tore open the covers and revealed the room in sections.

A partially bubble-wrapped stack of giant framed photographs stood against the wall, distant Asian women with their legs spread wide, frozen-faced Chinese girls in fetishistic corsets, unblemished teenaged girls sprawled on sofas with their pale buttocks raised invitingly. They were dream-people, consumer goods no more obscene than photographs of sports cars shot in dancing beams of Italian sunlight, or close-ups of unpeeled lipsticks in the windows of Boots.

No personal mark had been left in the room. There was nothing here that would incriminate for anything more than a lack of taste. I tried the bedrooms, but the beds had been stripped. In one room, shiny fake-silk bedding lay screwed up in a bundle. The sheets were fleshy mauves and purples, the unsubtle colours of arousal and intimacy. Empty boxes, polywrap and polystyrene sections littered the floor. There were hundreds of empty DVD cases, virgin discs waiting to be digitally inscribed with pornography. The acts that had taken place here left a stale trace in the air, a faint ghost-image you could glimpse in half-light, fading heat-marks of desire.

In the wardrobe, I discovered a safe with its electronic locking facility disabled, and inside, layered in more bubble-wrap, was a heavy stainless steel object with a long wide barrel that looked like something from the sleeve of an old rapper CD. I was surprised by the weight of it. I had never touched a weapon before, and it felt dangerous. There was a gold sticker on the side reading 'Smith and Wesson 669 Double Action Automatic', as though it was a museum exhibit. There was a cartridge box, too, and when I checked inside I noticed that twelve bullets from the top layer were missing, so it was safe to assume the gun had been loaded and was ready for use. There had to be a safety catch somewhere, but nothing looked very likely. It was tempting to peer down the barrel, but I didn't trust myself to do so, like standing at the edge of a cliff and trying not to jump.

I decided to take it with me, even though I wasn't sure where to keep it.

Petra had been here, patiently sitting on this bed or perhaps on the lounge sofa, to be filmed by digital low-light cameras, everyone just doing a job, waiting to get paid and hoping to get through the experience with some slight sense of respect intact.

Petra had come back to Azymuth's flat, either to rob it or to collect something she had left behind. It meant returning even after she had reached a decision to leave for good, but her need had overcome her fear. But they – one of Rennie's employees, Stitch-Head – had followed her into the building and killed her before she had a chance to collect what she had come for. Her punishment, and the silencing of the doctor, should have been the end of it. Instead, it had made matters worse. Because there I was, in the wrong apartment, on hand to see Petra left for dead, and the doctor had told his client about me.

No more extemporising; I needed a plan.

I went back down to Malcolm's flat and put the automatic in a kitchen drawer. It seemed to belong with other steel utensils. Besides, it was too heavy to carry about, and frightened me. I could now return to Azymuth's apartment and search the bookcases. If I was unable to find what the girl had left there, I would have to admit defeat and go to the police. The problem was that in Britain, at least, Petra didn't exist. She had no criminal record, no identity, no employment records. She paid no taxes, held no permanent address, had no family members resident in the country. I would have to prove she lived before I could prove that she died.

'Hallo, love, I thought you'd gone.' Mr. Ashe, the gas fitter, was standing on the landing of the stairs armed with Waitrose bags full of rubber tubing that looked like something out of an operating theatre.

'No, I was just... out shopping.'

'No luck?'

'I'm sorry?'

'No shopping bags. Unsuccessful trip?'

'Yes.' I hastily headed on up the stairs.

'You know we're testing the gas tonight. You can't stay in the building.'

I paused and studied him suspiciously. 'What about the other residents?'

'There's no-one else left here now. I've just been round the whole place. I only came back for these.' He indicated the hoses. I knew Elliot was home, but he would still be unconscious. Perhaps Ashe didn't have keys for all the apartments. 'Come on, it's dark, I'll take you downstairs.'

'I have to get something too,' I said, trying to buy time.

'Then I can wait, it's no problem.'

'Really, no, I'll be down in a few minutes.'

He watched me as I started onto the next staircase. 'That's the penthouses up there, love.'

'Oh yes. It's confusing not having lights.' I was forced to stop on the landing, but he showed no sign of moving.

'Wait, you said the gas is being tested? So the electric ignitions are all off?'

'That's right.'

An idea had occurred to me. But first I needed to search Azymuth's apartment; I had a feeling I wouldn't get another chance.

I waited until Ashe moved away down the stairs, then continued up toward Azymuth's flat. I found everything as I had left it earlier. The great lounge, guarded by its lugubrious yellow-green canvases, was sunk in crepuscular gloom. I should have collected a brighter lamp from Malcolm's flat, but there was no time. No sign of Azymuth's body, either, but the dark Italy-stain still faintly marred the floorboards where he had fallen.

Crossing to the bookcase that filled the far bedroom wall, I began trying the doors. It was too much to hope that I still had the little key; it had gone missing during my most recent fit of shopping dementia. There was only one thing for it. I pulled off my trainer and whacked the thin crystal panels with the heel, shattering one after the other, all the way along the shelf. My lantern wick died and darkness thickened around me. I found a box of long stove matches in the kitchen, and returned to wedge them along the shelves. Pulling the volumes down in twos and threes, I checked the mahogany planks that lined the case.

I was sure that it had to be something small and of great personal value, an object the girl could have carried with her all the way from her homeland. Elliot had said she was carrying something when she arrived, a religious book. I pulled down the anatomy hardbacks, riffling through the pages and throwing them onto the floor, emptying the shelves one by one until I could no longer see the highest titles.

The matches burned too quickly. I was down to the last few and no closer to finding what I sought. The volumes were all similar, medical publications bound in black leather and edged in gold, their exterior elegance masking the horrors of damaged humanity. There were research documents on rare diseases, psychological casebooks, volumes on grafting and surgery, the pages falling open at appalling injuries, sores, abcesses, cancerous growths – it was hard to believe that the body could be so corrupted and remain alive.

On the top shelf of the last cabinet I found a plastic-covered paperback, the only one, wedged in between taller hardbound tomes. I lit a match and held it over the inside page. Petra's name was scribbled across the flyleaf in the same handwriting I had seen on her documentation.

The book was not a religious volume. It was *Not A Penny More, Not A Penny Less* by Jeffrey Archer.

Worse, it was so scuffed and filthy that it might have spent most of its life stuck up a chimney. I tried to flick through the pages, but the copy was so old that most of them were stuck together with dirt. This was the big prize, the precious treasure she would not part with, the sole item that belonged to her, Petra's only reminder of family and home? To have so little was pathetic.

Even though I barely knew her, I saw that this was the link between myself and the girl. She was my opposite in every way, barely more than a child. She owned nothing, but had been brave enough to take a chance and head halfway around the world for an unknown land, with her sad little paperback clutched to her chest, something she couldn't read but which acted as the symbol of a better life. Filled with hope for the future, she had been cheated and lied to, set to work, used up, tortured – the scarred backs of her hands testified to that – and finally destroyed. Meanwhile, it had taken me over a decade to make a journey of about twenty-five miles. I felt worthless compared to her.

I told myself that whatever else happened, I would not let her death be in vain.

CHAPTER THIRTY
The Incinerator

I COULDN'T JUST stuff the book into my back pocket, it didn't feel right, so I put it in a plastic freezer bag first, then ran out to look from the end window of the hall. Oval patches of street light had illuminated most of the area, but the Ziggurat's quadrangle remained in darkness. I sensed, then heard, two cars pulling up below, matching navy blue Mercedes saloons that flicked off their headlights the moment they had parked. Three men climbed out of each vehicle. Even from here I could see that they were further up the corporate ladder than the skinhead I had wounded.

My mother always said you could tell the class of a man by the quality of his overcoat. To that advice I would add a 21st century coda: you can tell a man of means by the fact that he even bothers to own an overcoat, and these were men of means, suited, booted and coming to take care of business.

At least I was now attracting a higher rank of criminal.

I couldn't see police anywhere. I rather hoped they would be watching and waiting to make their move, so that at a senior officer's signal a hundred uniformed men and women in riot gear would swarm the building to rescue me. There would be a brief but noisy machine gun battle, and I would be carried out to safety wrapped in a Mylar blanket. Instead, I couldn't even be sure that they had bothered to hang around. But then, what cause had I given them to do so? It was beginning to look as if I hadn't handled any of this very well. If I had stayed in the right apartment to begin with and not involved Dr. Azymuth, and not stabbed anyone, and then not lied to the police, I might now stand a chance of getting out alive.

So by now I was a hair-trigger mine of suppressed panic. This state of hysteria allowed me so little focus that I could only run with my instincts. I needed to take evidence with me, proof that Petra and Azymuth had been killed. I thought back to the first conversation I'd had with Ashe. If the electronic ignitions had been off since Friday, the eco-system disposal unit wouldn't be working until midnight tonight. I was gambling everything on one assumption; that they thought they had incinerated the bodies, but had reckoned without the power being off. Petra and Azymuth would presumably still be where they had fallen, at the bottom of the incinerator shaft. How could they be anywhere else?

I couldn't see any way around having to check it out before I could finally leave the Ziggurat.

But first I had to get the hell out of Azymuth's flat – it was the one place they would head for. I lit the oil lantern with shaking hands. Pulling the front door shut behind me and pocketing the key, I ran to the back stairs and started my descent. I had reached the fourth floor when I heard them coming up, so I hurried to the end of the building and down the far staircase, knowing that I would still have to cross the lobby to reach the basement steps.

In the silence of the dark building I could hear men talking above me. There was no urgency in their voices. They could have been heading for a business presentation in a hotel. But instead of shaking hands and exchanging contracts, they would catch me, kick me to death and dump my body with the others. The work was less complex than signing a property deal or a bank loan, merely operating from a different moral perspective. At midnight the electricity would come back on, the incinerator would pop into life and any evidence would be gone forever. Another London disappearance would be added to the list. I had read that over 210,000 people were reported missing in Britain every year. How many more went unreported? I wondered if anyone would even bother coming to look for me. Lou, perhaps, if only to get her mobile and credit cards back.

Why wasn't Ashe here now? He had turned up when I didn't need him, and just when he could prove himself useful he was nowhere to be seen. I ran through the darkened cathedral knowing that just above me, just behind me, just ahead of me, were men whose lives were so shadowed and stained that I could not imagine how they lived from day to day without shaking into pieces. I swung the lantern from side to side, hurtling angles back and forth, expecting any one of them to jump into life.

They were shouting to each other now, some voices growing fainter as they spread out in their search. There were no echoes to be heard here; the Ziggurat absorbed all cries of pain or pleasure. I reached the ground floor and began to dart back through the maze of twisted glass, toward the other basement door that, according to my hazy recollection of the plans in the brochure, led to the incinerator. Twice I ran blindly into dead-ended service corridors. The building seemed to be working against me. Looking out through the lobby glass I could see someone standing in front of the cars, watching the building's entrance.

I tried to turn the handle of the basement door but it wouldn't move. The square steel incinerator chute stood beside it. I pulled open the flap to see in, but it was too dark to make out anything. A powerful stench of paint fumes and old cabbages came up at me.

And then the lantern – useless bloody thing – blew out.

The darkness slammed in like a suffocating wall. I could not see my own hands. *If you panic now,* I told myself, *you're dead. Think. You have to see. Where is the nearest working light?*

The crazy woman, the concierge. Madame Funes had an onyx desk lighter. I ran back to her office, listening for the voices above, and noisily forced the door behind her desk, hurling myself at it, knowing the sound would carry through the building. The bar fell off and the lock popped. Actually, it came right out of the wood and clattered across the floor, so much for quality workmanship. Grabbing the lighter, I ran back to the shaft and tried the hatch again, holding the slim blue flame before me.

This section of the shaft was so close to the basement that there was no holding container attached to the steel door, just an open chute. It looked as though there was a short drop inside, no more than eight or ten feet. Nothing at the bottom but brown rags and bundles of paper, nothing sinister, although who knew what the rags were resting on? Realising that I had probably allowed my imagination to spiral away, I lowered the lighter with a sinking heart.

I didn't even hear them coming up behind me. If I had, I would have screamed the place down and fought back. Instead, the hands that seized my ankles were raised so suddenly that I was tipped up and over into the chute. Moments later I fell into the shaft.

I landed on my back, my short fall broken by paper and wadded-up bundles of painters' cloths, but a sharpness jarred beneath my right shoulderblade, cutting the skin, and there was something sticking in my thigh. As my breath came back I tried to turn around. I was in the base of a fifteen-foot-square steel box, the bottom of the incinerator shaft. Reaching down with my foot, I could just feel the plates of the fire grate underneath me.

The claustrophobic darkness here was total and alarmingly warm, as though the thing was on a low light. *I'll never get out of this alive,* I thought, *whatever happens, there's no way back up.*

The lighter had been knocked from my hand. I had lost my charm bracelet in the fall. I touched dirty steel walls, kicked out with my feet, but there was nothing like an escape door. My fingers brushed something spongy and moist, like fat mushrooms. Recoiling, I dropped to my knees and felt for the lighter.

After agonising moments of digging through the foetid, slimy rubbish that had spilled from split Sainsburys bags, my fingers closed around the oblong onyx base. The shaft was full of paint-fumes, but I had no choice. I carefully turned the lighter upright and flicked it. On the third try, the flame caught with a pop and grew.

Azymuth's face was staring back at me, no more than three inches from the tip of my nose. His bulging, bloodshot eyes were wide open, and his lower jaw rested against his throat, his grey tongue thrust out absurdly. He didn't look dead at all, he looked like he was screaming his head off.

I tried to turn, but my legs were caught. I glanced down and found myself tangled in rolls of cloth. The more I twisted, the more enmeshed I became. A scarred hand was sticking out between my knees. As I twisted harder, Azymuth's head bounced up from beneath the sheets like some demented Punch and Judy character.

I'd meant to be brave, but instead I yelled with all my might, panicked and dropped the lighter onto the paint-soaked rags.

CHAPTER THIRTY-ONE
Bullets

'YOU MUST CALM down and stop screaming. I locked the top door from the inside but it won't take them long to find the other entrance. Give me your hand.'

Stefan held open the steel incinerator hatch, which was below me, not where I had been looking for it at all. I dropped forward into his arms and clung tightly until he had lifted me free, but then his strength failed and he dropped me. Pieces of fiery rubbish were falling all around us. 'You could have burned yourself alive in here, silly English lady, what on earth were you thinking?'

'I was looking for a way out. I thought you'd gone.'

'I could see them waiting for you through the front door. A policeman went upstairs looking for you. Did you not hear either of us calling out?'

'The building deadens the sound depending on where you are. It's dark even in sunlight – I couldn't see anyone. Azymuth's body is in there.' I was shaking so hard as he led me away from the incinerator that I couldn't stand upright.

'Are you hurt?'

'I've cut my leg. And my shoulder.'

'Let me see.' He examined the wound on my thigh. 'I have to clean it. There are men are all over the building. The place is swarming with them. But only one policeman. What did you do? How did these people know you would come back here?'

'Elliot probably told them. Or any of the residents, I'm sure they all know at least part of what's been going on. Stefan, did you warn them?'

'Thank you, I am not so bad as all that. There are different degrees of breaking the law, you know, it's not just one side or the other, like if you do some deals you'll also help commit a few murders, fucking hell, what d'you think I am?'

'I'm sorry, it's been a very confusing weekend for me.'

We were in the section of the basement where I had first talked to Ashe, moving under the lobby in the direction of the river. I could hear a commotion above, and wondered how we were supposed to get out.

'They let you in because you know them, don't you?' I asked Stefan.

'Sure, of course I know them. We must leave this way now.'

'You lied to me. You said you didn't know that man with the stitches across his head.'

Stefan shrugged. 'We talk about this later, okay? Let's get you out.'

'Petra – the girl I saw murdered– she hid a book in Azymuth's flat.'

There was no time to explain everything, although given what happened afterwards it would have been better if I had. 'I think they were trying to frighten the answer out of her before they realised I was there. Her hands were scarred. Why would they scar the backs of her hands, Stefan?'

'Those marks were nothing to do with torture. She... well, she had an accident. You don't understand how it was.'

'I interfered,' I explained, 'but Petra was dead when they came back up. They think I know where the book is and I do know, *I do know,* I just don't understand why anyone would want it. Look.' I pulled the freezer bag from my back pocket. The paperback had now broken its spine, and was in an even more ruinous state than when I had found it. I passed the bag to Stefan as he pulled me through the basement corridors. He turned the volume over in his free hand and peered through the plastic at the filthy pages.

'You know what this is?'

'It's an absolutely terrible novel.'

Stefan sniffed the cover. 'Couldn't you smell anything?'

'I thought it was musty, all that dirt.'

'It's not dirt, Mrs. English Lady. It has been soaked in heroin. A common transportation method used through the Afghanistan-Pakistan smuggling routes. Cheap paper absorbs a lot of liquid. All you have to do is soak the pages in water to recover the full amount of the drug. If you're travelling illegally, it's better than wearing a money belt.'

'I thought she was keeping it for sentimental value, as a family memento.'

'Westerners,' Stefan snorted. 'Your charming romantic notions about the East never cease to amaze me.'

'It doesn't make sense,' I said stubbornly. 'The street price of heroin has fallen through the floor. I saw it on Channel Four. It isn't reason enough for a company to take the risk of killing someone, not in this city. Can you talk us out of here?'

Stefan turned to me. 'If they get difficult I will have to give them the book.'

'Tell them to take the bloody thing,' I told him, 'just get us out in one piece.'

'All right. They will see us if we walk back into the lobby. But there is no other way.' He pushed open the door to the concrete staircase. 'You must stay quiet and let me do the negotiating.'

At first I thought we were in luck. The lobby looked deserted. Then I realised there was someone leaning against one of the pillars. Silhouettes split as he moved into the light from the street.

'Stefan, what are you doing?' A young man who looked alarmingly like David Beckham approached him. Slim featured, smart coat, with a pleasant if peculiarly high voice, he was entirely lacking mean-spiritedness or a sense of threat.

'Hello Josh, what are you doing down here? I thought you were going home after you finished filming.'

'I am. Just clearing up a few odds and sods, nothing very interesting. Can you walk away for a few minutes? I need to speak to the lady.'

'She cut herself. Took a bit of a fall. She's going to need stitches. I was just helping her out of the building.'

'You don't need to do that. Mr. Rennie's on his way over, and he won't want anyone to leave. Not even you, mate.'

'She's had a hard time, Josh. She's got no quarrel with you. Let her go home.'

I started to move away from Stefan, but he gripped my hand and pulled me closer. I didn't want him to end up at the bottom of the burning shaft with the others.

'I wish I could, Steff, but we can't have every fucking housewife in London nipping round the shops and telling the neighbours what goes on. We're trying to run a legitimate business.'

'What's your plan, then? Take her off somewhere? That will still leave me.'

'Not a problem, mate. We can sort that out as well. Please, just walk away from her.'

'Come on, what's she going to do? Who's she going to tell? Look at her. She's not worth the trouble.'

Stefan released my hand and started to close in on Josh, who was becoming noticeably agitated, shaking out his hands like a gunfighter preparing for a showdown. Stefan was distancing himself from me, charting a course according to some map in his head.

'Nobody's under my radar, mate. Everyone gets attention. There aren't any exceptions to the rule. I don't want to get trouble from my boss.'

When Stefan released a burst of movement it caught me by surprise even though I had somehow expected it. A moment later he was locked in a ridiculously awkward scuffle with the other man. He and Josh looked like they were dancing. I noticed the others arriving at the entrance doors just as he did. Then Stefan fell down so hard that I heard his skull crack on the floor.

'Run, June,' was the last thing he said, but I hesitated, and the opportunity was lost. I was forced back in the direction of the central staircase, taking the steps three at a time, heading for Malcolm's flat, the one place they still had no idea about.

It was harder to keep count of the floors without light, but I'd had plenty of practice by now and smoothly hit the landing, the corridor and Malcolm's front door, running into the kitchen praying that they would never find me. I would have made it, too, if two of them hadn't followed me straight into the flat.

They behaved methodically and rather gently, as though they were in a profession that required an absence of panic, like zookeepers intent on catching an escaped snake. They were armed with powerful, sensible torches, and asked politely if I kept candles. I pointed to a cupboard beneath the sink and they thanked me. I wondered how much they knew, how much I could bluff. I hoped they thought I was a resident of the block, nothing more than a nosy neighbour.

They asked me to sit on a high-backed kitchen chair, to be still and wait. I couldn't stop myself from fidgeting, so after a couple of minutes they tied my wrists and ankles to the chair-back with plastic tags. Obviously they'd bought a job lot.

My captors, whose names I was too frightened to catch but whom I had come to think of as Friends of Stitch-Head, or Foshes, checked their watches and talked to each other across me, discussing some kind of sports quiz on television, and a problem with the ignition on one of the cars. Actually, being held prisoner was as boring as it was frightening.

I wondered if the lone policeman had spotted something wrong and decided to send out an alarm, but the more I thought about it the less faith I had. After all, I was in one of nearly a hundred locked apartments, in a building everyone thought was empty.

All in all, it was the wrong time to get a nosebleed. They panicked a bit when they saw my shirt suddenly turning scarlet, but found a damp J-cloth and managed to smear it around, making it look like someone had committed an axe murder.

As I sat there, I tried to arrange the weekend's events in order, to work out how I ended up being tormented by a man with the charm of a drain. Some time later, as I watched Raffles the gargantuan skinhead fleshpod wedging a half-pounder with cheese into his mouth with the flat of his thumb, I remember thinking I'd prefer to meet a noble end at the hands of someone with manners, a surgeon with Parkinsons or a pissed Bentley driver.

I thought about dying. With so few people ready to miss me, I started thinking about reincarnation instead. I knew that we were supposed to come back in a lesser form if we disappointed our maker, but even so I decided that putting Beethoven into Doris Stokes was a bit of a jump, so at that point I stopped thinking altogether, and sat mesmerised as a Fosh unwrapped a second sweating burger from its foil and munched it at the window, peering out with his greasy hands cupped around his eyes, complaining that he couldn't see anything.

The other Fosh tried his mobile and swore when he couldn't get a signal, but kept doggedly trying. It annoyed me that they had the upper hand, considering they were so incredibly stupid, but then I decided that this was probably what really made the world go around, stupid, dangerous people acting violently behind the backs of ordinary folk. It was so obvious when you thought about it – why had I ever thought it would be otherwise? They acted as though I was just another customer, like nurses talking over a dying patient or Cassandra's prostitute friends in the pub chatting over the shoulders of their punters. After a few minutes, one of them went out into the hall and returned with Mr. Rennie.

I knew it was him because he perfectly looked the part: old money in a neat new format. Polished black shoes with pale leather soles, blue woollen overcoat, fine-striped Marc Jacobs shirt – new season, not a sale item – slim blue Armani tie, wavy brown hair just touching his collar, a hint of the young Rio Ferdinand about him.

Rennie immediately began to berate his staff. 'I've been wandering around in the dark for the last ten minutes trying to work out where you'd gone,' he complained. 'I thought I told you to put some lights on the stairs.'

I wondered what had happened to Stefan – it sounded as if he had fractured his skull. I shifted uneasily on the chair as Rennie approached. The tag cut into my wrist when I fidgeted and I could feel blood on my back from the wound on my shoulder.

'So you're the infamous Mrs. Cryer,' he said, finally turning his attention to me. 'I've been hoping we would get to meet.'

'I have what you're after, and you're welcome to it,' I told him, feeling no guilt about surrendering the drugs. 'Did you know it's in a book?'

'What do you mean?'

'She soaked a book in a solution of some kind. All you have to do is soak it again and get the residue, apparently.'

'Thank you for clearing that up. Nice of you to be so helpful,' said Rennie. He didn't sound too bothered. 'But then you did cause the problem to begin with. It's what she owes us, nothing more. I don't steal from people.'

'The girl is dead.'

'Whose fault is that? Not mine.' He raised his hands, questioning, then tapped at his front teeth. 'So, what to do, what to do? How are we going to resolve this matter?'

'I want to know what will happen to me.'

'Oh, bargains now, is it? We don't do bargains. Sorry.'

'Then I won't tell you where the book is.'

'I'll let you in on a little secret.' Rennie pulled over a chair and turned its back, sitting astride it to face me. 'I don't care about the book,' he whispered, smiling. 'Dealing drugs is an old-fashioned, high-risk way of making money, and to be honest it's tacky, a bit too Essex these days. The boys can have it. I'm more concerned with you. You're not helping this city. You're just someone's wife, you clean, you shop, you do the lottery and tut over things you read in the newspaper. You're not productive. Us here –' he indicated the others, '–we're little power stations, working night and day to keep London running smoothly. Why do you think the police leave us alone? We're public servants, providing essential services, clearing up the mess, making everything tick over. Raising profits, employing staff, rebuilding, reinvesting. If that dim little constable who's wandering around this place had to choose between the two of us right now, just judging us by our usefulness, he'd lock you up and let me go. We have a sense of corporate responsibility. That way we can be selfish and civic-minded at the same time.'

I didn't buy his line because I had to believe that people in public service had a better value system than his. Even so, it would have been nice if a crowd of them had burst in at this point to save me. Surely they should have called *someone* by now.

Rennie scraped his chair a little closer and smiled pleasantly. 'I'm not doing a macho number on you, Mrs. Cryer, I'm just trying to explain the difference between us. The law works on two levels. There are the written words, which are just scratchmarks on a wall, something to keep the public from fretting, something people like you obey, and there are the actual rules, like smoke in the air, the ones aimed at us, where practical deals are struck without court intervention.'

'That's not right,' I ventured.

'Things don't look right because you never see the other part of the picture, but we're always there, putting in the hours twenty-four seven, hard but fair, working for London, just like our mayor. So that you can have an easy life. Do you want a cigarette?'

'I don't smoke.'

'No, of course not. Whose flat is this, by the way?'

'It belongs to a friend.'

'Malcolm somebody,' said one of them, talking to his boss. 'Little bald bloke. He did the Marylebone clinic deal.' There were now three Foshes in the apartment, standing around with their hands in their pockets, as bored as bouncers on a quiet night in Swansea. Five men had arrived altogether. That left another one with Stefan, and I had to assume that the police officer had wandered off unseen.

'Right.' Rennie turned his attention back to me. 'Well now, let's see. The book is here in the building, because you couldn't have found out about it very long ago and you haven't been anywhere else. You can save these boys the trouble of taking the place apart.'

'I don't care what you do with drugs or anything else, I just don't want to die. I'm not important, you said so yourself. I'm even less interested in your life than you are in mine. So let me give these gentlemen the book and get the hell out. I'll go home and that's the end of it.' I was sure he had no intention of letting me go, but it was worth a try.

'Oh, go on then. Show them what you've got and I'll think about it. It's not the money, it's the principle.' Rennie couldn't be bothered to go rooting about in the gloom. He nodded to one of the Foshes, who snipped the tags from my wrists and ankles and let me rise from the chair. He had underestimated me. Trying to act as calmly as possible, I went to the kitchen drawer, but my heart was quivering. I turned back to them.

'You say I'm not worthy of attention, but I think I'm potentially dangerous. Do you know why?' I asked, digging noisily among the utensils, stalling for time.

'No, Mrs. Cryer, why are you dangerous?' asked Rennie, vaguely amused by my bravado.

'Because I'm a housewife with a gun.' I meant to pull up the stainless steel automatic in one smooth move but the trigger got caught in an egg-whisk. Shaking it free, I pointed the barrel at Rennie. 'I may be running low on estrogen, but I'm not out of bullets.' I flicked off what I hoped was the safety catch and squeezed the trigger.

The detonation was simply astonishing. It made my ears ring and nearly broke both my arms. There was a hole the size of a saucer in the wall next to Rennie's shoulder.

This, I thought dazedly, *is empowerment.*

I was amazed that I'd been able to miss at such close range, but then I realised that I'd been too nervous to actually take aim before firing. Rennie and the Foshes were looking at me in total bewilderment. One of them had dropped his burger on his shoe. Another had bent his knees and put his hands over his ears.

'That's my gun,' said Rennie, 'what the hell is it doing here?'

'I locked it in the safe,' the tallest Fosh explained.

'You fucking plimsoll-brain, the power's off,' said Rennie, taking a step forward as I held the gun at arm's length, closed my eyes tight and fired again.

This time the bullet ricocheted off the polished marble kitchen counter and went straight through the cupboard door under the sink, ploughing into ranked cans of highly pressurised cleaning sprays and flammable fluids. The resulting explosion sent a ball of flame across the room that felt as though it would melt our faces.

The tallest Fosh was standing nearest. The shoulders of his suit appeared to be on fire. The Fosh next to him had a fork stuck in his ear. Rennie had been knocked off his feet, and had fallen back against the far wall. There was a cake-slice sticking out of the sofa. I was still standing, but could barely hear my own voice above the singing in my ears. There was a very strange smell in the air. 'Nobody move!' I bellowed, shocked at my own power.

Flames crackled, popped and spat, spreading through the cupboards and blowing out partitions as further cans exploded.

'You don't have to shout,' Rennie pointed out. 'What do you want? Come on, you're the one with the gun, think of something you want fast, just keep your fingers away from the trigger while you're thinking.'

'I can't hear you.' I wiggled the gun between them, causing each to duck in turn.

'What – Do – You – Want?'

'I want to go home.'

I remembered my husband-less smashed-up house, my friendless, hateful street and my embittered neighbours.

'No I don't,' I carefully corrected myself. 'I want to go shopping.'

CHAPTER THIRTY-TWO
Shopping At Gunpoint

As we left, I looked across the car park to the river side of the Ziggurat. In the building's shallow front garden, Stefan was sprawled across a plastic lawn chair and appeared to be sunbathing. A livid bruise had spread from his left ear to his shoulder.

Mr. Rennie drove me in silence to the Westfield mall at Shepherd's Bush. From behind, I and my companion could have been any couple heading for the shops, except that we were periodically hitting fifty miles an hour on backstreets, speed-bumps included.

I knew I wasn't thinking straight. Right now, I couldn't tell if I was hosting a backfired kidnap or behaving like a Stockholm Syndrome sufferer on a shopping trip. Whenever we pulled up at the lights, I wondered if anyone could see the dark gleam of the gun barrel in my right hand, but I knew no-one would do anything, not with the dangers of road rage these days.

By now the Foshes would have taken Petra's book from Stefan in order to turn it back into its component chemicals. Despite the fact that Rennie's drones were clearly longing to hurt me, I found them almost endearingly silly, like Munchkins or body builders. Firing the gun had made them look a bit soft. I had shown them how to use Malcolm's fire extinguisher, and left them happily putting out the blaze in the kitchen. None of them seemed very bright, but they obviously made stacks of money, because they were all wearing designer suits under their smouldering overcoats. Call me old-fashioned, but it seems odd to spend over a thousand pounds on a suit and have your hair cut like a Turkish convict. I blame footballers for getting in touch with their feminine sides.

The Westfield car park was less than half full, so we didn't have to wait at the entrance. Rennie made no attempt to take the gun from my hand. The heavy automatic was now welded to me, its stainless steel casing matched to my body temperature. Actually, it was starting to feel rather sexy, if a little obvious in the 'I Haven't Got Much Of A Penis' way.

'Park in the Blue section of Level 3,' I told him, 'between numbers 245 to 253. That way we'll be nearest the entrance door to Zara.'

'Jesus, you could get a job as a buyer here.'

'That's right, and you're on my territory now,' I warned him. 'The amount of money I've put back into this country's retail outlets, they should give me an OBE.'

I loved the new store policy; open early, close late. My kind of place. I suppose at this point I had gone slightly mad. I just wanted the freedom to do it one last time, before my life came to an end – as I was sure by now it would.

Department stores have countless ways of easing the plastic from your pocket, but I knew all their tricks. They use the old casino ruse of hiding their clocks to make you lose track of time. They arrange their high-profit lines so that they're perfectly reflected in your fitting mirror. They dot their spaces with leather armchairs and copies of *GQ* because they know that men will rather sit than shop, not that I ever went shopping with Gordon. Shopping is self-pleasure. There's no point in going with a husband who races for the counter with the first pair of trousers he sees in his approximate size. Gordon regarded shopping as an SAS manoeuvre – get in, do the job, get out fast. It betrayed a carefully plotted commercial ethic. Retailers went to the trouble of constructing their food courts at the tops of buildings to keep the smell of fried meat from permeating their womenswear collections. They marked their UP escalators but hid their DOWN ones. They built their cosmetics bars with plenty of angles because research showed that women preferred to sit at counters with lots of corners. To them I was someone important, someone sexy and rich enough to be worth pursuing, and Gordon merely ignored all their hard work. I thought that was plain bad manners.

We walked into Zara half an hour before the mall was due to close. There was hardly anyone in the store. I kept my eyes on Rennie, who seemed vaguely amused rather than bothered by my behaviour.

'I just want some underwear here,' I explained. 'They do nice tops, but when someone else is paying you want something a bit pricier.'

He looked at me as if he'd been handcuffed to an escaped lunatic. In Dolce & Gabbana I gathered together a whole new wardrobe in black, jumpers and shirts, jackets, belts and pairs of jeans from the racks, and whenever Rennie turned around to complain or ask where we should go next, I allowed the gleaming barrel of the gun to become visible behind my bag, like a flasher exposing himself to a child.

There's always a prickle of electricity over my skin when I buy something expensive, a race of blood cells as I press my card into the reader and watch the assistant delicately folding tissue as if packing a rare dead insect for a long voyage by steamer trunk, running her scissors over the back of a piece of ribbon to make it curl.

I found a Mango outlet that unfortunately didn't have my size, so I picked up a trouser-suit and a pair of rhinestone evening pumps from Prada. I didn't care whether the CCTV could see us. On the one hand, if they did they might come and save me. On the other, it would put an end to my spending pleasure.

Rennie sulked like a fractious husband, thrusting his hands into his pockets. He was quite attractive in a degenerate way, but I couldn't see him as husband material; too arrogant, too restless. He seemed less concerned about being shot than being embarrassed.

'If I don't find the shoes that go with this dress, I'm going to kill you.' I was only half joking. I piled him with bags and headed for Marks & Spencer. I didn't care where I shopped. The mere act of exercising purchasing power was enough to restore me. It would be an ignominious end to a career as a crimelord, arrested at the M&S bra and knicker counter.

'What do you think, the grey or the blue?' I asked, holding different brassieres against my breasts.

'I don't know, I really don't care,' my hostage replied sulkily.

I let him see the muzzle of the gun again. 'Make a decision.'

'The blue. This is like being married.' Rennie shoved his hands into his pockets. 'Do you want me to sit down over there and leaf through magazines while you rob the till?'

I changed my clothes in the cubicle with Rennie standing on the other side and the gun trained through the door. Balancing on one leg like an armed flamingo was not an easy thing to do. Shopping had been my drug of choice, and I had gone for one final overdose, hoping it would now be out of my system.

I applied some lipstick while targeting Rennie in the makeup-mirror, Annie Oakley attempting a trick shot. As I did so, I caught sight of a cashier peering around a rack of remaindered skirts at us, but when I looked back the girl had vanished.

'Just stay close enough for me to shoot you if I have to.' I piled my hostage high and aimed him at the checkout. I was nudging him with the gun-barrel just as his mobile rang.

'Answer it,' I commanded.

He flipped open the phone. 'Hi... yes, we've sorted it out. No, I'm still with her.' He listened for a moment, then covered the phone. 'It's my director. He wants to know where we are. Where are we?' He took a look around. 'Marks & Spencer. We're in ladies' separates, but I think we're heading for tops and tights. No, why would I be joking?'

I was surprised to hear he had a boss. How high did these things go?

The counter girl was pretty, but heavily made up. She didn't seem to notice that I looked – quite accurately, as it happened – as if I'd fallen into an incinerator and been tied to a chair. She didn't see anything beyond the eyeline of her route between counter and screen. She could have been on the fourth quarter of her shift in a factory, filling bullet cases with powder.

We waited awkwardly as she detagged the items and folded them into carrier bags. I felt the burning panic that had been roaring about inside me receding as each purchase received its tissue-paper prepuce. Rennie withdrew a platinum Amex card and handed it to the cashier. I almost fell in love with him.

'What do you want to do now?' he asked as we moved toward the exit. Overhead, a soothing voice told us the mall was closing. I was disappointed because there was a perfume concession somewhere above us selling virgin rose-oil at £600 an ounce. Rennie had got off lightly.

'Give me a minute,' I told him. 'I'll think of something.'

'Dinner? Arson? Blackmail? When you abduct someone it's a good idea to have a plan.'

I had no answer for him. Now that I had shopped, the familiar thrill was fading to post-coital guilt. We reached the car with a trolley full of purchases and he began loading them onto the rear seat.

'You don't know, do you?' he pushed. 'Look in the back of the car, all the clothes you don't want. Are you planning a killing spree, or shall we just go and get your legs waxed? You can't go home, you can't stay here. You're stuck between two lives. There's no quick fix; shopping will never work again after this. I'll tell you, some of the people who work for me get into drugs. They're fine for a while, but after that they get so restless they don't know what to do with themselves, and that's when it gets dangerous, for me and for them. You're in the same state, I can see it in your eyes. You have to figure it out, June. What the hell is it you want? Until you figure that out, you'll never cure your addiction.'

'I'm not listening to you, Mr. Rennie, you kill people.'

'Give me a break, it's been an unusual week. I explained to you that the girl had to be punished. She was jacked-up all the time and useless at her job. She went missing for days. She'd have died young if she'd stayed in her own country.'

'Instead she ended up in an incinerator.'

'Don't preach to me. The guy you knifed in Lower Marsh market is still breathing, no thanks to you. He has to have a zipper in his stomach.'

'I thought I'd killed him.'

'Yes, you've blazed quite a trail, haven't you? Interfering here and there, stabbing one of my best men, forcing us to get rid of the doctor and generally screwing everything up wherever you go. Why don't you let me call your husband and have him take you home? Go and do some damage in the suburbs where it won't be noticed.'

'He's divorcing me. And he's sold the home. I've got nothing to go back for.'

'There are plenty more –'

'Don't say it. I'm nearly thirty. All the women's magazines agree that the odds of getting into a permanent relationship after the age of thirty are the same as being in a fatal boating accident.'

'Listen, thirty is no age at all. I have sixty-year-olds working for me who look fantastic.'

'I don't want to bleach my hair and be filmed giving blowjobs on the internet, thank you. Every woman looks good when you only see the back of her head.'

'Ah.' Rennie thought for a minute. 'I don't suppose you'd consider employment in a more legitimate capacity?'

I suddenly felt so very tired. I sniffed and wiped my eyes, swinging the gun into my right hand and causing Rennie to duck back. 'Doing what?' I asked, trying not to let my voice quaver. 'What can I do? I'm still a housewife, for God's sake, it's in my genes. I can't stop reading the backs of cleaning product packages because it's too ingrained in me. You're not even supposed to say "housewife" anymore, you're an "unwaged homemaker". But I was rubbish at homemaking, even at school. I dropped out right after we did meringues.'

'Nobody cares whether or not you finished school. You've got one major asset you've overlooked. You're respectable. Take a look at yourself. Anyone would trust you. Do you know how rare that is in our line of work?'

'Really?'

'Really. It could be a big help. Tell you something, June. I'll admit I was going to have this little business sorted out in the traditional manner, but that was before I got to know you. I wouldn't hurt you now. I think you could be an asset to us, I really do.' He looked over at me and his smile lit up the interior of the Mercedes. 'Put the gun down, for God's sake. Let's go back to the Ziggurat.'

We drove in silence for a while. I wasn't about to suddenly drop my guard just because he was being charming. But I lowered the gun onto the seat, and looked sadly back at all the ridiculous carrier bags.

'I don't want you to hurt Stefan.'

'He used to work for me. I don't hurt my own people unless I have to. It's up to him now.'

'Thank you for the clothes. I can't help myself.'

'We all have our obsessions, it's nothing to be embarrassed about.' He pulled up in front of the darkened building. The other car was still there, but there was no sign of any Fosh activity. 'They're up in the penthouse.'

'I don't think I should come up,' I told him. I was counting on the police not giving up on me, but couldn't see them anywhere. If I knew they had the place under surveillance there was a still a chance that I could get out, but the odds had fallen to around zero. 'You could lend me a few pounds, I could check myself into a hotel and think things through for a few days. Maybe come to some kind of decision about my future.'

'I think if you search your heart you'll find you've already made up your mind.' Rennie's fingers brushed my shoulder lightly. 'Tell me, June, when was the last time you had really good sex?'

'That's none of your business.' The question was impertinent, but the answer would have shocked him.

'I bet it was a really long time ago.' He reached back, and before I could see what was happening, he kissed me.

I remember that kiss. Body warmth, Cartier aftershave, a prickly chin, something else, something stony and secret, so different from Stefan. I broke free, flustered, trying to speak. 'Listen to me a minute,' I asked. 'You don't know what I'm like.'

'I think I do. If you'd fallen in with a wild crowd or done something crazy instead of trying to please people, you could have got away, but you left it too long and one day you woke up next to a man you didn't love. You lay in bed watching him sleep, wondering how you

313

could leave and survive. What you should have done was take a chance and walk. Life is too short to worry about what other people think.'

It was as if he could read my mind. 'Do you know how often I've painted my nails at home?' I asked him. 'Every day, while I watched the Living Channel. I thought I was addicted to the smell of polish remover, but since I've been here I haven't even thought about doing it. I don't think I even care about my cuticles any more.'

He turned to me and smiled. 'Scientists say we're shaped by our environment, June. There's hardly any hereditary influence at all. After all the social experiments, they discovered that the family no longer has a hold on us. It means there's still time for us all to change. So how do you want to do it? Benjamin Disraeli said that London is a modern Babylon. It's a tribal society. All you have to do is pick your tribe.' It sounded like a line worn thin with previous use, but I didn't care. He kissed me again, his warm, peculiarly large tongue searching my mouth. I thought of Stefan and felt ashamed, but closed my eyes as he embraced me.

This time he broke away first. 'I'm sorry, June.'

I opened my eyes. Rennie had the gun in his hand. He held it with the muzzle down, as though he felt it was inconsiderate and unnecessary to point it. 'Let's go upstairs and figure this whole thing out.'

This is a really sleazy way to die, I thought as we climbed the stairs into the Ziggurat, *my mother's worst fears will all be confirmed. You failed to have children, your husband walked out on you, of course you were bound to be shot in the head by gangsters.* I felt strangely calm, like Anne Boleyn going to the axe. At least I would never have to return to Hamingwell again, never have to spend arid days waiting for nothing in particular to happen, never have to hold dinner conversations so dull that they dried my mouth to sand.

Rennie guided me, his hand firmly pressed at the base of my spine as I climbed. When we reached the penthouse, I was surprised to see that the two remaining Foshes had revealed a flair for interior decoration. Perhaps they were a couple. The covers were thrown back from the lounge furniture and dozens of fat cream candles had been lit. The room looked positively cosy, although there was no disguising the vulgarity of the soft furnishings.

I hadn't expected him to hit me. The blow, the back of his hand across my face, caught me completely by surprise, so that I was thrown down onto the sofa. I tasted blood in my mouth; a tooth had cut my gum, nothing more, but it stung. One of the Foshes inexpertly slipped another plastic tag over my wrists. I studied Rennie, bewildered.

'That was for making me go shopping with you, that's all.' He checked the edge of his hand and rubbed it. 'You shouldn't get involved with things you don't understand.'

'I had to. I did it for her.'

'Who?'

'I couldn't let Petra go like that,' I explained, 'without anyone caring whether she even existed.'

Rennie considered the point for a minute. 'I think there's something I should tell you.' He shrugged at the Foshes. 'This wasn't about Petra hiding the book. That's not why she was punished. Your friend Stefan

315

knows the truth. You should have asked him when you had the chance.'

One of the Foshes strolled out of the room and re-entered with a thicker plastic tie looped over his arm.

'No,' I said quietly.

I tried to climb over the back of the sofa, but he snapped the thing around my throat in one smooth movement; it was an action made quotidian by repetition. He tightened the band, clicking it until it enclosed my neck tightly. Now I understood why Petra's hands had been tied. It had been to stop her from wriggling her fingers under the noose.

'You know why we use this, don't you, June?' asked Rennie. 'Everyone understands once it's on them.'

I did understand. It was not a method of torture but control, pure and simple. A dog, a slave, a subservient creature who would be forced to obey. Now that I could feel the edge at my neck, it was obvious.

Rennie slid his arms beneath me and carried me gently to the bedroom, laying me down on the bare mattress. 'You two, go and put some lights on in the kitchen, and bring Stefan up here.'

Rennie called the rest of his men out into the hall and said something to them. Even without catching his words, I understood what was to happen. The incinerator would start working as soon as the building works were finished. I twisted my head to read my watch: 21:46pm. I wondered if anyone would ever find me; I wasn't even wearing my wedding ring anymore. That had vanished in the ransacking of the house. Even my charm bracelet was in the incinerator.

It was becoming hard to catch my breath. It was as though someone had put a plastic bag over my head.

Rennie was arguing with the others about something. I sat up, then tried to stand, but the room was in darkness and my tied wrists made it difficult for me to keep balanced. My vision had started to spackle with orange dots, like phasing television reception.

I needed to conserve my breath. I remembered that the bedroom had sliding doors leading to the balcony, but couldn't find the handles with my hands tied behind me. Lost to a world of pain, I fell back and spread my fingers wide, distantly searching for the catch. When I found it, I pushed down hard. The door rumbled softly as I pushed it back. Night air swept into the room, cooling the molten band at my throat.

I can't do it again, I thought, *not now, I nearly killed myself last time.* As it turned out, I didn't have the option. The top of the yellow rubble pipe had fallen away. There was no other way down.

I had reached the end of my journey. I was never intended to leave the Ziggurat. Something had always drawn me back here, to my final resting place.

What would I have sacrificed in return for one more minute, one more second of breath? I was the stroke victim, the heart attack sufferer, the dying patient we must all one day become. The darkness drew choking blinds around me. I felt myself tipping and falling to the balcony floor.

The pain vanished as I lost consciousness. *This is my death,* I thought calmly. *It's not so bad. Nothing can hurt me ever again.*

CHAPTER THIRTY-THREE
Flight

I WAS AWAKE on the floor, and the scalding pain was back. The fall had twisted the muscles of my neck, allowing some small passage of air. There was nowhere for me to even crawl. I thought of throwing myself over the balcony, anything rather than the death I had seen Petra suffer, but the parapet was beyond my reach. Rennie wouldn't want me falling into the traffic-filled street, where someone might raise an alarm, not when the incinerator...

The incinerator.

I tried to clear my oxygen-starved brain. The gas was due to have been turned back on between nine and ten. Ashe had said it would be a while before they could sort out the electrics. No pilot lights. No flames. Someone would have to air the occupied flats because it would only take a spark –

Rennie's men had put out the fire in Malcolm's flat, but had filled the penthouse lounge with candles, and were now carrying lights into the kitchen.

I prayed for a combustive journey to oblivion, but nothing happened. The plastic loop seared as it cut the sides of my neck. The pain shot down my spine, trapping nerves, paralysing me. The least agonising thing I could do was lie very still.

Why wasn't the kitchen in flames by now? Ashe had been overcautious, a typical bloody gas board employee justifying his job. I fought to clear my senses through the hammering chaos of a neural firework display, but pain overrode all thought. There was still conversation in the kitchen, but now another voice was being raised.

Stefan was there with them.

I could no longer draw breath. I knew the small capillaries in my eyes were bursting, as they did in strangulation victims. The penthouse walls began to slide away in a sparkle of light. All sound was subsumed in the drumming of my blood. I could feel nothing now except the white-hot band around my neck. I tried to crawl, but my limbs refused to obey commands from my blood-starved brain. I knew I had only moments left to live, but I could think of nothing, not my parents, not love or happiness or regret, not my life with Gordon, no memories of my lonely childhood, nothing at all except the all-enclosing pain.

And then the collar opened. It was like being rushed into a bath of iced water. The force of my returning senses overwhelmed me as I looked up to see Stefan standing in the doorway with his finger to his lips. He had a penknife in one hand.

He lifted the collar off, and I breathed deeper than I have ever done before or since. Returning with water, Stefan squatted beside me and dribbled it into my open mouth. '*Juin*, I am sorry. They would not come in here. Very bad luck to see a woman die. You must get out of this place right now.'

'What do you think I've been trying to do?' I rasped. Confusion clouded my judgement. I could no longer tell who to trust. I rose to my feet and stumbled past

Stefan, out of the room, into the dark tunnel of the corridor, hitting the door frame as I fought to regain balance.

He tried to come after me, but was abruptly involved in a shoving match with the Foshes. I was momentarily forgotten as their old enmities surfaced. I had one advantage; over the course of the weekend I had come to know my way through the building's secret folds and angles without the aid of light. I flew out into the stairwell, pumping blood back into my limbs, amazed to be alive.

There was no other way down. Suddenly I was reliving a childhood nightmare, chased by some malevolent assailant from the top of a house toward the safety of daylight and the front door, knowing that even as I descended, the closing gap between us meant that safety was exponentially retreating.

'Wait!' I heard Stefan calling as he ran after me, 'don't go down there!' I was between the third and second floors, passing through a concrete box of angled shadow when the burger-shoveller made his grab for me, seizing a thick handful of hair. My banshee scream into his face must have shocked him because he looked like he had just sucked a live three-pin plug.

I lashed up at him, connecting at least three nails (plastic, pearlised, chip-resistant) with his face. One (index, right hand) broke off in his neck with a satisfying snap. He released my hair to pull it out, but I was wearing a lot of lacquer and it wasn't as easy to get his fingers loose as he'd expected. For a minute we grappled with my head attached to his hand like Perseus trying to rid himself of the Medusa or Magic Johnson taking control of the ball.

I lost some split ends and my glitter-spackled faux-tortoiseshell slide, but I made it around the next corner to the stairs below as he grabbed at me again.

This time, his reach was better. A fat hand clamped my upper arm and hauled me back. He slipped both arms under mine and lifted me from the ground as though I weighed nothing. I kicked back instinctively – sadly not in my lethal heels – but failed to connect with his legs. As he held me tighter, I couldn't help noticing that he smelled of vinegar. Still, he couldn't carry me downstairs like this because suddenly Stefan was hanging on to the back of his jacket, pulling him over. After a few moments, the burger-shoveller was forced to drop me onto the landing, and then I kicked back hard.

This was the first time I had ever hit a man in the testicles, and I was thrilled by its effectiveness. Burger-Boy seemed clouded by confusion rather than agony, as though recalling an unpleasant childhood memory of being sick on a long car journey. In the brief moment that he lost his orientation, Stefan showed surprising agility by dropping onto him from a great height and fixing his wrists into a pair of handcuffs. I was off down the stairs, taking them in threes, widening the gap between us.

When I reached the lobby I didn't mean to fall down, but my legs simply stopped supporting me, and I did a kind of slapstick drop to the floor. I remember laughing weirdly and asking Stefan where he had got the handcuffs from. He said something about keeping them under his bed, and only using them when someone had been very naughty.

'Well, I've been a very naughty housewife,' I heard myself saying as I passed out.

CHAPTER THIRTY-FOUR
Untraceable

I WAS ONLY unconscious for a few seconds, but it was enough to punch me back into reality. Stefan was shining a torch in my face and staring at me in great concern. Part of me knew we should get out of the building while we still had a chance, but for some reason we stayed in the darkened lobby, whispering.

'None of this would have happened if I had explained properly,' Stefan admitted, holding my hand and pulling me to my feet. 'But you were off on your crusade, running about – I did not mean things to go so far.'

'I don't understand,' I said, leaning on him.

'You said you want people to know that this girl Petra existed, but you see... she did not exist. There was no Petra. I wanted to tell you, but the next time we met you'd taken her cause to heart, imagining some poor refugee girl.'

'What are you saying?'

'This can wait until later.'

'No, I want to hear,' I insisted.

'Okay, they told you how Petra survived, travelling from a war zone halfway around the world. How do you think a penniless young kid could have managed, a beautiful teenager smuggling drugs through borders by herself, making her way here? Elliot lied to you. So did Rennie. Perhaps they all forgot how it was.'

'*I don't understand*,' I repeated stupidly.

'Look, it's true I used to meet immigrants in the coastal towns. I thought I was helping them make connections to better lives. There was a young Kyrgystani man, sixteen years old, he was wanted by the police in his own country and had come across China, selling himself to anyone who could help him reach these shores. His body, you know? Very dangerous there, not legal. As soon as I saw the boy, I knew that Rennie would want to groom him for work. He was very pretty, small and slim. He had a special quality. His name was Piotr. Dr. Azymuth thought he was beautiful, but too – *effemine*, you know? This is why he had been arrested in Kyrgystan, for going with men and taking money. Elliot was brought in to make an assessment of his mental state, and he reported that Piotr was psychologically more girl than boy, so...'

'Oh God, they didn't.'

'When Azymuth made his standard cosmetic changes, he was instructed to make some extra ones. Nobody told Piotr what they were going to do. I had no idea what they had planned. All I know is that Piotr went to sleep as a boy, and woke up a girl. They tried to make his hands more feminine, but it didn't work and left scars. Rennie said he would make it up to him, give him a starring role in his very first film. Or rather I should say 'her', because Piotr was gone. It was foolproof – no-one could ever trace Petra because 'she' had no past. It left her free to become famous, to make a fortune for the company, and to be Rennie's special private girl. But then he fell in love with her, this beautiful, strange being the three of them had created, and that was when everything started going wrong.'

'Piotr didn't want to be female.' I now knew the picture of Piotr in Azymuth's file had shown him as a boy. It had been cropped tightly around his face, which had barely changed in his transition to a female. It's amazing how asexual teenagers can appear.

'She threatened to go to the newspapers. She did the work because she loved the money and the attention, but she got drunk and wasted, and could no longer be trusted to keep her mouth shut in public. The book was just her emergency fund, in case she needed to get out of the city. On Friday evening she came to get it. I think also she came to take revenge on Azymuth, but it was too late. Rennie found out and ordered her to be punished, but you accidentally saw them. Rennie's man slipped back when you left and removed the body.'

I had interfered from the moment I stepped into the building. They had lied to me, and lied again. Rennie, Elliot, Azymuth the middle-man –

– Azymuth, a private joke about the morality of his profession. I should have known just by thinking about that name, an azimuth, an arc from North to South, a meridian passing through any given point, a neutral zone.

We were still talking in the centre of the darkened lobby, but now it was time to get out. At the entrance, I looked back and saw Stefan stall like a child caught stealing. We hadn't seen the other Foshes gathering ahead of us in the shadows, but now I could make out at least six of them. As they closed in, I realised that the biggest mistake I'd made was thinking they might be remotely scared of anything, anywhere, ever.

My previous night on the town had brought me to a new level of self-assertion, but even that was of limited use now; if we had made a run for it, we would probably have managed four steps across the quadrangle before they landed on top of us like the Leicester Tigers piling onto the ball.

'Can't we find that policeman and get him to call for back-up?' I whispered.

'This is London, not Los Angeles,' said Stefan, grabbing my arm. 'What are you expecting, a fleet of helicopters?'

The Foshes slowly turned like crocodiles twisting to face their keeper at feeding time, and I thought *we're going to die,* which is why I seized my chance, running away from the building as fast as I could.

I put this move down to lack of experience in such situations. When you've spent half your lifetime making sure that the armchair legs go back into the same carpet indentations after you've vacuumed, tackling a scrum of thugs with shoulders like bookcases doesn't seem a viable option.

I ran, or at least I would have run, if two things hadn't happened in quick succession. First, the car park lit up like a night baseball court as *yes, thank you, there is a God,* a police helicopter actually shone its billion candle-power beams down on us. Well actually it was a traffic helicopter, but it was blasting leaves and rain in every direction with an eardrum-pummeling roar. Then I fell over the bonnet of a car as someone ran me over for the second time in one weekend.

CHAPTER THIRTY-FIVE
Time Limit

'You really are an absolute fucking cow,' shouted Lou as she leaned across the seat. 'I just needed to tell you that and then we're straight, all right? I had a *horrible* row with Hadrian and needed to get out before I drank bleach and set fire to the house. Then I discovered you'd stolen my purse and my mobile. You stranded me. You're not the only one who's going through a crisis, you know.'

'I'm really sorry, I didn't know what else to do.' I glanced nervously back as all hell broke loose on the steps of the Ziggurat. It looked as though Stefan was being thrown into the air while the other Foshcs ambled toward us. I think they were laughing.

'Get in, hurry up. You've got terrible bruises on your neck, are you all right?'

'It's an allergic reaction,' I told her, forgetting that I could stop lying now. 'I think I'm coming down with flu. Whose car is this?'

'I borrowed it from Hadrian's last girlfriend.' She reached across and yanked the door of the miniature emerald-green Smart car shut behind me. 'She left him but didn't bother taking the car with her because she didn't like the colour, can you believe that? Middle-class children have far too much money nowadays. I haven't quite got the hang of the gearshift yet.'

Rennie's glittering Mercedes skewed to a stop in front of the building, and the Foshes piled in. They were laughing at our little car, like it was all a game. I realised they were probably enjoying themselves. In their world this was comic relief. A moment later, they were pulling out of the car park ahead of us, steamrollering through the floodlit puddles. A very young bat-eared constable was standing alone on the steps gesturing to the men in the overhead chopper. I couldn't see where Stefan had gone.

'Can we go now?' I begged as Lou tried to get the key into the ignition. The boxy vehicle reversed sharply, kangarooed to a halt and took off just as the Foshes roared away. A second Mercedes pulled up behind us, and more men were attempting to cram themselves inside as we overtook them. I suddenly realised how many of them must have been in the building.

'It's roomier than it looks, isn't it?' Lou spun the wheel and grinned at me as we swung onto the Embankment. I couldn't see that the interior capacity was important because there seemed every likelihood of us flying off the road and being flung into the filthy freezing waters of the Thames. Every time we went around a corner, a hail of cigarette butts and empty doughnut boxes flew past us as though we were in zero gravity.

'Put your seat belt on,' Lou warned. 'I have to tell you that I am not entirely sober, but I'm going on the wagon after tonight. Is there any reason why a helicopter would be following us?'

'Yes, I rather think there is.' I searched for the seat-belt buckle. 'Where are we going?'

'I can't believe you've forgotten. You've got to get the key back to Malcolm's safety deposit box, remember?

The time-lock shuts at midnight. If you don't return the keys on time he won't be able to collect them on his way to work, and Julie will have broken her promise, and he'll have issues with that, and the finely-wrought web of trust she has built between them in New York will be broken, and she'll go on another high-fibre diet which will probably kill her, and everyone will blame me. You *do* have the front door key, don't you?'

I checked the back pocket of my jeans and was faintly amazed to find it still there. 'Yes. Where do we have to take it?'

'To the night deposit box at Malcolm's bank. Didn't you read the letter Julie wrote you?'

'What letter?'

'It was in the envelope with her note to the concierge. She should have headed it 'Sale Preview', then you might have bothered to read it. She wrote out all sorts of anal middle-class stuff out for you, like where to buy those organic loaves that weigh the same as paving stones.'

'She did tell me, I just forgot. I've had a lot of my mind. I have to get the key back to his *bank?*'

'And it seals off at midnight. I'm glad one of us has been paying attention. It's all right, it's only Holborn. Just the other side of Waterloo Bridge. If we don't return it, darling, you don't get paid.'

I looked at my watch, but realised I must have smashed the face when I lost consciousness. 'What do you make the time?'

'Ten to midnight. We're cutting it a little fine. The traffic's awful.' We swung out of the junction and onto the busy Embankment road, a fiery fairground of cones, tape, red and white plastic barriers, ditches, plastic drainpipes and mounds of paving stones. 'Actually, don't take this personally, but the traffic's not the only thing that looks rough. You could use some foundation and lip-liner.'

'You haven't been through what I've been through tonight.'

'No, it's just a bit severe, this new look of yours. Where are those nice sunflower earrings, they'd go nicely with that top.' Accessorizing was the last thing on my mind right now. 'I think your new friends are following behind us,' Lou warned, checking the mirror.

The second Mercedes was closing fast, trying to cut into the inside lane, spinning cones from beneath its wheels as it did so. 'They're not my friends, they're Foshes,' I pointed out, although it was hardly time for semantics, especially as we seemed about to rear-end the Mercedes in front. I could feel the vibration of the helicopter above us.

'Do you know the people in the Mercedes?'

'Which one? Behind or in front?'

'Either. Both.'

'They'd all like to kill me, but right now I think they just want to get away from the helicopter.'

'So they're friends of yours as well? Is there anyone in London you *don't* know?'

'I'm beginning to wonder.'

'I want you to understand that I'm only driving this fast because I'm plastered,' said Lou reassuringly. 'Shit, we just went past one of those camera-on-a-stick things. I saw the flash go off. That's three points on Hadrian's ex-girlfriend's licence and a hundred quid fine winging her way. It'll teach her to dump my son because she wanted to take a gap year. We know what that means

– two months in Thailand and a summer spent pouring tequila shots in Ibiza.'

Suddenly we hit heavy traffic and were forced to slow. Ahead, the traffic lights started to change to red. The cross-lane was gridlocking.

'Hold on,' warned Lou. There was a lurch like a ship hitting an iceberg as she geared up and the car shot through a gap so narrow that we would have lost the wing-mirrors on a conventional vehicle. The Mercedes behind slammed on its brakes and fell back.

'It's got some acceleration,' I managed to shout above the engine noise.

'Hadrian put a different engine in. He wanted to surprise her. He warned me that if you accelerate too hard, it's actually possible to do a somersault. Where are the wipers?' It had started to rain again.

We heard a scream of tyres from behind, but no crash. Seconds later, the Smart car was forced to stop in a chaotic funnel of traffic as the coned-off lanes narrowed. 'Look at these roads. Cairo has a better traffic system than this, and they have donkeys carrying hay on their motorways for God's sake. At least your friends are blocked in behind.'

'I do wish you'd stop calling them that.'

Lou looked back at the Mercedes as its rear doors opened and two Foshes climbed out with their right fists clenched. They were carrying skateboards. 'I *simply* don't believe it,' she said, 'they've waving guns about in the street. Where do they think they are, Nottingham?'

If the Foshes were chunky and ungainly standing on firm ground, they developed grace and poise once they jumped on the boards, swiping themselves through the traffic with extraordinary dexterity. They cut on either side of the stalled vehicles, snubby dark weapons ill-concealed in their fists.

Lou spun the wheel, bumped over the kerb and scraped the Smart car through a slim space between an Audi and another Mercedes that had appeared behind the second one, taking the paintwork off all three vehicles. A pair of Sikhs leapt from this third Merc and started shouting, but I realised they had nothing to do with what was going on, they were just a couple of shouty motorists. We were approaching the Waterloo Bridge roundabout. Ahead, the traffic was picking up pace.

I think one of the Foshes fired at us, because there was a sound of puckering metal, and steam started pouring out of the Audi. The driver was surprised; Audis look unstoppable. He went to get out, but another bullet cleaving the air between us changed his mind. An amber traffic light exploded, and something pinged off a right-lane filter sign.

'Marvellous, there's never a cop around when someone's firing a gun,' Lou complained, 'but they'll appear out of nowhere when you're trying to take a pee behind a hedge.'

'You were in your next-door neighbour's front garden, Lou,' I pointed out, recalling her last drunken misdemeanour. 'There was a children's Harry Potter party going on.'

On the left, Waterloo Bridge appeared to be clear of Northbound traffic. The Foshes had nimbly come racing up around us on their boards like sea-lions cutting through water.

'The gradient up to the bridge must slow them down,' I shouted at Lou. 'Put your foot down.' The Smart car bounced and skidded on the roundabout, fighting for purchase on the rain-slick road, and then we were skimming over water in a clear lane.

The downpour was wind-driven, sweeping across the bridge as Lou lost control and hammered the Smart car along the side of a parked coach. We ricocheted off like a green snooker ball and bounced over the central reservation into the oncoming traffic. Behind them, both Foshes had made the short slope with ease, leaping easily over the kerbs. They followed us over to the other side of the bridge with ridiculous dexterity. Now that they were running parallel, they had time to take aim.

'What are they, Olympic medallists?' asked Lou.

The surprised driver of a Bill & Ben Office Plants van coming from the north side slammed on his brakes when he saw the overpowered Smart car and the Foshes heading for him. His tyres air-pocketed and failed to grip tarmac as several McDonalds boxes catapulted forward and hit the inside of his windscreen. I was glad we weren't the only ones in an untidy car.

We carried on across the lane, losing a headlight and wing-mirror against a lamp-post with a metallic bang. Reversing sharply, we mounted the pavement as the two Foshes, barrelling too fast to turn, tipped and halted within inches of the van's radiator. A skateboard shot through the air and bounced through the open window of a fried chicken van. We heard a screech of brakes and a crunch of metal as something big ran into the back of the van, and a hubcap overtook us, but we didn't dare to turn around.

Lou had decided that it was safer to stay on the pavement. The battered Smart car was just wide enough to make it between the balustrades and the traffic lights.

We shot up Kingsway on the sidewalk, scattering a group of horrified tourists who had just had their worst fears about traffic in London confirmed.

'Look out,' said Lou, 'Canadians.'

'How do you know they're Canadians?'

'Well, you just *know*, don't you? Look at Celine Dion.'

By now, the jumbo Mercs had vanished into the side streets, and the helicopter seemed to be tacking between the office blocks in some confusion.

The cross-current of traffic by Holborn Tube would have killed us, but luckily Lou began applying the brakes the moment she saw the bank looming. Even so, we only stopped when the car's front bumper hit the wall of Barclays. I leapt out and searched for the private safety deposit box.

'Around the side!' yelled Lou. Behind her, I could see a couple of constables starting to take an interest. I remember thinking they were very short for policemen, and that the Met must have changed their height regulations, or perhaps it was the new helmets.

I tried to yank open the deposit box drawer, but it wouldn't budge.

'You need the pin number,' Lou called.

'I have no idea what that is.'

'You must do, it was –'

'Don't say it was in the letter.'

I looked up at the wall clock. One minute to midnight. A row of asterisks appeared on the readout above the deposit drawer. It was asking for an eleven digit number.

'Eleven digits!' I shouted.

'Don't ask me, you're the one who watched *Countdown* every afternoon.'

I don't know what made me do it but I entered 16121202193, and the drawer opened. Afterwards I had time to consider, and came up with the numerical version of the word PLASTIC, A equalling 1. It was instinct, you see. At that moment I just knew that Malcolm and Azymuth were acquainted, and were probably good friends. Malcolm had worked on some kind of clinic, Azymuth was a doctor and they were neighbours. They made their money through plastic. No-one is without taint, that's what Rennie had told me.

I threw the key in, slam-dunking it to the bottom of the wedge-shaped drawer. A moment after it clanged shut, the wall clock above my head clicked over to midnight. Lou let out a rebel yell.

'I don't know about you, but I need a Mohito,' she warned, pulling a plastic Simpsons flask from under the seat and unscrewing the cap. 'I couldn't find fresh mint so I made it with toothpaste.'

'Let's put some distance between us and them first,' I pleaded as the constables spoke to the driver of a patrol car. It pulled out of Great Queen Street and flicked on its lights, like a toy fitted with new batteries. The helicopter was still drifting overhead.

As the traffic lights changed, the patrol car fell in behind us. Lou swung the Smart car, which had now developed lumpy steering, around in a jerky arc and cut back into Sardinia Street, then gunned it until we hit the comparative desolation of Lincoln's Inn Fields. Here we slammed to a halt behind a skip (actually thumping it with a hollow boom) and doused the lights. It took the police car longer to make the turning, and then it carried on past us.

'It's a good job we stopped when we did,' said Lou. 'The steering wheel's come loose.'

I fell back into the seat and opened the window, feeling the rain on my face. The raindrops were so light that some were actually drifting upwards. I love it when they do that. I had one of Lou's cigarettes. Neither of us spoke for some minutes. Lou poured a Mohito into an empty cigarette carton and handed it to me. I tasted it and winced. The bottom fell out of the carton and the rest went in my lap.

'So, what's your verdict on the luxurious riverside lifestyle?' Lou searched the glove box for a fresh packet of Rothmans.

'Interesting. That very respectable building turned out to be a wonderland of liars, psychopaths and deluded criminals.'

'I don't suppose Jeffrey Archer will want to buy one of their penthouses now then,' sniffed Lou, flicking her lighter.

Rain tumbled on the roof and the car cooled.

'Why were you so anxious for me to return the keys on time?' I asked. 'It makes no difference to you. Tell me the truth.'

Lou watched her cigarette smoke roll along the ceiling. 'One of us has to get out of Hamingwell for good. It isn't going to be me, is it?'

I could have hugged her then.

Later, though, when I mulled over all that had happened, I thought of Piotr. I imagined him as a boy, skinny and pretty, his aqua eyes drawing pederastic glances, outcast for his coquette effeminacy but willing to fight his way to a free life, trusting his new English friends and waking from a chemical slumber to find himself betrayed and transformed for the pleasure of others.

I wanted to kill Rennie with my bare hands. His speech about keeping the wheels of commerce turning was nothing more than an attempt to justify murder. His only concern was building enough wealth to get away with it. Poverty is still the greatest mark of guilt against any criminal.

I had walked in the poisoned river ground that Nalin had warned me about, and had left behind a bloodied footprint, adding to its darkness. It was easy to discover places in London so rotten with centuries of greed, corruption and sins of the flesh that no amount of restoration could return them to a humanistic whole. I'd failed to change anything, and had hastened a lost innocent to an ugly death, merely adding to the city's criminal record. I was disgusted with the way I'd behaved.

If you're really going to get involved in urban life, I decided, *surviving it suddenly becomes a tough trick to pull off. It's hard to stay clean. And it must have always been that way.*

As I walked alone through the bare night streets, I realised that for the first time in my life I owed a real debt, and had no way of paying it back. I wasn't brave or foolish enough to return to the Ziggurat, and could think of no way to make restitution by bringing the man responsible for its secret miseries out into the light.

CHAPTER THIRTY-SIX
First Day Back

THE POLICE WERE told not to disturb the Ziggurat's residents while their investigations were being carried out, or they would sue. Madame Funes wouldn't even let them use the front entrance. Despite Lou's protestations, an officer managed to get through to Malcolm Phillimore while he was waiting for his luggage at Heathrow, just to warn him that there was a forensics team taking the flats apart and bagging evidence. He went mad, apparently.

I gave a statement at Vauxhall police station, and they asked me to start going through Azymuth's patient files, to see who I could identify. Material witness to two murders and all that, I could hardly turn them down if I wanted to get away with the self-defence thing. I knew that Rennie's people were just going to evaporate as soon as they started looking for them. He would already have gone to ground, his office rerouting calls, his mobile number changed, and he'd be calling his well-placed pals and briefing his lawyers, way ahead of the police. The Foshes would all perform vanishing acts because they knew how to do it, and although the police would make a show of listening to me, I would eventually be branded a runaway housewife with a big imagination.

What the police didn't know was that I could disappear, too. I was still planning to get paid for flat-sitting, and knew I would have to collect the money at some point. But I had Lou to help me, and she knew a thing or too about dealing with the police.

Still, I thanked God that our little constable had managed to call in the helicopter. We wouldn't have stood a chance without something to panic them. I suppose it was simple law of scale, you wheel out something bigger and more dangerous than the people you're dealing with. But I knew – and the police probably knew – that they would never get Rennie's organisation to court. They'd end up arresting some of the little people, but not him. Perhaps someone else would decide that he was too much of a risk to stay in business. These people tend to take care of their own affairs.

I read in the paper some time later that the Minister of Defence was furious about the go-ahead being given for his brother-in-law's new mega-million-pound building to be pulled apart. Vauxhall's murder squad was allowed to tear up the brand new beechwood floors looking for body parts.

But of course, they didn't find anything.

One other odd thing happened. The following December I was standing on the Strand looking for a taxi one night. I'd like to tell you I'd been doing something sophisticated and cultural but we'd just been to see *South Pacific*. And someone exactly like Piotr walked past me.

I recognised the look at once, because I'd spent so much time staring at that angelic face. She was dressed in a beautiful white Agnes B coat and scarf, and very high heels, and I like to think she was going to dinner at the Savoy. I wondered if there was any way that it might really have been her. After all, I had only seen Azymuth dead. From Eastern Europe to the Savoy via near-death in an incinerator – wouldn't that have been a story to tell?

CHAPTER THIRTY-SEVEN
New Life

'WHAT ARE YOU doing here?' I asked, opening the door. 'I thought you were in Barcelona.'

'Hilary had to do a double, so there was no point in me going with her. Can I come in, June?'

'Of course.' I opened the door of the loft apartment wide and stepped back to let him pass. Gordon had put on weight around the midriff, and now looked as I had always imagined him, older and more settled, operating from a lower centre of gravity. I had trimmed off a fair amount of body fat, but was still wearing one of my old baggy tops. Even so, he kept eyeing my slender new form oddly, particularly when I bent down to pull the back of my shoe over my heel.

'It's not been going very well between us, to be honest. Hilary doesn't seem so interested now that I'm single. She enjoys her job and says she doesn't want to be tied down. She's thinking of going long-haul. The money's better. She never used to be so –' I think he was going to say 'independent' and stopped himself. I mentally threw an air-punch.

'I've just made coffee. Want some? Make yourself comfortable, if you can find somewhere to sit.' The apartment was a tip. Bare boards, half-plastered walls. I pulled over a tea-chest and upturned it for him. I still felt a spark of emotion when I looked at Gordon, but it wasn't love. Sadness, really. I found it hard to imagine that I had once depended on him for everything.

'It's bit of a rough neighbourhood, isn't it? It took me a while to track you down. I understand you've changed your name. Alaska Dash is a bit melodramatic, don't you think?'

'I named myself after a programme on the Discovery Channel,' I explained. 'Something to do with a snowmobile race. I don't feel like a June Cryer any more. Part of me will always be her, of course. You can't entirely erase a personal history.'

'You look so different with your hair cut short and coloured like that. I've never seen you in jeans. I nearly didn't recognise you.' He looked uncomfortable and out of place in this great sunny modern room.

'Don't you like it?'

'Not really. It makes you look like a lesbian.'

To Gordon, any combination of jeans and short hair suggested lesbianism. This was a bit rich coming from a man who looked as though he'd been knitted. 'How did you find me?'

'Your horrible friend Lou phoned up to have a go at me over bin bags. I didn't tie them up properly or something. She let slip where you were. She sounded a bit drunk. I think she's having an affair with some young police officer.'

'So you still haven't moved out.'

'No. After the burglary, word got about that there was trouble in the area and the sale fell through. Whatever happened to you on that weekend you went away? I heard there was a fire or something. I've asked Lou about it, but she won't tell me.'

'It was nothing. The insurance company sorted it out.' Rennie's men had wiped away their trail by torching several of the apartments and blaming it on the gas company. Malcolm and Julie had split up, and he had gone back to his wife. At least she was eating normally again. 'It gave me a chance to think things over, that's all.'

Gordon went to the window to check on his car. 'The company bought me a new Rover. V6 engine, two-tone leather interior, SatNav, all the optionals. A very nice motor. There are some unsavoury characters hanging around outside.'

'They're okay if you stay on the right side of them.'

'Whose flat is this?'

'It belongs to a friend of mine. I'm looking after the place for a few weeks. Doing it up in lieu of rent.'

'A friend, eh?' Gordon walked around, unsure what to make of the airy open space. I knew that in his eyes it wouldn't count as a proper home because there weren't enough walls. 'You've got no curtains up. Anyone can see in. I was going to ask if you wanted to come back to Hamingwell for a few days. I felt bad about leaving you broke.'

'No, it's okay, it was good for me. Besides, I'm quite comfortable here.'

'Are you sure?' He looked uncertainly at the chaos of the room, the half-painted walls and boxes. 'It doesn't look safe outside.'

'It's the little kids you have to watch out for, they're buggers.'

'One of them wanted money for minding the car. He couldn't be more than ten.'

'I hope you gave him something.'

'I certainly did not.'

'Then I wouldn't stay up here too long if I were you. Gordon, I saw some of the websites logged on your PC.'

'What are you talking about?'

'When I stayed at the house overnight. I went on your computer. All those adult sites. Don't look so innocent.'

'Oh, those?' He laughed, but I could tell he was embarrassed. 'They don't mean anything.'

'I don't mind what you do anymore, Gordon. It's your life to enjoy as you see fit.'

Gordon looked at me in genuine puzzlement. 'So you've no plans to move back to Hamingwell? I thought you'd stay in the area. You loved it there. Apart from anything else, it's so much safer.'

He knew that wasn't true. Only a couple of months ago, some Hamingwell schoolgirls had stabbed a classmate to death and set her body ablaze because she had dissed them on Facebook. It had been in all the papers. Neighbours were busy silting up the street with plastic-wrapped flowers and teddy bears. All kinds of inexplicable things happen in suburban neighbourhoods, but men like Gordon pretend not to notice.

There are a lot of people out there who refuse to help. There are victims who have no recourse to the police, and no-one to protect them. It made me start thinking.

'What about your little house, your nice garden, all the neighbours you could chat to?' Gordon asked.

This was particularly insensitive, I thought, seeing as he was sleeping with one of them. The only other neighbour I had ever spent time with fantasised about burning the town down.

'No, Gordon, it's really much easier for me to be here.' I thought of Virginia Woolf's comment on

London, that it takes up the private life and carries it on without any effort.

There was a clatter of paint cans and a cry of '*Merde!*'

'Who's that?' asked Gordon.

'This is Stefan. He's helping me paint the apartment.' Stefan came in from the bedroom. He was naked under his overalls and appeared to have tipped yellow paint over his chest. He reached over and shook hands awkwardly.

'Pleased to meet you,' said Gordon stiffly. 'Well, June, you seem to have everything under control. Your new life must be agreeing with you. You've certainly lost a bit of weight. It makes you look ill.' His attention strayed to the window again. 'I think I had better go and keep an eye on the car. Well.' He jangled the change in his pockets. 'I guess it's a divorce then. You could have half of the house, save getting messy in court. I hope you're ready to handle the financial side now.'

'Yeah, I can handle it. I'm not fussed about buying stuff any more.'

'Why not?'

'Once you've done it at gunpoint, regular shopping loses its appeal.'

'Oh. That's a pity. I bought you these. A sort of peace offering. For old times' sake.' He set down the shiny white bag before me like an appeasement to the Shopping Gods. Inside was the pair of beaded evening shoes I had lusted after on the day of my last spree on Gordon's money. 'I'm not very good with this sort of thing, as you know, so Hilary chose them for me. She thought you'd like them.'

'Perhaps you'd better let her keep them,' I said gently, handing back the bag. 'I don't think they'd suit me.'

He looked hurt. 'I don't understand you anymore, June. There's something different about you. You seem colder. Too much like a fella for my taste.'

'You don't have to like it. There are a lot of things I still have to figure out. I only know that I don't miss our old life. It was comfortable, but it made me so spineless.'

'I wouldn't say that. You were certainly the mistress of the house. Hilary's away all the time and I can't find where she keeps anything. And I never seem to have any clean pants. Don't ask a man to do a woman's job, eh?' His bluff joviality faded. 'Listen, I know I left you, but for many years you had everything you could ever ask for in Hamingwell.'

'That's the point, Gordon. I don't ever want to have to ask for things again, or sit there making up ways to fill the hours. It's time to give myself a different kind of credit.'

'Would it make any difference to say I miss you?'

'That's to be expected when you spend ten years with someone. But at some point you have to ask yourself, what was it for? Did we learn anything from each other?'

'I don't see how you can talk like that. I looked after you.'

'I know you did, Gordon. Maybe you protected me a little too much.'

'Fine, go ahead and live this way, but I think you're making a terrible mistake. People aren't nice. They're out for everything they can get.'

There are a lot more good ones than bad, I thought, *but you'll never see it.* I watched from the upstairs window as he left, disappointed and bewildered. He didn't stop to look up. He checked the Rover for scratches, then hastily hopped inside and started it. He couldn't wait to get out of the area fast enough.

Me, I like it here, but I won't stay. I'll move around. Whitechapel, Hoxton, King's Cross, Shoreditch, Lambeth, Borough, Pimlico, Deptford, Bayswater, I haven't decided where next. I'm learning new lists.

I've taken a new job, rather an appropriate one. I've become a personal shopper for the wives of the wealthy, and I'm damned good at it. The first thing I'm going to do is get Mrs. Rennie to spend her way through her husband's fortune. How we'll laugh as we burn a path through the laundered cash of the corrupt. What's more, I'll be able to keep an eye on her husband's mysteriously transmuting network of alliances. So long as respectable people require someone to do their dirty work, he and his companions will continue to make their fortunes. I desperately want to hurt him, to make him pay for what he did, but I no longer know which side I'm on.

I wouldn't exactly say I've faked my death, but changing my name will be the first smart move, and if I ever do get another credit card it'll have that new name on it. I'll have been reborn.

My old life as June Cryer has officially ended.

I am a former housewife, an ex-housewife. Like the Monty Python parrot sketch, I have ceased to be. To put it another way, I am one mean mother of an ex-pelmet-hoovering Sainsburys-shopping dishwasher-loading housewife who can no longer remember which leading shower spray gets rid of stubborn limescale and which attacks unsightly soap-scum, and doesn't give a flying rat-fuck, pardon my French. I'm just glad I came out of my coma long enough to build a new life.

When I finally do have a child – a girl, I feel sure – she won't be bullied into doing what's best for her by her parents or her peers, by suitors or salesmen. She'll be free to choose the life she wants. Of course, I'm realistic enough to know that her choices won't be mine. You set up home on solid ground and tend it, or you move to shifting sands. It's a hard decision. The most important thing is discovering you have a choice.

The housewife is dead, but the woman is doing just fine.

ABOUT THE AUTHOR

BORN IN LONDON, Christopher Fowler has written for film, television, radio, graphic novels, and for newpaper including *The London Times*, for more than thirty years. He is a regular columnist for *The Independent on Sunday*. Fowler is the multi-award-winning author of more than thirty novels, including the lauded *Bryant & May* mystery novels. In the past year he has been nominated for eight national book awards.

For more information visit
www.christopherfowler.co.uk

NON STOP.
ONE WAY.
STRAIGHT
DOWN!

HELL TRAIN

CHRISTOPHER FOWLER

UK ISBN: 978-1-907992-43-8 • US ISBN: 978-1-907992-44-5 • £7.99/$8.99

Imagine there was a supernatural chiller that Hammer Films never made. A grand epic produced at the studio's peak, which played like a cross between the Dracula and Frankenstein films and Dr Terror's House Of Horrors...

Four passengers meet on a train journey through Eastern Europe during the First World War, and face a mystery that must be solved if they are to survive. As the Arkangel races through the war-torn countryside, they must find out:

What is in the casket that everyone is so afraid of? What is the tragic secret of the veiled Red Countess who travels with them? Why is their fellow passenger the army brigadier so feared by his own men? And what exactly is the devilish secret of the Arkangel itself?

Bizarre creatures, satanic rites, terrified passengers and the romance of travelling by train, all in a classically styled horror novel.

 WWW.SOLARISBOOKS.COM

Follow us on Twitter! www.twitter.com/solarisbooks